THE HAPPY PEOPLE

THE

HAPPY

PEOPLE

BY SARA JENKINS

PEOPLES BOOK CLUB

CHICAGO

For my brother Dan, and Celeste, the sister he gave me

THE HAPPY PEOPLE

CHAPTER I

STEPHEN ELLIOTT stood perfectly still by the heavily carved, mahogany lectern until he had the attention of the entire congregation. This was one of hundreds of small dramatic tricks which he used to lend importance to the order of service, and this morning he took a bit longer than usual so that his new congregation might satisfy their curiosity about his appearance. When exactly the right moment of tension arrived he began to recite the Scripture, his dark blue eyes moving from face to face as if they said, "You, and you, and you."

His voice was deep with an actor's range, and as Stephen read the words of the familiar King James version, he gave them a freshness. He had reached the third verse of the second chapter of Isaiah, "And many people shall go and say, Come ye—" when he faltered an instant and the muscles of his face tightened. Probably no one in the congregation noticed it except his sister, Elizabeth Marsden.

After that one second of hesitation he went on

smoothly, "—and let us go up to the mountain of the
Lord, to the house of the God of Jacob." His eyes moved
carefully away from the spot where he had been looking
when the small break in his reading had occurred.

It was a hat which had startled him, a woman's hat,
saucy and veiled, and made of yellow pansies. He had
gone shopping with Claire and picked out that hat, and
she had worn it the last time— He took a quick breath
in the middle of a phrase, brought his mind sharply back
to the business at hand, and looked elsewhere. As if any
woman would be wearing the same hat after a lapse of
more than two years, he jeered at himself. Besides, Claire
lived in Macon. She wouldn't be here.

The words of the Old Testament rolled out majesti-
cally. "Their land also is full of silver and gold, neither
is there any end of their treasures."

He had found the hat once more, his eyes seeking it
unconsciously. Butter yellow hair curled up about it—
Claire's hair. The heavy shoulder of one of the officials of
his board hid the face beneath. He read on, but something of the unique quality of his reading of the earlier
verses was gone now.

"And the idols he shall utterly abolish," he concluded
at length, and closed the Book gently. In the same gesture he moved slightly to the left and peered about the
obstructive shoulder.

It *was* Claire. His heart lurched even before his mind
would admit that it was she.

Her eyes had been fixed on his face and now their
glances met across three pews and the chancel. When
she realized that he had recognized her, she smiled
faintly, looking just as she had the week they had both
left college, just as she had the first time he had ever laid

eyes on her, and every time in between—cool, and poised, and the most beautiful thing in the world.

He reached out and put his small Bible on top of the big one which belonged on the lectern. It surprised him that his hand was trembling. Claire Collins, his heart was saying, then corrected itself painfully. Claire Winthrop!

The organ pealed out the offertory. Stephen turned to the altar, lifted the collection plates and moved to meet the ushers in their white linen suits, a red carnation in each left lapel. When he returned to his pulpit chair, the offertory became no more than the unnoticed music which makes background for a movie climax. He was once more running from the college library, a cold autumn rain driving into his face as he bowled over a tall, slender girl in a yellow slicker.

When he had set her on her feet, her face almost on a level with his, she had laughed and said, "My goodness!" in a breathless voice.

"I'm sorry. I didn't see you. I hope you aren't hurt," he apologized in the same instant and she had laughed again.

"How sorry?" she demanded. "I was simply starving and nobody in the Delta house would come out in the weather. Sorry enough to keep me from eating by myself which I purely loathe?"

He had sat wet and adoring while she ate him completely out of pocket that night. And on countless nights afterward she had shredded the slender budget on which he and Elizabeth lived. She had worn his fraternity pin. She had threatened laughingly to change from psychology to domestic science when the second semester began. But they had never spoken seriously of marriage until commencement week.

Sitting here in his pulpit chair two years later, he seemed to feel her lips against his as they had been in that long moment before he had raised his head and asked the shaken question.

"When are you going to marry me, Claire?"

She hadn't answered at once. She had looked away and swallowed. Then she had turned back and opened her eyes very wide in a way she had. He was sure that she could hear his heart beating but her voice sounded unstirred, her hands lay relaxed in her lap. And she had said, "I couldn't marry a preacher, Steve."

"You—" He choked on the unexpectedness of it.

She went on in the same cool way. "I'd be a terrible preacher's wife, darling. I couldn't butter up the ladies of the Women's Society. I probably couldn't even sit through their meetings. I certainly have no intention of trying all my life to live on a church-mouse salary."

He gulped, could say nothing.

After a little she went on. "Look at me, Steve. I'm beautiful. I've never had any money of my own but one of these days I'm going to—like my sister Paula. She married J. G. Kinsman, III, a man who already had it to burn. If I didn't love you better than anyone in the world I wouldn't gamble on you. But I will marry you if you'll take that personnel job you turned down with Kinsman Mills. You're brilliant, Steve. You'd get on and make money if you tried."

"You love me better than anyone except *yourself*," he had retorted bitterly. "That is, *maybe* you do."

They had quarreled until daylight, and that afternoon she had married Bruce Winthrop, who at thirty-five owned two cotton mills and wore the mark of future millions like a coat tailored especially for him.

As the tenor solo ended, Stephen shook his memories from him. He forced himself to take the collection plates from the ushers and pray briefly for the use of the offering and for those who had given it. His self-discipline did not relax throughout the sermon, nor until he stood at the door with the benediction on his lips.

Afterward he remained there shaking hands, looking into faces he did not see, repeating names he would not remember. He forced himself to outward steadiness but inside he shook as he sometimes had after an icy shower. Any moment she would be there, offer him her hand, and smile as if they had never meant anything to each other.

His widowed sister, Elizabeth Marsden, came and stood near him waiting but he did not realize it. The crowd was thinning and Claire had not come.

J. G. Kinsman, mill owner and chief member of Steve's church, with whom he and Elizabeth and his nephew Bobby were to have the midday meal, had hung back among the last and now the great man was introducing his wife. Steve looked at Mrs. Kinsman, startled. He thought her very like her sister, Claire, only paler and less beautiful. Surely he had not made such a mistake as to think— At that moment he saw Claire herself, standing tall and proud and somewhat amused at a little distance in the aisle.

"And my daughter," Kinsman was saying, introducing a small, dark-eyed girl.

Steve took the proffered hand, found it small and cool, and said, "Miss Kinsman," politely but he could not have told whether she were fifteen or fifty, tall or short, pretty or otherwise. He was looking over her head at Claire.

"My sister-in-law, Mrs. Collins Winthrop," Kinsman continued.

Of course that's why they are alike, Steve thought. After all Claire and Mrs. Kinsman were sisters. He cleared his throat and murmured, "Mrs. Winthrop."

"Steve, you silly, I do believe you've forgotten me." She moved closer to him. It was the same hat, or one exactly like it. The perfume was the haunting one of two years ago. And she was laughing at him just the way she used to. "I almost graduated from college with you, only I—something happened and I left a few days before the exercises."

"I'm glad to see you again, Claire," he told her awkwardly. It was no polite phrase. He was glad, indecently, uncontrollably glad. And she was Bruce Winthrop's wife. He dropped the soft hand which he had already been holding much too long.

"I'm devastated I can't go to Paula's for dinner with you today," she was saying in the old breathless, exaggerated way, "but perhaps you and— Hello, Elizabeth. It's good to see you again. I used to know you when you and Steve had the trailer, back at the university."

"Of course. I remember," Elizabeth answered, her voice a little flat and less cordial than the words.

"I've a new little house here in Kinsman and I'm having my first guests Tuesday night about eight. I do hope you'll both come. It'll make up a bit for my having to miss the visit today." Claire moved her eyes from Elizabeth's and let them linger on Steve's.

"We'd like to," Steve assured her gravely.

"Paula will give you the address," she called over her shoulder. " 'Bye until then."

Kinsman was leaving too. "We'll be outside in the car," he said.

"I'll only be a moment," Steve promised, unbuttoning his robe.

The others were scarcely out of hearing when Elizabeth spoke fiercely. "I think I hate her."

Steve turned about, astounded at the words from his usually gentle sister. "A girl's got a right to marry whom she pleases, honey," he told her.

Elizabeth's gloved fists did not relax. Her nostrils flared. "I don't care. You ought to have a wife, children, lead a normal life. But there *she* is."

He did not argue the point. "I hope that she and Winthrop are happy. She looks happy," he added wistfully.

His sister snorted. "Honestly, Stephen Elliott, you are so *unworldly*. They're divorced, she and Bruce Winthrop."

"Divor— When? Who told you?" He did not believe it. Not yet.

"No one. But Mr. Kinsman made it clear when he introduced her. Mrs. Collins Winthrop, he said. Mr. Winthrop is named Bruce, and Collins is Claire's maiden name. That's the way Emily Post says a divorced woman should refer to herself. Mrs. Maiden-Name-Husband's-surname. Mrs. Collins Winthrop."

Steve stood there shaking his dark head, his lips parted, his dark red vestments half off. His pulse beat thickly and his throat hurt him. Claire was not married to Winthrop. She was free.

But not free to him. The two thoughts were almost simultaneous. He was a minister of God and of the Methodist church— Adultery! The word flamed through his mind. That's what his church taught about marrying a divorced woman. He was not even allowed to perform a marriage ceremony for a divorced person. He could certainly not make Claire his wife and stand in the pulpit.

"The Kinsmans are waiting," Elizabeth reminded him.

He looked at her as if he had forgotten she was there, then disappeared into the vestry to hang his robe on a padded hanger.

CHAPTER II

THERE were six at the table in the big Kinsman dining room: Kinsman and Paula, Steve and Elizabeth, and the two boys, eight-year-old Kinny, who was Joel Garner Kinsman, the Fourth, and Elizabeth's Bobby, aged nine. As they took their places J.G. turned to ask his wife, "The girl's not coming?"

Steve had already noticed that Mrs. Kinsman rarely spoke and even more rarely smiled. Now she did both, rather briefly.

"I believe she has guests of her own. They're being very gay down at the guest house."

Kinsman frowned. "She's supposed to have Sunday dinner with her family. That's one of the conditions I made when I let her have a place of her own. Don't approve of a young girl living by herself. Elliott, will you say grace?"

The prayer was short, and when it was over Elizabeth turned to her hostess. "It's unbelievable that you should be Miss Kinsman's mother—"

Paula shook her head. "I'm not. We're very good friends, though."

"I married before," Kinsman explained. "One of the follies of my youth. My first wife was rich and spoiled, and I was too busy to run around with her the way she wanted me to. After it was all over, she let me keep the girl."

Elizabeth's face burned. She had thought Mrs. Kinsman rather young to be the mother of a grown daughter and that the two looked very unlike, but her remark had been purely a social one.

"Joel is—I believe she thinks she's *my* mother," Paula said softly. "She's been doing her best to take care of me ever since J.G. and I got married, when she wasn't much more than Kinny's age."

"Joel—?" Steve repeated. It seemed an odd name for a girl yet he felt sure that Mrs. Kinsman had been speaking of her husband's daughter.

Kinsman's booming laugh rang out. "Both my kids are named for me. When Connie and I were expecting the girl—well, we weren't expecting a girl, if that makes sense. I named the baby for me the minute I knew it was coming. Connie was equally determined to name it for her father. When it turned out to be a girl she said, 'Well, name her for yourself, you conceited ass.' So I did. And Joel she is."

Elizabeth thought of the name and of the girl she had met that morning. "It fits her, I think. She seems an interesting person and I hope that we'll get to know her better."

Once more a frown crossed Kinsman's face. "Not much for church, our girl isn't. Nor any of the things we're interested in. Sometimes I worry about her and that crowd she runs around with. Atlanta folks mostly and I don't know anything about them. Couldn't figure out why she came along to church this morning. I suggested it, but usually she just laughs at me."

Elizabeth, deciding that Joel Kinsman was an unfortunate subject, was searching her mind for something different to talk about when Paula asked the question which Steve and Elizabeth were to hear many times during the next month.

"And how do you like the town of Kinsman?"

Elizabeth smiled. "We only came last night," she reminded her hostess.

"We haven't really seen it yet," Steve answered. "The church is a gem in every way, however, and the parsonage is comfortable and attractive."

Kinsman beamed.

"That parsonage," Elizabeth closed her eyes and sighed ecstatically. "All new. And convenient. I had to keep going over it last night to convince myself. Such things just don't come in parsonages."

"Modern," J.G. said proudly. "The best of everything, like the factory and the town. I didn't name the town for myself, as some people think. Named it for my grandfather who was born here when it was called Bitter Creek. I have often thought grandfather must have been some sort of war profiteer. Anyhow he had enough money left over after the Civil War to build a factory and buy machinery. He founded the first Kinsman Textile Mills right here in 1865."

His guests murmured their interest and he went on. "He wanted my father to go in with him but Papa was set on being a minister. Grandfather never forgave him, only son and all that. But I was interested in the mills and the old man sent me to college to study textiles. Just as I graduated, Grandfather died and pretty soon after that the depression came along. I didn't know enough to keep things going even if there had been a way. I went North when things were at rock bottom, invested what he had left me and— Do you know what is happening now to textile mills in New England?"

Steve and Elizabeth shook their heads, each of them feeling that it was tactless to come to dinner with Kinsman without knowing all about his business. Paula sighed, gave a little shrug and murmured with humorous resignation, "Here we go again!"

"Going to the dogs, that's what. Half an eye can see that the New England buildings are ancient, the machines outmoded, taxes and labor too high, production too low. Guess I can't claim all the credit for thinking of the South, born here as I was, but I was one of the first. I began buying up land in Bitter Creek Valley twelve years ago, put up my first building the next year. Ten years ago things began to hum. I brought a city planner in. No two houses alike. Parks. Swimming pools. Golf course. Recreation Hall. You'll see it."

Steve nodded. "I have already seen some of it. When I was in college there was a field trip in one of my sociology courses to show us what an ideal mill town was like. Kinsman was chosen, naturally. But I didn't realize then that it was quite so new. Only twelve years and you've accomplished so much!" He was filled with honest admiration.

Both boys were looking at Steve with wide, accusing eyes. It was Bobby who spoke. "But Uncle Steve, you've told a whopper. You *said* you hadn't ever seen this town. Just a little while ago you said it."

Steve chuckled. "I meant *this* time, son. You ask Mr.
Kinsman. I'm pretty sure he'll tell you that seeing as
fast growing a town as this one two years ago wasn't
really seeing it at all."

"That's right," Kinsman agreed, flattered. "Two new
factory buildings, more houses. The Recreation Hall.
The church. Your uncle's right that he never really saw
the place, Bobby. And the money it's cost." He stopped
to whistle. "Still, the move has paid me, or will once I
get to where I don't have to put every single penny back
into the investment."

"You sound as if the South might be in for some long-
delayed prosperity, sir," Steve suggested. He was excited at the thought of his own world with money in
its pockets.

"It is! It can't miss. Contrast production in New England and here. A hand won't operate but two looms
there. Why should he? His daddy didn't. Nor his grand-
daddy. Here he'll take three or even four and pride himself on being able to handle more than the other fellow.
On an average, labor costs thirty cents an hour less here.
I'm getting my cloth on the market twelve cents a yard
cheaper than before. All my machinery is practically
brand spanking new. The buildings are new, full of
windows from ceiling to floor, and one story. They are
air-conditioned. Pretty different from the old ones, any
way you look at it." He seemed to have forgotten the
food cooling on his plate.

Elizabeth was thoughtful. "I suppose the better living conditions offset the difference in wages."

The mill owner leaned toward her, emphasizing his
words with thrusts from his fork. "That's not the point,

Mrs. Marsden. Everything's cheaper here. The wages don't need to be as high. We have carefully scaled them to living costs." He turned to his dinner with reluctance.

"You like music, Mrs. Marsden?" Paula asked, her face lighting momentarily.

"Very much. The music in the church this morning actually raised goose pimples on me, it was so wonderful," Elizabeth answered. "Unfortunately I'm just a listener. I took piano lessons when I was a little girl but I hated to practice and never seemed to get anywhere with them. It was so much easier just to listen to the radio."

Kinsman's proud laugh sounded again. "I guess I ruined the career of a promising young radio star—or opera, maybe. Paula was studying voice when I came up to New York to buy the machinery for the first factory here. And I couldn't come back without her. Just stuck right to that same spot until she married me three weeks later. I usually get what I go after, don't I, hon?"

Paula smiled a smile which never quite reached her eyes. "You're very dynamic, J.G. And I was just a kid who *hoped* to become a professional singer."

Steve had been watching her still face. "You must be in great demand around here, Mrs. Kinsman. We have very few real voices in this section of Georgia."

She was so like Claire, he thought, yet like her shadow —her hair silver blond instead of yellow, her eyes gray instead of blue, even the small show of animation which had come with her first mention of music dimmed now. He remembered, on that night when they had quarreled so bitterly, that Claire had mentioned a sister who had married for money. If this was what would have happened to Claire, he was glad, very glad, that she had thrown her marriage off.

"No," Paula Kinsman answered him. "I rarely sing now."

"It's hard to keep up a thing like that when you've got a family and a house to see to," Elizabeth suggested easily. "Does your sister sing?"

Paula shook her head in silence.

Kinsman was grinning. "You know, that Claire's a smooth one. I had forgotten until this morning that she'd known you folks before. I remember now that she talked me into offering Elliott here a job the year she finished college. Something in the line of—of—"

"Personnel," Steve completed the sentence gravely. "I turned it down. She hadn't told me you were her brother-in-law."

"M-m-m," Kinsman agreed. "Made me promise I wouldn't tell you. She said you were just the one for the job. I thought maybe—but I guess not. She married Winthrop about that time, and you went on into the ministry."

"Yes," Steve answered briefly. His face felt stiff, as if it were made of steel wool. He could sense Elizabeth's eyes on him, and Paula's, and he longed to be hidden where no curiosity could touch him. He had spent much of the last two hours forcing Claire from his mind, had not allowed himself to wonder how many times she had sat at this table, had kept himself from asking questions about her. Yet now that Kinsman had mentioned her, he wanted to shout a demand that he "shut up."

But Kinsman went on talking. "Way she acted, I could have sworn she was gone on you. Just goes to show how little I understand women. All the time, right under my nose there was that fellow Winthrop and her acting indifferent. Never saw a man crazier about a woman. Reckon he still is. He wrote me, after she left him, that she was to have anything she wanted." He shook his head, puzzled. "I always heard you could treat a woman *too* good."

Both Paula and Elizabeth started to speak at once. It was Elizabeth who got the words out first. "Mrs. Winthrop doesn't live with you?"

"Oh, no," Paula hastened to say before her husband could break in with something even more tactless. "She hasn't since she married, and before that she was usually away at school. She was in Florida for her divorce and then she rented a place until her own house here was finished. She's taken such an interest in that house, keeping the road between here and Atlanta hot to make sure that she had the exactly right thing for every corner. She hasn't even let me see it inside. Wanted it to be complete before anyone could comment."

Kinsman looked at his wife in astonishment. He had never known her to make such a long speech.

"What fun it must be," Elizabeth said, "to do a house from start to finish, just the way you'd want it. I suspect it's really every woman's dream."

"Perhaps," Paula assented indifferently.

"What beats me," Kinsman went on insistently in spite of the fact that the others tried to divert him, "is how she fooled me again. 'I hear that young man in Augusta is young, a good preacher, ambitious. Sounds just your sort, J.G.' She said it like she didn't even remember your name and didn't give a hoot what I did about it. Sly. Twisting me around her pretty finger."

He sat there smiling, rather flattered at being duped by an attractive woman.

Steve's throat closed so that he could not swallow the pie in his mouth. It was one thing to have J. G. Kinsman come and hear him preach; another to owe this enviable appointment to a woman who had scorned and humiliated him.

Paula moved her head languidly until her eyes met her husband's. "Mr. Elliott and Claire were college friends, J.G. So naturally she'd want to interest you in a man who would do well in Kinsman, one whom you'd like. And she knew that the indirect approach always works better with you." She smiled to show that the comment was affectionate.

Steve did not hear any of this. He felt sick and swallowed the piece of pie with difficulty, looking with distaste at that which remained on his plate.

"We goin' to sit here all day talkin'?" Kinny inquired with an injured air.

Steve, Elizabeth, and Paula sighed. Kinny had voiced a thought they all had shared.

Kinsman rose and put his napkin down beside his plate. "I know how things are with a preacher on Sunday," he said, linking his arm through Steve's as they left the dining room. "You've already had two services and got another coming up tonight. If you're tired, and would like to eat and run, we'll understand why."

Paula was shocked. "J.G., you sound—really inhospitable."

Kinsman laughed and shook his head. "Best kind of hospitality, understanding that a man's got work to do and might like to rest first. You folks know you'd be welcome to stay. We'd be glad to have you."

Steve nodded. "It's most kind of you. Preaching's exhausting business, especially a first sermon at a new charge. It's nearly three o'clock, and, if we may, I think we'll take you up on our going now."

Paula was still embarrassed at her husband's unconventional behavior. "At least let Bobby stay. We'll bring him home late this afternoon."

And Kinsman offered, "I'll call the chauffeur. He'll drive you over to the parsonage."

In the car Elizabeth and Steve sat in replete silence. After a while she spoke softly as if to herself. "I don't believe she's really happy."

"Of course she's not," Steve answered with unexpected violence. "Divorced. Her whole life—"

Elizabeth broke in with the complete disgust which one can feel only toward a loved one. "I was speaking of Mrs. Kinsman—Paula, I think her name is."

CHAPTER III

THE NEXT two days passed with a rising tension. On his return from the Kinsmans, Steve had difficulty reviewing his evening sermon. Claire in a bewitching yellow hat with softly smiling lips and earnest, rather unhappy eyes, kept floating between him and his carefully prepared outline. Yet she was not present among the sparse congregation that night—nor were any of the Kinsmans.

Monday, which he usually set aside for golf, fishing, or some other purely personal recreation, he spent helping Elizabeth get settled in the new parsonage. But neither his mind nor his heart was in the job. Before noon he had smashed a forefinger with a hammer, dropped a leatherbound, first edition into a damp pile of trash, soiling several pages beyond repair, and dropped a corner of a sectional sofa on his foot. So when, in the middle of a scorching afternoon, he knocked his sister's cherished wedding-present vase from a table and broke it into pieces too small for mending, she burst into tears and turned on him like a fury.

"Get out of here, Stephen Elliott. Go hunt up that woman. Keep on ruining your life over her," she told him fiercely. "But get out of here, acting like a bull in a china shop."

Steve flushed, stood awkwardly a moment, then took a very soiled handkerchief from his work trousers and mopped her wet face.

"I didn't mean to break it, Sis. You're bone tired. Go lie down for awhile. We can finish this room tomorrow. And I'll rustle up something for supper."

By this time she, too, was ashamed of her outburst. She took the handkerchief from him, laughed shakily at its filthiness, and blew her nose on it.

"I'm not a bit tireder than you are," she said. "But I didn't sleep much last night and I worry about you, Steve. You were just beginning to get over her and now she's come back to upset you all over again. I wish she—" She broke off without finishing, but her tone made the wish a dire one.

Steve's lips had grown tight, his eyes blank and distant. "You know, Elizabeth, I have to manage my own life." The words were softly spoken but they might have been said to a stranger.

Elizabeth flared afresh. "If you'd manage like a man! You've mooned about that woman like an adolescent for two years, three really. She doesn't care about you. She showed that. Get over it, Steve."

Steve stared down at the bits of vase scattered about his feet, swallowed an anger which choked him, and spoke evenly. "Her name is Claire Winthrop. I'd just as soon you stopped calling her 'that woman.'"

He had meant to sweep up the vase. Instead he let himself out of the house, banging the screen door behind him.

Maybe he had acted like a teen-ager, he told himself numbly. But he'd had no adolescence to speak of. He'd been interested in athletics in high school, had been intent on keeping his grades high enough to help him get a scholarship to college. There had been little time for girls and his interest in them had risen late. He had gone into the army the week he was graduated, had eyed girls at USO centers wistfully only to have them snatched up by bolder and more experienced fellows. Before he had known it he was in India where he'd remained nearly five years.

He'd come back and entered college, with the widowed Elizabeth and her son not financially dependent on him but with a need of him that was always there. Study had not been easy after the years in the army, there had not been much money, and he had kept an evening job. There had been no girls except an occasional blind date, until that night he had knocked Claire off her feet.

Now he thought resentfully of the past, of Elizabeth

and Bobby. He had had no youth. But if he'd been Casanova and Don Juan rolled into one, he'd still have loved Claire, have loved her truly, not just in passing. Hang it all, Elizabeth always said she didn't care about men because none of them was Bob, that she could never marry as long as her first thought was a comparison in Bob's favor.

"I just don't see them as men, Steve," she had said once. Couldn't she realize that that was how he felt about Claire?

The quarrel did nothing to clear the air. Steve and Elizabeth were all the more unhappy because they never got on one another's nerves, hadn't since they were children. The night was hot and there was no breeze stirring. The sheets, even the air which closed in on them, seemed to scorch and sting.

Elizabeth tossed on her twin bed and listened to her son's even breathing from the other. Steve lay still and tense on his wide one and hated himself. He even hated Claire who should have given herself and him a little more time that other hot early summer.

Tuesday morning he sat in his study going over the church roll with a map of the town in his hand, arranging the nearly three hundred members according to neighborhoods to facilitate his calling on them. He did not complete the task. His mind was all thumbs. His breath seemed to stick in his lungs.

By two in the afternoon the study in the church had begun to give him claustrophobia. He washed his face in cold water and ran a paper towel about his damp neck inside the collar of his open sports shirt. He decided against putting on his linen coat until he was at the door of his parishioners, took a map and a list of housebound members which his secretary gave him. Talking to the sick would take his mind away from the evening before him.

Steve halted in the cloisters which ran between church and educational building to study the town which was still strange to him.

Kinsman lay in a small valley like a broken cup, rounded red hills forming the sides of it. Far below the church, the flats were split by a winding river so sluggish and muddy that only the sun on it made it different to Steve's eyes from the earth which formed its banks. He remembered that the guide, when he had come from college nearly three years before, had told them that the stream here had once been Bitter Creek which joined the Tinsley beyond the valley. But the state, in its eagerness to attract new industry, had built a dam which coursed the bigger stream here to give power to Kinsman Mills.

The river, like railroads in other towns, divided Kinsman into two parts. The factories, rambling one storied, and glass walled, were on the east side, and beyond the houses of the mill hands climbed so that each row of pastel colored, wide-windowed houses peered over the flat roofs of the one below it. Steve's eyes followed the streets which went up and up the hillsides, then remembered that his parish did not lie there with the workers.

He brought his eyes back to look down on Main Street where the company stores, the hotel, the restaurant and the movie house faced the river. From that he followed the road which brought him back to his present surroundings, the church, exclusively small, and ecclesiastically Gothic, set in its own five acres of wooded land. All about it, from the lesser officials who lived below, to J. G. Kinsman himself, whose estate was at the very top, dwelt the members of his congregation. Most of these houses were hidden in trees and behind walls but already he thought of the people within them as his own though he knew almost none personally.

Remembering the directions the church secretary had given him, he moved his eyes from the break in the hills where the river came in to where it went out again. Just above him and three blocks to one side was the Phalen house, and Mrs. Phalen was old, blind, and ailing. He would call there first.

He soon found the address, and as he braked the car he noted that a small, dark girl, loaded with tall bags was climbing up the sidewalk almost even with the Phalen house.

"Nice legs. Proud walk," he said to himself, smiling at his own maleness as he reached for his coat.

"Mr. Elliott, how perfectly divine of you," a pleasant drawl was exclaiming and before Steve could turn and look at her the girl had dumped her bundles in beside him.

Steve hoped she was not aware of his surprise, and his lack of recognition. "U-uh— You didn't think I was going to let you *walk* on a day as hot as this one," he managed to reply.

He didn't know her at all, had no consciousness of ever having seen her before. She had blue-black hair which curled damply about her face, a golden, sun-washed skin as innocent of make-up as a baby's, a pointed, pixieish face with oversized dark eyes, and a miniature though perfectly scaled figure. He itemized each of these facts in a quick sweeping glance but not one of them helped him recognize her.

Steve started the car once more up hill. The girl had been going in that direction and she probably lived somewhere up there, though the plain, faded cotton dress she wore looked more like factory town. He was on the verge of asking her name, saying that he remembered only her face, when she ruined that escape.

"To tell you the honest truth," she was laughing through long, tangled lashes, "I didn't think you saw me at all Sunday. I am ashamed of myself for misjudging you."

"Oh, I remember all the *interesting* faces," he retorted. That at least was the whole truth if he did not mean it to be interpreted with complete honesty. He had been interested only in Claire's face.

"I kept wondering all through the sermon why you hadn't gone on the stage, or into television," she went on when she had wiped her face on her sleeve and taken a deep, relieved breath. "You don't—look like a preacher."

"What is a preacher supposed to look like?" he countered, smiling.

"M-m-m," she considered the question, tilting her head to one side and studying him. "Older. Though I suppose that he has to be young in the beginning."

He nodded. "Is that all?"

"No. Paler, I think. A lean and hungry look like fasting and prayer. And deep, burning eyes."

He laughed aloud. "You're thinking of a Middle Ages monk, aren't you? And by the beard of the prophet, if I were thinner, my sister couldn't hold her head up in public. When I try to marry her off she says that no-

body will have her because all the eligible men think
she starves me to death."

The girl's small-boy chuckle surprised him. "Oh,
you're not fat, but you don't look *wasted.* A minister
ought to look wasted, I always say. He ought to at least
look spiritual. And your sister should stop blaming you
because nobody has married her recently. I think you
look very well fed but as if you exercised it off. How
are you on sleep? A really spiritual man ought to walk
his cell by night, thinking soul-shaking thoughts."

Steve began to wonder if he could ask her where
she lived. He was nearing the top of the hill and she
had not suggested that he turn a corner nor given him
any other clue as to her destination.

Instead he asked another question. "Hollow chest?
And stooping shoulders?"

She grinned. "By all means. A slight tremor of the
hands might help, too. There was a time Sunday morning when I thought your voice wasn't quite steady but
I can't imagine it now. You hadn't stage fright by any
chance, had you?"

"I have had, but not Sunday morning," he said, still
amused. For the moment he had forgotten Claire, and
that his voice had trembled as his eyes met hers.

But now he looked again at the girl beside him. There
was a tear in the sleeve next to his shoulder. Her shoes
were scuffed. There had been nobody so shabby as this
at the morning service, he was sure.

She was looking at him strangely and he could not
tell whether it was in girlish admiration—she did not
seem quite that young—or whether she was poking fun
at him. He decided that it was the latter, not really ridi-
cule but banter.

"I spend my mornings under a sun lamp, since you've found me out," he said. "And to keep my voice in trim I practice my pear-shaped vowels. You won't give me away? Promise?"

She laughed. "You don't *sound* like a preacher, either. The quick come-back is decidedly un-ministerial. You can turn in here, and if you don't mind, all the way around to the back. These," she indicated the bags which she was picking up again with her chin, "are dinner tonight. Jack Baylor has the station wagon on an errand, the boss took the big car to the factory, the lady of the house is at a bridge party with her car, and the little one is in the garage for a repair job. So—"

It was the drive of the Kinsman house they had turned into. Steve opened his mouth, then closed it again without saying anything. He stole a sideways look at the girl. She couldn't be—

Almost before he had come to a stop at the service entrance, she had opened the door and slipped out. With that movement she seemed to have changed her entire personality. The laughter had slipped from her eyes and her voice seemed suddenly distant and formal.

"Thank you, Mr. Elliott. I don't know what I would have done if you hadn't picked me up, sir. It was most kind. Well, back on the job." She hitched the bags higher and disappeared into the kitchen.

Steve took out his handkerchief and mopped his wet face. That was no daughter of J. G. Kinsman, that shabby, small girl. Kinsman was blond and as tall as himself, besides weighing, Steve would judge, more than two hundred pounds. The Kinsmans had white servants but she had not sounded in the least like his conception of a servant girl until right there at the last.

He turned and drove out into the streeet, still per-
plexed. Suddenly a thought struck him. People like the
Kinsmans would not be likely to send their boy to public school with mill hands. She must be some recently
graduated college girl acting as governess to young
Kinny. He grinned as he remembered her baiting him.
She was—cute—as—a—button.

He drew up before the Phalen house a second time
with a smile still hovering about his mouth. He hadn't
thought of Claire once in twenty minutes.

CHAPTER IV

A NEGRO girl in a crisp, white nurse's uniform answered Steve's knock.

"Is Mrs. Phalen in and able to see company?" he asked.
He had not understood that she was ill enough to need
a trained nurse. Her son, Drew, the chemist, had not
told him much about his mother's physical condition.

The girl smiled. "You're the new minister, aren't you?
Come in, sir. She'll be especially glad to see you, though
she loves company, generally."

He followed her through a somewhat formal and old-
fashioned living room to a shady porch, pleasant with
iron and chintz furniture and luxuriant plants. A thin,
white-haired woman lay on a chaise, her head propped
up by a rose-colored pillow, her hands busy with knitting.

"It's a stranger, isn't it?" she asked as he came in the

door, and her voice was young and singularly sweet. "Is it the new preacher, Lucy?"

The girl laughed softly. "The new preacher. Mrs. Phalen, Mr. Elliott."

Steve went to her and took the hand she held out in both of his. "I hope you are feeling very well today."

"Quite comfortable and happy, thank you," she answered. "You're very prompt to come to see an old lady, Mr. Elliott. Won't you sit down? Here, close to the couch. If Lucy has left the book there she was reading just now, put it on the table."

"It's already on the table, Miss Laura," the nurse said softly.

Mrs. Phalen smiled. "It's a game we play, Mr. Elliott. Lucy has been with me five months and I'm still trying to catch her leaving something out of place."

The nurse looked a little embarrassed and moved a dark hand toward an empty black bag surrounded by instruments, medicine, and first aid paraphernalia lying in the middle of the floor. "I'm afraid I've made an awful mess. We don't really keep house like this, Mr. Elliott."

On her knees, she began to repack and to explain. "The express company just delivered it and I—I had been saving every penny I could get my hands on—"

"And could keep from giving away," Mrs. Phalen broke in.

"—ever since I left nursing school to buy it, and I couldn't resist showing it to Miss Laura the minute it came."

Mrs. Phalen smiled at her indulgently. "I wanted to give it to her. She's needed it ever since she came. But she wouldn't have it that way."

The girl shook her neat, capped head. "This is the most important thing I've ever owned. I guess I was silly but I had to buy my 'doctor bag' myself. *You* understand, Miss Laura."

She finished the task and touched the pillows gently to plump them up. "Now if you and Mr. Elliott will excuse me, Miss Laura—"

Mrs. Phalen patted the brown hand. "Never rest a minute!" she accused.

"I was resting when I was reading to you," the girl said, smiling as she withdrew quietly.

Steve sat down by Mrs. Phalen. "This is my first pastoral call," he said.

"That's nice," she replied, turning a bright face toward him, "though I'm not at all surprised. I'm accustomed to being spoiled. Everyone has always been very kind to me."

He picked up the book, *A Man Called Peter*, which had been lying open and face down at his elbow. "I hope I haven't interrupted."

"Books? I love 'em but they're only a substitute for living, after all. I prefer people. And don't get the notion because I have a nurse that you have to whisper and walk on tiptoe. It's a notion of my son, Drew's. A very good notion, since the nurse is Lucy."

"She seems a superior sort of person," Steve said and realized that his words had a stuffy sound.

"She's a miracle," Mrs. Phalen added warmly. "You should hear her read. It's like—she doesn't go in for drama or—they called it 'expression' when I was a girl —but she never mispronounces a word and her voice is—"

"That of an educated and cultured person," Steve offered.

"All of which her family has been for generations, really. Her great grandmother was a slave of the first J. G. Kinsman's, a children's nurse. Lucy tells me that she could read and write, and that she spoke English like the folks in the 'big house.' It was she who urged the second J. G. Kinsman into the ministry. She had two sons of her own. One became a doctor, the other a minister."

"The first Kinsman was not pleased with her influence on his son, if I remember correctly," Steve said.

Mrs. Phalen smiled. "That's what J.G. tells me. But he also says his grandfather admitted that his old nurse taught him to run the original mills with justice and kindness. As I see her, that slave woman was not only a very great lady, but something of a saint. And both her sons held college degrees."

"Lucy's grandfather? That's more than mine did," Steve exclaimed. "He was the doctor, I suppose."

"No. The minister. Like her father, also a college graduate." She paused and went on with her knitting in silence for a bit.

"And Lucy?" Steve prompted. The girl's dignity and poise had interested him and now that he had learned something of her background he was even more curious. All the Negroes he had known belonged to the servant class.

"Lucy received a degree in science from Meharry, and then went into nurse's training. If there had been more money in her family I think she would have studied medicine but she has two brothers."

Steve had been wondering about something else. "Lucy's very attractive. She's not married, or interested in marrying?"

Mrs. Phalen shook her head. "She has a sort of passion for service to her people. She considered settlement house work, thought of being a deaconess in her church but decided against it. The way she explained it to me was that her people have a sort of spiritual perceptiveness that is unequalled. Even when they aren't moral, they manage to live very close to God."

"That's true," Steve agreed, "they have a sort of gift for religion."

"Well, Lucy felt that her service to her people ought to lie in another field. She always speaks of Negroes as a sick people."

"I suppose that's true," Steve said thoughtfully. "I hadn't thought of it just that way. But they certainly have short life spans."

Mrs. Phalen laughed indulgently. "You should get Lucy started on the subject. She'd tell you about the high rate of infant mortality, the ignorance and filth of midwives who deliver them, the deaths of mothers, the prevalence of tuberculosis and social disease."

"But they used to tell us in sociology classes that those weren't specifically Negro problems, that as long as a part of society suffered from them, there would be a constant seepage from the bottom to the top," Steve said.

"Lucy goes and tells white women's clubs just that whenever she can," Mrs. Phalen added.

Steve looked about him questioningly. "But she's nursing here?"

"Yes and no," Mrs. Phalen answered. "She wanted to

work in rural Georgia. She tried to get a job with the state but was unable to. Finally she applied to J.G. He's a good man."

Mrs. Phalen's description surprised Steve. "Good" was not an adjective he would have chosen for the mill owner. He would have thought him rich, successful, egotistical, tactless, even philanthropic, but he would not have said "good."

Laura Phalen seemed to feel his doubt. "Of course he's not like his father, Mr. Elliott. His father was a good man and a spiritual man. But J.G.'s his son and he couldn't escape high morals and a deep sense of social responsibility. When Lucy put it to him he promised her a hospital here, a wing of the one he plans to build next year. It will not only minister to the mill employees but to the countryside, white people and black. Lucy will be head nurse of the colored wing. J.G. will bring a Negro doctor here and there'll be a nursing school for colored girls."

"And Lucy's waiting meantime?" He did not know whether to admire the girl's patience or feel that she was wasting her time.

Mrs. Phalen laughed. "Dear me, no. She lives here and is a slave to all my whims only in the afternoon, for which I pay her a salary. J.G. gave her a car. Mornings she scours the countryside, talking to women, showing them how to live more healthily. That is, except the two mornings she teaches classes in hygiene at the mill. J.G. pays her for that, of course. But she gives it all away."

Neither of them spoke for a bit. Steve pondered a word Mrs. Phalen had used at least twice—spiritual. He had not heard it often, even at theological school;

it was an old-fashioned, out-moded word. He used to
hear it applied to ministers occasionally when he was
very small, and remembered the rest of the words that
went with it, "a truly spiritual man, though he never
had very good appointments." It was a sort of apology,
almost an alibi, as if being spiritual were a reason for
lack of success.

"Have you read Mrs. Marshall's book?" Laura Phalen
asked suddenly.

Steve's eyes went to the volume he still held in his
lap. "Not yet. I have meant to."

"It's a beautiful story," she said. "I hope you will. It
is about a man who walked with God. It seems to me
strange—" She was silent for a moment, then went on
with a different thought. "I suppose that there are no
easy answers about religion. We are so fortunate, so
blessed—and so busy."

"You mean now? In the world today?" She had surprised him deeply.

"But of course. It's such a *good* world." The young,
enthusiastic voice was as out of keeping with the age of
the woman who spoke, as the words were with the world
in which Steve lived every day.

"B-but—" he began, then broke off. Perhaps she was
not conscious of the things which went on about her.
Perhaps she was even—

"I'm no Pollyanna, Stephen. You will not mind my
calling you Stephen, will you? I'm old enough to be
your grandmother. You must be about the age of my
Drew. I didn't say a *perfect* world, I said a *good* world.
Who'd want to live in a perfect world anyhow? Only
the lazy, for there'd be nothing to do." She chuckled
softly, amused at his astonishment.

He made no answer. J. G. Kinsman was good. The world was good. He could see how Mrs. Phalen believed the former but the world had never been so evil, so lost.

"It's like God promised through His Son when He walked on earth. Don't you remember? 'The blind receive their sight, and the lame walk, the lepers are cleansed, and the deaf hear—' In our world, Stephen."

He was frowning. It was a new conception—a good world, his world, now.

"You know that I am blind?" she asked him gently.

"Yes. Someone—told me." He was embarrassed.

"Perhaps that's why I see it so clearly," she went on calmly. "I've always been especially interested in science and in medical discoveries. There's an operation now that could restore my sight if I were younger. Have you seen the work they're doing teaching spastics, legless people and other cripples to walk? Have you read of the new treatment for Hansen's disease? It's a wonderful world!"

"Y-e-s," Stephen agreed doubtfully.

"My parents, and probably your grandparents were slave holders. But doesn't selling a human being horrify you?" she pressed on.

"Yes." This time the word was said with certainty.

"That was nearly a hundred years ago but think about the condition of labor when I was a young woman. If I am tempted to feel that the working man has got too big for his breeches I remember back to fifty years ago. Do you ever estimate the money that's raised each year for the relief of miseries of every kind? It's a *kind* world, Stephen."

This interpretation wasn't easy for Stephen to swal-

low. "But Mrs. Phalen, the corruption in high places,
the moral irregularities, the—"

She laughed at him gently. "How much history have
you read recently? Or biography? Corruption in high
places is not a new thing. Pick any biography of a states-
man, Stephen. Read it for your soul's good. Nor immoral-
ity. It seems to me that you young people today think
you invented sex. And almost any of you believe that
if we could go back to the days of the Puritan— Recently
I read something that is supposed to be historically
authentic. It was about an indentured servant whose
master raped her. He was called on to repent in the
church. She was given ten lashes in the public square
because she had been a fleshly temptation."

"That's horrible," he said.

"It was the best morality of that day," Mrs. Phalen
insisted.

"But—wars. Civilization is going to be destroyed by
wars," he went on, somewhat weakly defending his
stand.

"Perhaps it is," she agreed, "but I don't think so." She
put down her knitting and turned toward him, her face
serene and intent. "Don't you suppose there was fear
like this today when gunpowder was first used for a
war? There's a letter written during the War Between
the States, written somewhere in New England, planning what to do when that part of the world was utterly destroyed by the Southern forces. It was a comfort
to me to read that in a book recently."

"I-I'll think about it," Steve promised, then laughed
self-consciously. "I haven't heard anybody defending
this present world in so long that it seems a totally new
idea to me."

"It's a good world, Stephen, believe me. The very fact that we weigh a better world than anyone ever knew before, against the thought of a still better one promises that."

He ran his hands through his hair, still frowning his doubts. "I hope so."

Mrs. Phalen let him think that over for a little, then spoke again. "I always forget that mentioning blindness embarrasses people who see. And I am about to ask you something else. Would you mind—letting me see you with my fingers? I know your step and the sound of your voice already. I'll always know them."

"Certainly not," he said, leaning forward. But he felt rather ill at ease.

Light as a butterfly's passing, her pointed fingers memorized his broad forehead, high cheek bones, and square, stubborn chin.

"There," she said when she had finished. "Now I have the advantage of you. I know what you look like just as you know me. And in addition I can feel your thoughts and tensions as only a blind person can."

Steve straightened and blurted the words which rose in his mind. "You sound as if being blind were one of nature's gifts, like—being musical or being able to write poetry."

She lay there smiling, searching for exactly the words she wanted to express her thought. "It's life that's a gift, Stephen, any life, on any conditions. We aren't usually allowed to ask those fairy godmothers who bring gifts to our christenings for particular ones. But almost anything is a gift if you make it so. I have been blind since I was very small but I don't believe it has been a real handicap. Perhaps if my people had been poor— But my life has been very full, very happy. I think I have had *everything.*"

Steve sat looking at that fulfilled old face, and thinking of his own feeling of emptiness. He had thought her beautiful from the first, with her firm, aristocratic features, her clear skin, and her dark eyes which, even now, he could hardly believe were sightless. More than that, the beauty of contentment and right living marked her. Right now she seemed to glow.

"You are too young ever to have heard of me, but I was a concert violinist when I was young. A good one, I think. After the age when love usually comes to a woman, I married a very wonderful man. I had not expected, had not dared hope for children but I bore two. I lost my husband and my daughter. I have had music, and love, and birth, and death. And I have walked with God. Blindness! It's just an incidental thing, Stephen."

She spoke quietly as if of bread, or clothing, or a roof over one's head. Only her face shone, transfigured with her memories. "And I have walked with God." The words exploded in Steve's mind. People he had known didn't talk like that. Perhaps they did not walk with God. *He* did not know.

"There's Drew now," Mrs. Phalen went on happily. "I hear his car climbing the hill."

"Already!" Steve exclaimed, looking at his watch. "It's after four. I hope I haven't tired you too much. I hadn't dreamed—"

She laughed at him. "I have enjoyed every minute of it. Stay a little longer and speak to Drew. And pray with us before you go."

"I'll be glad to," he said gravely. What he wanted to say was, "Pray for *me*, Mrs. Phalen."

CHAPTER V

ALL OF the town of Kinsman was modern in its architecture, a thing of glass and open spaces, but the small house of Mrs. Collins Winthrop made the rest seem conservative by comparison. Elizabeth was a bit startled by the shut-up look of its entrance even in the dark.

The living room was still more dramatic. Gray and black, pointed with jade, Claire had chosen for her color scheme. The high wall which opened on the back garden was entirely of glass, its curtains of an elephant gray exactly matching the two walls which ran into them. By artificial light the color became mysterious and shadowy and cool. The fourth wall, a gray brick so light as to seem almost white centered a fireplace with a jade-green, free-form figure not distinguishably male or female above it.

Furniture in the room was sparse and of a gray between the light and dark of the walls except for a luxurious divan of black which matched the carpet. Jade cushions and a great jade bowl of white camellias completed the furnishing.

"Claire would!" Elizabeth thought as their hostess came toward them. Then she admitted honestly, "But it is beautiful."

Steve was not conscious of the room, but the same adjective filled his mind. Claire in her favorite yellow, a ballerina length organdie which might have been an evening gown or a simple afternoon dress, was beautiful!

"Elizabeth! Steve!" she was saying in her gay, throbbing voice. "My little house is perfect in my eyes now that you have come to warm it for me."

She slipped a white hand into the elbow of each of them and led them toward the other guests. "Paula and J.G., you know. And Drew Phalen, who is chemist for the mills, tells me he saw you this afternoon when you called on his mother. You met Joel at church Sunday, and—"

Steve found himself looking into the great dark eyes of the girl he had taken to the Kinsman house that afternoon. He supposed that her dress was expensive but it did not suit her nearly so well as the shabby one she had worn earlier. It was the sort Elizabeth called "fussy," hiding slim hips and slender legs. She wore a great deal of make-up and her pointed face looked thin and sharp. There was no welcome, no secret laughter, none of the witchery of her daytime personality about her now. Steve, ready to laugh with her over the joke she had played on him, felt his face stiffen with a smile only half formed.

"Mr. Carleton," Claire was going on with her introductions. "J.G. says he's a brilliant statistician but I wouldn't know about that. I can scarcely add two and two."

Steve noted that Mr. Carleton, a pale, rather nondescript man, rewarded her claim to stupidity about figures with a look of adoration. "Young idiot," he thought in jealous disparagement.

"Mr. and Mrs. Potter," Claire continued. "Mr. Potter is general superintendent of the mills, and if you're very nice to Mrs. Potter, perhaps she will invite you to dinner. She's the best cook in this part of the world."

They were a colorless pair, Steve thought, not quite middle aged but already carrying the mark of it.

At that moment a Negro man and a slim café-au-lait girl appeared with trays, drinks and hors d'oeuvres. Claire touched Steve's elbow lightly.

"The tomato juice is for you, darling. I had thought of tea but I knew you'd want to avoid the appearance of evil."

The touch on his arm, the tenderness in the eyes raised to his, the softly murmured endearment, intoxicated Steve as a cocktail would not have. Talk swirled about him, but he stood with a glass and a small open sandwich in his hand, neither eating nor speaking, only trying to swallow the tightness in his throat.

Claire moved away and stood talking to Elizabeth and Drew. After a moment young Carleton drifted into the group. For a little Steve's eyes had lost Claire and went seeking her. It was Joel Kinsman they found. She looked tiny and lost, and when her eyes met his they seemed inexplicably accusing.

Dinner was gay with Claire sitting between Steve and Drew to see that conversation was general and that everybody took part in it. Only with Joel was she unsuccessful.

"What ails the girl?" Steve asked himself irritably. "She was certainly high spirited enough this afternoon."

But even without her, there was laughter and chaffing about the long, slender table. Steve could not remember when he had had such a pleasant evening. And afterward, as soon as Claire's serving man set out two tables and eight of her guests sat down to canasta, she linked her arm in his and made an announcement to the party at large.

"I haven't really seen Steve since college days and we're going out on the sun porch to catch up on the long years. Robert will see that you have everything you want and I'll bob back and forth every few minutes."

That light-hearted remark angered Steve. All evening he had wanted to be alone with Claire but a contrary mood held him now as she led him across the small music room to the jalousied sun-porch beyond. He could hear only faintly the chatter of those about the card tables and it seemed to him indecorous to have left them. Besides, it was presumptuous of Claire to think she could throw him aside, then, after her marriage failed, pick him up again until something better came along.

But she was not so gay once they were alone. She sank down on a bright-colored wicker love seat and patted the place beside her. He smiled a brief mechanical smile and sat at some distance from her. "You've a beautiful house here," he said, formally.

She turned an almost woe-begone face to him. "You're still angry, still punishing me for the mistake I made, Steve. Or—maybe you're not— It was vain of me, when I found you hadn't married, to think that you might still care for me. You see, I—"

His anger boiled over into speech. It was Elizabeth's words which came almost as she had said them. "So you thought I had mooned about like an adolescent for two years over a woman who had jilted me."

She did not say anything, only sat there looking at him with hurt eyes and trembling mouth.

He went on, no less angry sounding because his voice was low and controlled. "Not satisfied with that, you had to tamper with my work. I suppose you thought if you wheedled one of the best appointments in the conference for me, you could whistle me back until you were tired of me again."

She leaned forward, her face strained and pale. "Oh, Steve, it wasn't like that. You must know it wasn't."

He was hoarse with anger. "I suppose you think it is nothing to let me believe I was chosen to come here because I had done my work well. Only to find you got me the appointment, teasing it out of Kinsman—for some whim of yours—to prove to yourself you could make a fool of me again."

Twice she had opened her mouth to speak, only to close it again. At last, almost as if she did not believe that he would listen, she said, "I thought—that I would be here. And—if you came to Kinsman—in a year I could—You hadn't married anyone else, Steve. I hoped you still thought of me. I couldn't get you out of my mind."

"How could I marry? It would have been—sin, with you always eating away at my heart and mind!" His words were explosive, then he went on more calmly with the sadness of fatality coloring his tone. "I've never thought of marrying, really, except to think I need a wife, that I ought to be married. I've never once thought, 'This woman,' but only that I am lonely and thirty years old."

She lowered her head and turned her face away. Her

voice was thick with feeling. "You should have beaten me that night, Steve, beaten some sense into me."

He clenched his big hands into fists between his knees, his knuckles cracking loudly in the silence about them. After a moment he spoke again. "God knows I was half crazy, even before I knew that—that you had married Winthrop. I prayed. I walked the floor. I didn't sleep. I didn't see how I could go on without you, in the ministry or out of it. I came bursting out of our trailer on my way to you, to tell you that I'd take the job with Kinsman Mills, do whatever you wanted when— It was Elizabeth who told me. She had met a sorority sister of yours down the street who was all excited about the wedding they'd just had in the house parlor."

He stopped and drew a breath that was like a sob. "Oh, Claire, why couldn't you have *waited?*" He beat his hands together. The old pain was there as it had been that first day—stark, unbearable.

There were tears on her face when she turned back to him, but her eyes shone, alight with the knowledge of his love.

"I was a fool—just a fool, Steve. Bruce came to Atlanta on business and called me that morning. He had been wanting to marry me for—I guess two years. I was sort of engaged to him when I met you. I had never really— You hadn't asked me to marry you, Steve, and—" She was stumbling badly.

He turned hurt, horrified eyes on her. "But you knew I loved you. And you loved me. I would swear that you loved me."

She nodded miserably. "I know, Steve." She was silent a moment, her hand reached out to him in a mute plea, then she went on thickly. "I've never talked to anybody, even to you, about how I was brought up. We were poor. Not the kind of poor people talk about who can't afford a new fur coat, but desperately poor. My father went away one day to hunt work. We never knew what became of him. There were four of us already and I was born not long afterward. It was in the middle of that depression J.G. likes to talk about because he rose from its ashes with a cotton mill in each hand." Her words were bitter, her voice unlike he had ever heard it.

Neither of them spoke for a while. Muffled laughter drifted to them from the game in the living room, laughter and gay nonsense which passed over them unheard like familiar noises in the street. Finally Claire spoke again.

"Paula could sing. When I can first remember she was singing with dance bands, anywhere they would pay her a dollar. Mother sewed, or helped out when people had parties, or kept small children. Do you know, Steve, how hard it is for an untrained woman to get work in a community where all the untrained work is done by Negroes? Paula and I both—and I guess the boys too— were never so young that money did not seem the answer to everything. I was seven when Paula got her first radio job. It was like—like finding a wishing carpet. She bought me a new dress. I'd never had a new dress. And shoes. Two years later she won an audition and went to New York. The next year, when she was twenty, she married J.G."

Again they sat silent, Claire evidently lost in her memories, Steve digesting this strange story of her childhood. A car passing in the street backfired. A burst of hilarious accusations rose from the card tables in the room beyond.

"J.G. was thirty-six and—and— If he hadn't been so cock-sure of himself he'd have known it was for his money. Even now I don't blame Paula. Mother was sick. The boys had jobs but they didn't make much. Living in New York was expensive and so were her voice lessons. She was still going hungry unless somebody took her out. I remember how things were even if I was only ten."

She stopped to take a long jagged breath, then went on again. "I don't like J.G. I never have, but I must say this for him. He did everything for us. It was too late for Mother. He had the best doctors, sent her to the hospital, got her a private room, everything. But she died. J.G. sent the boys to school. He sent me to the same one Joel went to. Summers Joel and I went to camp. Vacations all of us came home to that place up on the hill. I had everything money could buy but I was a poor relation. Nobody ever told me so, but J.G. liked to talk about what school cost, what camp cost, what six children cost. You know how he likes to sound off."

Steve could see how it all was, even J.G.'s side of it. "He likes spending money though, likes having it to spend," he told her gently.

"Yes," she agreed unhappily. "But it made me feel— poor, in a way poorer than I had been before. He kept me thinking money was more important than anything. And I'd heard him talk about how poor he'd been as a minister's son."

"His father was a good man," Steve remembered. "He was pastor of the church at home before I was born but they still talked of him. He never had decent appointments. He served circuits and small stations. I guess they never did have any money." Almost unconsciously he rose from his chair and went over and took the place beside her.

She nodded slowly. "I'm not afraid of anything but poverty, Steve, but I'm deathly afraid of that. I still am. That's why I married Bruce without giving myself time to think. I knew that if I didn't put something final in the way I'd give in and— But I wasn't happy. Every time he touched me, I thought of you. I couldn't *be* married to him because he wasn't you." Her blue eyes were dark, remembering.

"I know," he said heavily.

"When J.G. told me that you really were coming here to be pastor I hunted up that little hat you had helped me to select. I had never worn it except that one time we—quarreled so. It made me physically sick to look at it. I started to give it to Paula but I couldn't do that either. So I wrapped it up in tissue and packed it away. Sunday I got it out, and the perfume I used to wear— though I don't suppose a man would remember either of them."

He was smiling. "I did remember it. The hat I mean. It nearly gave me heart failure right in the midst of reading the Scripture Sunday. And the perfume turned my knees to water when you came along after the service. Or maybe it was the way you smiled. Or just your being there."

She moved closer to him so that their shoulders touched. "Oh, Steve, you do love me, don't you?"

She was in his arms then, her hair brushing his cheek and forehead, her lips soft, warm, and ardent under his.

The kiss was long, at first only tender and sad, then hungry and fierce with the thought of the wasted years. It was wonderful to have her there once more, Steve thought, dear and familiar, almost like a part of himself, yet strange and exciting, too.

There was a sweet, silent interlude then. Claire sat with her head on his shoulder. Their hands were clasped. Neither of them spoke. Speech would have broken the spell. It was as if the past two years had never been, as if they were once more in the midst of first love, untroubled, without doubt or flaw. The guests in the next room did not exist. The world was theirs and they were alone in it.

At last Claire sighed deeply. "I won't be so selfish this time, my darling. I'm going to be the best preacher's wife the Methodist church ever heard of. You see if I'm not."

"Claire, I— Oh, God in Heaven, if—" The cry was hopeless.

She drew away from him, her eyes anxious, her face whitening at the look in his. "Steve, what—?"

"You—honey, you're divorced." The words were flat, dead.

"I know. I'm free. Free as I ever was. I'll marry you any day you say. Tomorrow." She was still puzzled, still anxious but she tried to conceal it. The effort wasn't a success.

His eyes were pained, his face drawn. He took her hands once more in his and they were cold like his own even though the night was hot.

"I'm a minister, Claire. A Methodist minister. They won't let me marry a divorced woman. Not and continue my work."

"Oh," she said. It was a cry of pain. They looked at each other aghast.

When she could answer him her voice was full of tears. "I'm sorry I did this to you, darling, but—maybe I wouldn't have made such a good preacher's wife after all. Maybe it'll be better this way. I'll be the wife of whatever sort of work you can get."

"Claire—" He couldn't go on. His thoughts choked him.

She searched his face, her own pitiful and uncertain. "But, Steve, you said that day at school—you were on your way to tell me you would give up the ministry when you learned—"

He shook his head as if to clear it of the chaos of his thinking. "That's it, Claire. I would have given it up, but you were married and beyond my hope. So I went on with my work. Four times in my life I have planned to do something else instead, and every time the road was blocked. I never had a call like a voice from Heaven, even a certainty within me. I doubt, and I flounder, and I sometimes despair. But, Claire, God stops me when I plan to do something else."

She drew a long breath and looked at him unbelievingly. "Steve, you don't really believe that. You can't. It harks back to the dark ages. It's just superstition."

Steve nodded, but his face did not change. "I know it sounds like that, Claire. But I've stood in the pulpit and preached that God has a plan for every man. I believe that. And I believe that he means me for the ministry. Besides there is a Bible teaching about divorce, Claire. About divorce and remarriage. I've been brought up to believe it."

She was as stricken as he. Her careful make-up stood

out in a ghastly mask as she drew away as far as the narrow seat would permit her. "You'd feel, Steve, as if we weren't— Even if you left the ministry and married me, after a while—after the new had worn off—you'd think we were living in sin."

Her feeling went too deep for tears. In that moment he saw what she would look like when she was old. He was trembling as he took her in his arms and hid his face against her shoulder. She sat unmoving, not touching him, her body stiff.

After a while he raised his head. "Claire," he begged, "it's all so sudden, so unexpected. In there a while ago, I wondered if you were interested in Phalen or Carleton. It did not seem to me that you could have loved me all this time. You were out of reach and I— Darling, don't do anything foolish now. Wait. Give me time to get used to— I can't give you up again, but—Claire, *this* time, give me time."

Her look was somber but she reached out her hand and put it in his. "I promise. I don't think it will make any difference, but I promise."

At that moment Paula appeared at the door. "It's been a marvelous party, honey, but it's a little after midnight. Come give out your prizes so we can go home."

Claire rose and was instantly all hostess. She even laughed convincingly. "Once you get to remembering your school days, the time does get away. Sorry I've neglected my guests."

A moment later, she was speaking to the card players, was collecting scores and checking them. Elizabeth's anxious eyes found Steve lurking in the shadowy doorway and grew more anxious as she looked at him.

CHAPTER VI

STEVE was long afterward to think of the next few weeks as the most difficult of his life. A soul-stirring decision hung over him, impairing his work, his appetite, his sleeping, his disposition.

He determined not to see Claire again until he had solved his dilemma but Kinsman was too small a town in which to avoid anyone. On Wednesday evening, demure and reverent, she sat through a prayer meeting. He spent much of the hour wondering if she had ever been to one of these poorly attended services before.

At night he gave himself over to a sort of civil war that tore him two ways. He wondered why it seemed impossible to leave the ministry. He could not remember any definite time when he had decided that he would follow that calling. The idea seemed to have grown in him slowly. He was a good speaker, a good mixer, tactful and efficient in the management of finances. He was serving his fourth charge, if one counted the two he had had while he was still in theological school. In the eyes of the conference, he was very successful. They didn't know, he thought with bitterness, that he owed his job to Claire.

That was not the only reason he was far from sure of that success. The ministry was not like other jobs. Success wasn't just counted in salary and demand—or it ought not to be. As he had never done before, he tried to evaluate now what he was doing. Did he actually bring comfort to those in sorrow? Did he lead the members of his church to a more abundant life? Did he banish fear, strengthen, lead his people to something better?

Was he able to do these things for himself?

He could not answer an unqualified, certain yes to any of these questions.

What, then, was he doing that he could not do equally well in a hundred other professions? Yet, argue as he would with himself, seek as he would to find a really convincing reason for remaining in the ministry and failing, the conviction grew that it was his destiny, that any deviation would be his undoing.

But then there was Claire. Without her his life was meager, colorless. By Friday evening he was so driven by his need of her that he went to her house and found her alone. She led him to a chair on the front terrace where they were in the full view of every passer-by and she did not allow the conversation to turn into any but the most impersonal channels.

Only when he was saying goodnight in the foyer did he take her in his arms and hold her hungrily close to him. He was surprised to find her weeping.

"Oh, Steve, decide something quickly," she begged, her face close against his shoulder. "I can't bear much more of this, I really can't."

His voice was broken. "I know, my darling. I can't either. But there is so much to see to. I have thought of no other way to earn a living. I've got to take care of you somehow. It means our happiness."

Suddenly she was as pleased as a child. "You *do* mean to marry me, Steve. You *love* me. As for money, well, right in the beginning while you're getting started, I have my settlement and—"

His hands gripped her shoulders and he shook her violently. "Claire! You'll have to give it back, every penny. Do you think I'd be able to live on that man's money?"

She looked at him with wide, wondering eyes. "But it's *my* money, Steve. Bruce wanted me to have it. I don't believe he would take it back and anyhow it's my security, my—"

He dropped his hands, rushed out of the door, and was gone into the starless night, not waiting to hear the rest of her defense. Once again he could not sleep but all of his thoughts were concentrated on one side of the argument. He would give her up, have none of her. He would go on with his life in the path which he had chosen, he and Elizabeth and Bobby.

He did not see Claire the next day, but did not think it strange since, for the most part, he kept to his study, polishing his sermons. Nor did she appear on Sunday. All through both services his eyes sought her in the pew where she had been the Sunday before. She was not there. Nor was she elsewhere in the church. On Monday he learned that she had gone away to the mountains and might not be back all summer.

That news made him utterly miserable. Yet it was a relief, too. He would not be seeing her around every corner, in every living room. He had reached his final decision. Now he would put her out of his mind as he had learned to do—had almost learned to do, he corrected himself honestly—before she had come back into his life.

And having so resolved, he found himself thinking of her constantly.

Meantime he drove himself unmercifully. Most of the women of his congregation were away at summer resorts. The heat was breathless and heavy. Night brought no release. The sun-baked air dried sweat before it had time to cool one's body. But the church work continued.

There were the sick to visit. Rarely was there an evening when something was not going on at the church where he was expected to be present: A Sunday School council meeting, a committee planning programs for the next quarter for the Young Adults, the sponsors of the Methodist Young People giving a picnic, a Women's Society affair at which he was expected to lead the devotional. He was coaching a baseball team among the older boys and calling square dances which were held in the church basement on Thursday evenings. He played golf with the men of his congregation, spoke at the Rotary luncheon and accepted its bid to membership.

Also he had a new project at the factory, a family problems clinic. He was working in his office there one day, almost a week after Claire's departure, when there came a knock on the door. Joel Kinsman, her face white and anxious, was framed in the doorway.

"Do you have your car?" she demanded without any greeting.

Steve gave her a startled "Yes."

"One of the children in the day nursery is very ill. I'm taking her to Dr. Mims. She's Opal Hughes. Her father and mother are new here, came last week. Will you go and bring Mrs. Hughes to the doctor's office?"

She didn't wait for his answer but went running down

the hall, taking it for granted that he would do as she asked.

He turned to the files, found that George Hughes lived on Elm Street, just above the flats, and that George and Mattie were both training at Number One Mill. But today was Mrs. Hughes' day off. He closed the files and went out to the car.

Before he climbed the stoop of the yellow, flat-roofed house, a full deep voice singing inside came to him. "When the roll— Is called up yon-der, When the roll— Is called up yon-der, I'll—"

The singing broke off suddenly as he knocked on the blue door and the same voice rang out cordially. "Step inside, do. Door ain't fast."

He turned the knob and looked in on a postage stamp of a living room and through a wide opening to the kitchen beyond. A tall, rawboned woman with a Lincolnesque face stood behind an ironing board set across the doorway, ironing a small blue and white checked apron. Beside her a refrigerator door stood wide open.

"She's sixty if she's a day," Steve found himself thinking. "She must be Opal's grandmother."

Aloud, he said hesitantly, "Mrs. Hughes?"

She shifted the snuff brush from the left corner of her mouth to the right and said, "Yessuh. Mattie Hughes."

"I'm Stephen Elliott, pastor of Kinsman Memorial Methodist Church. I—"

She spat resoundingly into an empty tin bucket, set an electric iron carefully on its end and came out to greet him. She was barefooted but her calloused soles hit the tiled floor as noisily as shoes.

"That's neighborly of you, preacher. Set, won't you?

Course, us Hughes is all Baptists but that don't matter
to us when it comes to keepin' the preacher. I reckon
we done slep' all kinds of preachers in the loft of our
place up the cuntry."

Steve saw that she was about to sit down and with
a householder's uneasy feeling for mounting bills, he
was unable to tear his eyes from the open refrigerator.

"Did you realize that the door was open?" he asked
instead of going on with the message he had come to
bring.

She smiled so that her poor and blackened teeth
showed. "Lawdy, yes. Don't it make ironing a sight
easier? You ask your wife. She'll know. Times when it
was hot like this, I have kep' my sad-irons on a hot stove
and the sweat a-runnin' down me. An' now I jest open
that there door an' stay cool as a cucumber. An' I don't
have to tote water, nor yet draw it out'n a well." She
sighed blissfully.

Steve was still eyeing the open door. "I should think
it would run your electric bill up terribly," he suggested
mildly.

"Hit do?" she asked, wide-eyed. "Well, I never." She
went over and closed it.

"You've a little girl? Opal?" he asked then.

Her face went stark and colorless. Her voice was
harsh. "What ails her?" she demanded, clutching at his
arm.

"She was taken sick at the playground," he told her.
"Miss Kinsman took her to the doctor's office. She asked
me to take you there."

The desolate voice went on. "She hain't dead then?
Not yet?"

"She certainly wasn't when I left. Miss Kinsman only

told me that she was ill," Steve comforted. "I have my car here. Will you come with me?"

She followed his guiding hand, moving like a sleep-walker. Her dark, tragic eyes had sunken further into her head and the long lines from the bridge of her nose to her chin seemed more deeply etched.

"You'll want your shoes?" he asked.

She got them and a shapeless straw hat with faded cotton roses on it. He helped her into the car and she sat there with her long arms tight about her flat, bony chest, and rocked back and forth as if to ease a pain.

"Opal is your own child?" Steve asked, hoping that it might help her to talk.

"My least one. My onliest," she said. "Nine of 'em I left up there by Harmony church up yonder, babies and little 'uns, they was. But Opal—I thought to keep her. She was five." Already she spoke of this least one as if it were sure to go the way of the rest. "Forty-five, I be. Won't be no other'ns." And she began to rock her angular body once more, dry-eyed as fate.

Only once did she speak again before they came to the doctor's office. "Did they tell him?"

"Mr. Hughes? I don't know. He's at work today, isn't he?"

She did not answer the question, but leaned out the car window and spat out brush and snuff as if suddenly it had sickened her. "Set a awful lot of store by the young'un, he done," she said.

A man as lean and weathered as herself was the only occupant of the doctor's waiting-room. He sat on the worn leather davenport, his face buried in his gnarled hands, his sobs dry and raucous in the empty room.

The woman went to him, put her hard hand gently

on his grizzled head. "Don't take on so, George. This is
the last one. We don't never have to bury nary n'other
one." Her words were like dust.

"The doctor—?" Steve asked.

"He's got her in there," the man said. "He's tryin' to
make her breathe but it ain't no use. She's done took."

The door of the inner office opened and Joel came
out looking sick and spent. "Lucy has come," she told
them. "She's better at artificial respiration than I am."

The four of them sat and waited, staring at their
hands, the rug, anywhere except at each other. And
finally the doctor came. He led the father and mother
into the inner room, his voice soft and explanatory, his
eyes full of the tragic impotence of medicine. After a
moment Lucy came from the hall, her black doctor's
bag held against her side as if it comforted her. But her
face was stricken.

"We've got to have that hospital," she said hardly
above a whisper. "We've got to have it soon."

Steve cleared his throat. "She's dead then?"

"Dead," Lucy said. "If we'd had an oxygen tent— Of
course, she had malaria, and hook worm and was under-
nourished. But if we'd had the hospital—"

They were silent for a while, weighing ifs as people
will in the face of tragedy.

Steve, who in his brief ministry had known only the
inevitable deaths from age or disease that came as blessings, prayed that he might say the wise and comfort-
ing thing when he drove the Hugheses back home. But
when they joined him in his car, he might as well have
spared his awkward phrases. No voice could penetrate
the deafness of his passengers now.

CHAPTER VII

STEVE was still in the process of getting the family problems clinic in order when, one morning, Kinsman knocked on the door. Steve turned from the files to greet him.

J.G. looked about the room inquisitively. "Heard it looked like a parlor," he commented.

Steve did not know whether this was a criticism or not, but he felt on the defensive. "People talk with more ease, I think, when a place isn't too much like an office."

J.G. nodded and sat down in one of the comfortable chairs. "And the personnel man says you've got a file on every person employed by the mills," he went on.

"If anybody does come to talk to me, I believe it would be a help to know as much about him as possible," Steve explained.

"Sounds sensible," J.G. agreed. "But what I wanted to see you about wasn't this thing at all. You called a stewards' meeting for tomorrow night. What's it for?"

Steve frowned slightly. He had known when he came to Kinsman Memorial that it was a one-man church, as the town was a one-man town. He was not at all sure that he approved of either. "It was to discuss the barbecue pit the young people would like on the church grounds. They are willing to pay for half of it."

It was J.G.'s turn to frown. "No need of that. Let 'em keep their money. No need of a stewards' meeting

either. I'll think about it and if I decide it's the thing
to do, I'll give it to 'em," he announced crisply.

Steve hunted for words with which to be tactful. "Do
you think that gifts are as good training for young
people as letting them do their part, J.G.? It seems to
me that Christians—and people in general—need training in generosity, in giving. Won't they be prouder of
the recreation grounds if it's part theirs?"

"It isn't," J.G. snapped. "Kinsman Memorial's mine.
I've spent two years building it. Cost me nearly a mil-
lion dollars, every penny of it out of my own pocket.
Looked after every detail myself."

"And you don't think that it would have been better
for the church itself if you'd let them share the responsibility?" Steve pressed his point.

"I do not," the mill owner stated flatly. "No telling
what a mess we would have had on our hands if every
member of the board had expressed his opinion. As it is,
we've got a regular little cathedral, perfect. Do you
know what a salesman tried to fob off on me? Some sort
of gray benches, plain as a wall. Said that it was what
churches were buying these days. I told him to go back
and tell 'em I'd be up there in two weeks to look over
the stock myself, and I was. Sat in pews until I found
the most comfortable ones, told 'em to put red velvet
cushions in 'em and there aren't finer church pews in
America."

Steve merely nodded.

"Pew ends were plain and of oak. I ordered carved
ends, lilies and a cross in a crown. My poor old dad used
to dream of a pew like that, but he never got a church
big enough to afford 'em. Chancel, lectern, pulpit of the
same."

"They're all beautiful," Steve agreed. But he was still thinking about the million dollars all this elegance had cost when there were already two churches in Kinsman. Would not God have been better pleased if the manufacturer had chosen to worship Him by building a hospital where there was none?

"Wanted the stained windows dedicated to the family. I don't know much about art and when I don't know about a thing I hunt for somebody that does. Found a man in New York through the Metropolitan Museum, took him to Tiffany's and we picked 'em out, six of 'em, dedicated to Grandma and Grandpa Kinsman, Papa and Mama, my sister who died when she was a baby, and my brother who died in World War I. Cost fifteen thousand each, but when I see the sun through 'em I think they're almost worth it." He chuckled softly, recalling the violet, blue, yellow, and green that sifted through the church on sunny days. "Colors of sanctity, those windows are."

"I never saw windows so beautiful," Steve said. "Or a more beautiful church."

"That choir is the best double quartette in Georgia," he went on. "Paula picked 'em and they drive out every Sunday for service. I reckon the church itself is small but I don't expect the congregation to grow. Don't encourage the folks from across the river to come. Gave them their own building and all, finished my church just before the conference, got me the best preacher I could find. It's exactly what I want." He chuckled in pleased acknowledgement of his own acumen.

"I see," Steve said, and felt that he was beginning to.

J.G. patted him on the shoulder. "You forget that stewards' meeting, boy. I'll have my secretary call the fellows and tell 'em we don't need to meet after all. And I'll let you know what I decide about the barbecue pit. Sounds like a good idea at the moment."

It was not until Kinsman had gone that Steve was aware of the bitter taste in his mouth. He had been brushed aside as though he were a child of twelve and his ideas of no importance.

"Not God's church, nor my church, nor the church of the membership, but J. G. Kinsman's church in no uncertain terms. 'I'll let you know what I decide,'" he quoted bitterly, and turned again to the mill-workers' files.

But he was not done with the Kinsmans that day, for that afternoon he met Joel on the golf course and went around with her. She played like a demon, her score so much less than his that it could hardly be said that they played together at all. Yet it was not her trouncing him so soundly which angered him. It was because she seemed so formal and distracted. The tragic afternoon they had shared with the Hugheses had in no way removed the barrier she had put up between them. Nor could he laugh with her as he had on the afternoon he picked her up.

She seemed to have closed the door forever on that other and more delightful person, at least in so far as he was concerned. But on several occasions he saw her with people he did not know, about the club house or the course. Then she always seemed to be laughing and full of repartee but *he* could never find that Joel.

He tried. "I'm sorry I didn't recognize you that first afternoon. Truly sorry. But I did think you were fun."

"Thank you," she retorted in a clipped sort of way, addressed herself to her ball, and made a birdie.

He tried a different angle. "You're always the center of a group of people who are laughing and having a wonderful time. They don't live in Kinsman though, do they?"

She said, "no," and swung her bag over her shoulder. She did not seem to want to talk to him about anything, though she had been quite willing to wait for him to bungle his way around the course.

Finally he screwed up his courage to ask about Claire. "She's away. Do you know where?"

The girl's eyes went expressionless and hard. "Hendersonville, perhaps. It's where she usually goes in summer. But Claire's restless. Even if she went there in the beginning, she's probably moved on somewhere else by now."

"You've been friends for a long time, she tells me," he went on.

At first he had thought that she was not going to comment at all. Then she spoke indifferently. "We went to schools together, and camps in summer. Ever since J.G. and Paula were married. Claire's two years older, of course, and that makes a good deal of difference when you're kids."

That would make Joel twenty-two, Steve concluded, subtracting. She seemed younger, somehow, and older, too. Anyhow, not twenty-two.

"You think Claire'll be gone from Kinsman until the cool weather?" he asked then.

Joel shrugged. "Nobody knows, with Claire, not even she. She may be home tomorrow or maybe not until after Christmas."

Tomorrow! Steve's heart quickened. On his ride back to town later, he thought of his loneliness, how empty

Kinsman seemed without Claire, what a fool he had been to get angry with her.

He could scarcely conceal his agitation when he drove by the Kinsman's to pick up Elizabeth and Bobby. And he was doubly upset when he allowed himself to be persuaded to stay for dinner.

That evening was the first time he saw the mysterious box. It had been delivered at the parsonage that afternoon while all of them were out, a plain wooden box, nailed and heavy and unaddressed. On each end was printed Pinadex, Inc., New Orleans, La. and it was sitting just inside the front door when the three of them returned from the Kinsman's. The door was not locked and Steve stumbled over the box when he fumbled for the light as he entered.

"What on earth is this?" he demanded. "Bobby, I have told you a thousand times not to leave things in the way. I'll have to punish you severely if this happens again."

Bobby, already tired and sleepy, burst into tears. "I didn't. I didn't leave anything."

By that time the light was on and Steve was bending over the offending object. Elizabeth came and looked, too.

"That wasn't here when we left," she assured him. "Bobby had nothing to do with it. There wasn't anything here in the entrance when we went out. I know there wasn't."

"Sorry, boy," Steve muttered. By this time he was thoroughly ashamed of himself for yelling at the child. All too often these days he felt he ought to apologize for his behavior.

But the apology did not entirely appease the youngster. He was still sniffling as he turned toward his room.

"You're getting to be more like a father than an uncle," he remarked in disparagement. "Hollerin' and fussin' all the time."

Steve promised himself that he would not be so irritable. "I'd sure like to know where this thing came from," he growled, kicking at it and finding it heavy for its size.

"Somebody'll appear tomorrow and claim it or tell us it's a present of some sort. Just move it out of the middle of the floor for now and leave it there," Elizabeth soothed. "Get some sleep, Steve. You're tired."

He obeyed, stifling an impulse to deny his fatigue in a loud and irritable voice.

But nobody mentioned the box and after a few days Steve began to ask everyone he met, "You didn't leave a box at the parsonage last Monday, did you? A box about so big?"

Nobody had and the crate became the center of all his ill humor. Finally, one noon when he returned, hot and weary, he delayed lunch while he jimmied the box open. He scattered sawdust all over the entrance and came up with two dozen bottles of a thick yellow liquid. "Pinadex," the label stated modestly. "A vitamin-packed, pleasant-tasting tonic for those aches and pains which attack the human race after forty."

"Somebody's idea of being funny," Steve decided, not at all amused. "Bobby, get those things out of here."

"Out where?" the child asked helplessly.

"Anywhere. Just out. And don't whine," Steve ordered, sharply.

Bobby met his look with defiance. "You got to tell me where. If I put 'em some place I think is good, you'll say nobody but an idiot would've put 'em there."

Steve was about to explode when Elizabeth came to

the rescue. "In the garage, Bobby. Take two at a time and be careful not to break any of them. They aren't ours and somebody is sure to be wanting them."

When the little boy had gone and Elizabeth was sweeping up the mess which Steve had made, she spoke to her brother quietly. "He's right, Steve. I've never known you to be like this except—" She broke off sharply, remembering that the cause the other time had been the same as this. "Can't you get away for a few days?"

"How can I? There's something going on at the church every waking minute," he answered glumly.

"Then see Dr. Mims," she advised. "You aren't well. All this irritability isn't like you."

He tried to bottle up his feelings after that but the results were not happy. He was brooding and lonely, remembering Claire as the girl he had pictured to himself during the first months of their going together, someone mobile and sweet whom he could make in his own image.

Then suddenly, one Sunday morning she was in her customary place in church, sitting between Joel and Paula. After the service she moved out with the rest of the congregation, gave him her hand, and her sweetest smile.

"You've been away, Claire," he said hoarsely.

"But I'm back, Steve," she said.

He clenched his teeth until the muscles of his jaws knotted. He was to dine that noon with the Potters. He wondered if she would understand his not rushing to her at once, or if she would think he was still sulking like a child. He hoped she knew why he could say nothing now, with all these people standing about. He had never been one to use casual, light words to her. He could do nothing—not now, not here.

CHAPTER VIII

As STEVE left the church, he had no idea it would be evening before he saw Claire again. Sunday dinner at the Potter's was heavy and long in the serving. Afterward they insisted on taking their guests to inspect Kinsman Dam, and they delivered them back home barely in time for Steve to glance over his sermon outline and wash his face before the evening service.

He had hoped that Claire would be there but she was not, and afterward he walked through the hot, star-filled night to her house. The screened porch where they had sat the last time he had seen her was filled with laughing young people now. He could hear the sound of silver on plate, see the flare of matches lighting cigarettes. Once Claire's voice with the familiar throb which never failed to excite him came to him clearly, one phrase out of what was probably a longer speech.

But he could not join a crowd, could not talk to Claire with all of them there. He turned, sullen and frustrated, and went home.

Monday morning Steve entered the kitchen to find Bobby arrayed in a cowboy suit Paula had brought him from New York. He could hardly be separated from his lariat and pistol long enough to eat breakfast.

"Kinny's got a suit just like this," he announced, "and he's coming over to spend the day."

"That's fine," Steve stood in the doorway with his coat hanging on one finger over his shoulder. "By the way, Sis, I'm going to that preacher's meeting in Dalton today. Anything I can bring you when I return?"

"I don't think of anything just now. Will you be back for lunch?"

"I—doubt it. Probably eat with some of the fellows. The meeting will last until noon, I imagine."

She smiled at him. "All right. I'll look for you when I see you. Have a good time."

Steve hurried to the church and called Claire who answered sleepily.

"Claire, I must see you," he began earnestly.

"Of course you must, darling. Have lunch with me," she answered indulgently.

"I've got to go out of town, Claire. Probably won't be back before three. May I come at once, now?" he went on urgently.

She laughed. "You're very flattering, Steve, but you waked me, you know. In an hour, if you insist."

"An hour!" he repeated aghast. "Claire, I have to be in Dalton in an hour and ten minutes."

"Oh," she said, then after a moment, "Steve, I'm a bear until I've had coffee. And of course you can't come into the house of a woman who lives alone until she's clothed and in her right mind. Come when you get back instead."

"You aren't punishing me, Claire? Because I rushed away like that?"

She chuckled. "I'm not exactly pleased with you. You made me pretty unhappy, you know."

He whistled. "And how I know! See you at three, then. And I love you."

Steve had always enjoyed preachers' meetings. His parish work was largely with women and this break, this talk among men whose problems were much the same as his, was stimulating.

But this morning his mind was not on the meeting, the reports, the discussions. His eyes wandered to a beautiful old face with the look of a saint. Brother Fraser was a *spiritual* man, he thought, harking back to his first talk with Mrs. Phalen. Perhaps he himself could never be one even if he stayed in— He broke off, unwilling to give the thought actual words. He hadn't fully made up his mind, had he? And in the ministry—he had not found real satisfaction there. He was empty, unsatisfied. His work had not brought him the deep joy he had expected. He had begun to believe that he had nothing to give his congregation. Yet the thought of leaving the ministry tore at him, left him desolate.

The meeting was interminable. It was almost one when they were dismissed, and Steve turned down several invitations for lunch so he could hurry back to Kinsman.

There was a car in the driveway of the parsonage when he arrived, a black convertible which seemed vaguely familiar. He braked his car with such suddenness that his neck jerked painfully. Then he heard the back door slam and turned toward it.

Drew Phalen emerged from the garage. There was a small, limp figure in black cowboy jeans in his arms and Phalen walked carefully so as not to jar it.

"Bobby—" He tried to cry out to Phalen, to ask questions, to demand facts. No sound came. His throat was tight and throbbing. His ears seemed full and he turned dizzy.

Then he was taking great strides across the lawn to open the back door for Phalen, to stand there with agonized questions in his eyes.

But it was not Bobby. It was Kinny, his eyes half open with the pupils rolled back, his lips pale and his skin blue, his hair wet with a dank sweat. Steve took a long ragged breath and asked the question that had been pushing at his lips from the first.

"What happened?"

Drew shook his head and turned toward Elizabeth's room. "They were vomiting when I turned in and before I could get to them Bobby had passed out. I called Mrs. Marsden and she has her boy already in the house."

Steve's heart lurched. Bobby, too. Bobby who had never been sick. Kinny looked like death.

He swallowed before he could speak. "Feel pretty rotten, don't you, fellow?" he asked with a false joviality.

The child made no answer.

Drew Phalen turned sideways to ease his burden through the doorway, pushing the door back with one foot. "He's not conscious, Elliott. They're both—like this." The voice was calm but forebodingly serious. He laid the boy on Elizabeth's bed, straightening the thin legs gently.

Beyond, Elizabeth was wringing out a towel in icy water and putting it on Bobby's forehead. Then she took a second and repeated the process for Kinny. She seemed quiet and efficient but there was a small twitching in her cheek and her face was white.

Elizabeth did not appear in the least surprised to see him there. She turned to him with a calm authority. "We don't know yet, Steve. Go call Mrs. Kinsman. Tell her Kinny is ill. And ask her what doctor she has."

She moved back and forth, touching cheeks and small wrists.

Steve made no move, but stood there looking at the two still figures, listening to heavy, almost raucous breathing. He had never been so frightened. His hands were cold, his whole body numb. He was remembering Bobby as he had been that morning, excited about the coming of Kinny. He hadn't been decent to Bobby of late. He—

"Yes, of course," he answered in a voice not recognizably his own.

"There's only one doctor in Kinsman," Drew was directing. "Mims at 8720. Maybe you'd better call him first."

Behind Steve, as he moved toward the phone, he could hear Elizabeth asking Drew to bring more ice. His fingers were slow and fumbling on the dial but after a moment he heard the drawl of Florence Colter, the office nurse.

"Dr. Mims' office."

"It's Stephen Elliott, Miss Colter. Bobby's quite sick. And the Kinsman boy who was here playing with him. Can Dr. Mims come at once?"

The voice was regretful. "He's out on a call, Mr. Elliott. Are the boys vomiting?"

"They have been," he answered, not surprised at her omniscience. "They fainted and they're still unconscious, breathing very heavily."

"Yes. They're all like that. I'll try to get Doctor for you as soon as I can," she promised. "Meanwhile put ice caps on their heads and keep them as quiet as possible."

"They're quiet enough," Steve told her despairingly.

He had dreaded calling Mrs. Kinsman but he was
equally disturbed when no one answered the ringing.
After what seemed a very long time, a rather crisp voice
announced, "Joel Kinsman. May I take a message? The
servants seem to be off the job for the moment."

"It's about Kinny, Joel," Steve explained. "You know
he's spending the day with Bobby. Well, they're both
ill—"

"Paula's in Atlanta for the day," she broke in. "I'll be
there as soon as the car'll bring me. And don't worry
too much. Kids can seem pretty sick one minute and be
perfectly O.K. the next day."

He turned away from the phone comforted by the
warmth of those encouraging words. Joel Kinsman was a
strange person, never twice the same, he thought.

Back in the bedroom Drew was replacing the ice
wrapped in towels. There were no icecaps in the parsonage. Elizabeth had brought warm soapy water and
was washing the boys' dirty faces. Steve went in and began to take off their boots and blue jeans.

The doorbell rang after a little and he hurried to answer it, leaving Drew to ease the boys into pajamas.
It was Joel, serious, yet somehow cheerful. Without
make-up and in blue denim shorts and weskit, she
seemed more like the girl he had first met.

The next hours were dim—unnatural. Drew Phalen
and Joel remained, doing with amazing skill the hundreds of small services which Elizabeth suggested. Steve,
too, took her orders, his hands and feet seeming not like
his own, his joints stiff and unwilling.

At length Dr. Mims arrived, his round face as placid
as if this call were not a matter of life and death.

"Quite a little epidemic you're having in the neighbor-hood," he commented as Steve led him and his bag to the bedroom.

"Epi-demic?" Steve echoed.

"M-m-m. Florence said vomiting, then unconscious-ness."

"Yes," Steve corroborated.

"Seven cases in a boundary of four blocks," he re-ported. "Can't get a word out of the boys. They're all asleep. Mothers don't know anything."

"Seven cases!" Steve repeated. His face whitened as he asked, "Doctor—could they have gotten hold of some poison?"

"Doubt it," Dr. Mims replied. "I've got another theory but don't want to make a statement until I'm sure. Whichever it is, vomiting is the best treatment for the trouble and they took care of that themselves."

In the bedroom he put his bag on a straight chair and looked about him. "Clear out of here, all of you, except Mrs. Marsden. They're just like the others and I have five of them sleeping naturally. Nothing serious enough to worry about."

Steve, Drew, and Joel found themselves in the kitchen, sitting about on gay, colored stools, their eyes vacant and wandering. Drew lighted his pipe then let it go out, and sat nervously chewing on it.

"I still don't understand," Joel began.

"Nobody does," Steve answered. "Phalen, how did you get into this?"

Drew had to think a minute before he could remem-ber. "I was bringing Mrs. Marsden a book Mother prom-ised to lend her and as I was driving up I saw that both kids were being pretty sick outside the garage. I came into the drive and asked them what was the trouble. Neither of them answered and about that time young Bobby folded."

Elizabeth came in then to take away a kettle of water. In answer to their queries she shook her head. "We don't really know anything. Dr. Mims thinks they're going to be all right but he's washing out their stomachs just to be sure."

More time crept by. The doctor was about to leave when Paula arrived. Tears were running down her cheeks and she staggered as she got out of the car.

"How is he? Is my baby all right? I shouldn't have left him. I—" She was near to hysterics.

Joel went to her and put her arms about her. "There. It's not that bad."

And Dr. Mims offered gruff comfort. "He's really all right, ma'am. It's nothing too serious. He's asleep but I think you can take him home in your car. Mrs. Marsden will let us have a pillow and a blanket."

It was dark by the time they had gone and the house was quiet. Drew Phalen made no move to go, but sat on, smoking in silence. At last they heard the bedroom door close softly, and in a moment Elizabeth, who had been so calm and self possessed, was standing in the kitchen door weeping with abandon.

"He's g-going to b-be all right," she sobbed.

It was Drew who was nearest the door, Drew who held her against his shoulder, who patted her back and murmured comfort.

At that moment the phone rang shrilly and Steve tiptoed down the hall to answer it.

"Darling, why didn't you call me? Or let me know

some way? Maybe I could have helped." It was Claire's voice, sympathetic and anxious. "Is Bobby all right? Kinny seems to be."

"Sleeping quite naturally, Elizabeth says. Snoring, I calls it, since I'm not a doting parent," Steve reported. "It's been very hard on her, of course. And Claire, I'm ashamed not to have gotten over. I—"

"Forgot about it, as you should have under the circumstances," she assured him. "I was sitting here blazing mad at you, I admit, but you had a reason, not just an excuse."

"But when—" Steve began.

She did not let him finish that sentence either. "Tomorrow night, Steve. I'm going to be frightfully busy all day. Good-night, dear."

CHAPTER IX

DREW left the laboratory at the factory early for lunch the next day, intending to stop by at the parsonage.

Steve met him at the door and answered his inquiry with a grin. "Much better. Come and see."

They found Bobby sitting up in bed, propped against a nest of pillows, working on a jigsaw puzzle and complaining between the placement of each piece because his mother was insistent that he remain where he was.

"Besides, it's too hot," he was saying as the two men came down the hall.

Drew poked his head in at the door and greeted the invalid.

"Hi, Mr. Phalen," Bobby returned, smiling delightedly so that two over-large front teeth dominated his small face. "Don't you think it'd be all right for me to get up now?"

Drew considered the question gravely. "That depends on what your mother and Dr. Mims say about it, I should think."

The smile did not entirely disappear but Master Marsden was quite disgusted. "Aw geezil! Grown folks always stick up for each other."

The boy was, Drew thought, still somewhat pale with blue shadows under his eyes and a white line about his mouth.

"How are you feeling now we've settled the getting-up business?" he asked, covering a very real anxiety.

Bobby screwed up his face, thinking that over. "O.K., I guess. Only it hurts my head if I move it too quick."

Drew winked at Steve. "Sounds like an old-fashioned hangover to me."

Steve nodded, amused. "Uncommonly."

At that moment Elizabeth bustled in with a loaded tray. Drew took it from her and she and Steve began to clear away the lapboard on which the half-completed picture lay.

"Don't spill it, Uncle Steve. Don't even tilt it. If you don't keep it level, all of it will get messed up and I've worked so hard. What's to eat, Mom?"

Elizabeth snapped out legs to the tray and took it from Drew. "Milk toast, Sonny. And jello."

Bobby eyed the tray being laid across his knees without pleasure. "Aw, geezil. Sick stuff."

Elizabeth ignored that remark and straightened up, facing Drew with earnest eyes. "I don't remember thanking you for all you did yesterday. You were wonderful through the whole thing, even to letting me weep all over you."

Drew smiled at her. "Any time," he offered.

She laughed at that. "I promise it won't happen again. I don't cry once a year."

"One of the things I stopped by for was to ask if you thought young Hopalong could eat ice cream if I brought it when I came from work this afternoon." Drew let himself down into a chair on the far side of the bed as if he meant to remain a while.

Elizabeth seated herself, folded her hands in her lap and took a deep, weary breath. "I should think so. If it were vanilla."

"How would that suit you, boy?" Drew asked the small patient, now very occupied with the food which he had scorned a moment before.

"Swell. I'd like it swell if there was a heap of it," Bobby replied, licking milk from his upper lip with a long, pointed tongue. "You know, some ways, bein' sick ain't so bad. Uncle Steve gave me that puzzle I was doin', an' Mom gave me two horse books, an' now ice cream. An' Uncle Steve ain't mad at me any more an'—"

Elizabeth's color had risen a little. "Bobby, I don't know whether to reprove your grammar, your greediness, or your giving away family secrets."

"But I was pretty sick, though," the child went on as though she had not spoken, his eyes fixed dreamily on the rosy jello which danced on his spoon before it disappeared into his wide mouth.

"Just what happened to you and Kinny before I came

along yesterday?" Drew asked casually, taking his pipe
from his pocket, filling it, tamping it carefully, then
lighting it.

The little boy's face became secretive, and his piping voice was evasive. "We were just playing."

"Cowboys?" Drew prompted.

"Yep. Mom, I'm through with this and I'm still hungry. Isn't there a choc-late bar in the refrigerator?"

Elizabeth rose and took the tray from him. "Dr. Mims
said this was all for now. You get a cold drink at two
o'clock."

"That's two hours off?"

"Yes," she agreed, turning toward the kitchen.

"W-e-l-l," he submitted to the inevitable reluctantly,
then brightened. "Mr. Phalen would you like to read me
some out of my horse book?"

"I'd rather you told me a little more about yesterday,"
Drew countered.

"And I'll read to you when Mr. Phalen goes back to
the factory," Steve promised. He too was curious about
what had happened yesterday.

"W-e-l-l," Bobby said, "we had on our cowboy suits
and we were playing saloon. Like in the movies, you
know, only no girl stuff."

"Saloon!" Steve echoed. Kinny and no telling how
many other small fry of his congregation had been a
part of the game. It wasn't, he thought wryly, a game
in which the minister's nephew should have been involved. Nor was the parsonage garage exactly the place
for it.

"Yep," Bobby went on more freely now that he was
launched on his story. "You know that long bench that
you pile stuff on? The one against the back wall? We

pulled it out and played takin' drinks, puttin' our boots on that piece of board runs along the side the way they do."

"And what were you drinking?" Steve inquired, holding himself to a calm he was far from feeling.

"Well, at first, before we had lunch, it was water. There were some glasses out there in a basket, ones used to have cheese in 'em. We drank out of those. But after we ate, Mom said she didn't want us traipsin' in and out the kitchen, and then Sammy Shields and Butch Wylie and some other kids came over and they said 'What are you playin'?' an' we told 'em an' 'en we told 'em why we quit an'—" Suddenly the easy flow of words came to a halt and he eyed his uncle in uneasy silence.

"And what?" Steve prompted.

Bobby looked away, swallowed manfully, and finally brought his glance back to Steve. "You won't be mad? I been pretty sick, you know."

Steve barely repressed a smile. "No. I promise."

"Well, you remember those bottles?"

Steve didn't. "Bottles?" he repeated.

"M-m-m. Those you got so mad about because they were left in our front hall an' you couldn't find out who left 'em or nothin'. An' you wouldn't tell me where to put 'em an' Mom said the garage an' be careful not to break any for somebody would be sure to claim 'em. Those bottles."

"Oh!" Steve recalled the whole matter. "Pine—pine, something, I think."

"Pinadex," Bobby supplied loftily. "Only Mom was wrong. Nobody did claim 'em. There they were high on the shelf where I'd put 'em like Mom told me, an' Butch pointed at where they were and said, 'What's them?' an' I said, 'I dunno. Don't anybody know.' "

Bobby stopped and looked all about him as he approached the climax of his tale. "An' Butch said, 'Looks like good likker.' "

Steve did not know whether to laugh or groan. He turned a rueful face to Drew and shook his head.

"You *said* you wouldn't be mad, Uncle Steve. You promised!" Bobby re-emphasized, then receiving Steve's nod, went on with fresh relish. "Well, we took down one of the bottles and I got an opener out of the kitchen. Mom hadn't said I wasn't to get can openers, only water. And we opened it and smelled it all 'round."

Once more the boy paused for dramatic effect, then took up the story once more. "It smelled all right, so I went back of that bench place and poured some in a glass and drank it right down, like cowboys do." He lifted a hand as if there were a glass in it and snapped his head back sharply, then moaned, "I reckon my head don't feel so good."

Drew took his pipe from his mouth. There was a glint of a smile about his eyes. "And how did it taste," he asked.

"It was all right. It made my tongue feel sort of funny but it tasted all right. Sort of sweet and like pineapple juice Mom uses in punch for the Women's Society, but sort of funny, too."

Drew leaned back in his chair, put his pipe into his mouth and pulled on it. He grinned as he waited for the inevitable end of the story, but Steve wore a rather grim look.

"Does you're not being mad mean I don't get punished, Uncle Steve?" Bobby interrupted himself to ask somewhat anxiously.

Steve continued to look grave. He took the rearing of his sister's son very seriously. "Do you think you deserve to be punished?" he asked.

Bobby squirmed against the pillows. "Makin' me say is worse'n a spanking, Uncle Steve. Seems like I ought not to have to decide." Then, under his uncle's unrelenting eye, he went on slowly. "I reckon I took something that wasn't mine. Only nobody did claim it, Uncle Steve. But I knew it wasn't mine, sir." The formality of that "sir" was an acknowledgement of the seriousness of the occasion.

Steve nodded. "As long as you know that it seems to me you've already had your punishment."

Bobby opened his eyes as wide as he could. "You mean God—made me sick because I drank that stuff that wasn't mine, Uncle Steve?"

That took some thinking over. "N-no," Steve decided finally. "Not exactly. It's more like this. When we break one of God's laws, the likelihood is we suffer for it."

Bobby looked very solemn, then said, "I guess I don't understand that. What's laws, Uncle Steve?"

"There was, I'm pretty sure, alcohol in that Pin—Pinadex. You drink it—it really *is* like your Butch's likker, Bobby— You drink much of it, it makes you sick, and you have a headache, like you have."

"You mean like in the movies, drinking makes cowboys sick?" the boy asked in wonder.

Drew took that up. "Remember who does the drinking in the movies, young fellow? Is it the good cowboy or the mean one?"

Bobby gave the matter his best attention. "The mean one," he admitted. "I guess it's all right if *he's* sick, huh?"

"There are other kinds of laws," Steve suggested. "You ask Mr. Phalen what happens in his laboratory when he puts the wrong things together."

The boy's steady, inquiring eyes swung from his uncle's face to that of the other man.

"I might blow up the place," Drew told him.

"What's a lab'tory?" Bobby asked. Then wriggling down into the bed and sighing, he added, "I guess I don't want to know what one is today. I guess I'm sleepy."

As soon as Drew had taken his departure, Steve went to the phone and called Dr. Mims.

"All your patients still improving?" he asked.

The doctor laughed. "They'll all be able to get into fresh mischief tomorrow."

"Ever hear of Pinadex?" Steve asked then.

Dr. Mims tried that one over on his tongue. "Some sort of patent medicine. A tonic. High-alcohol content that makes a fellow think he's a lot better, if I'm talking about the right thing."

"Sounds as if you were," Steve answered.

The doctor laughed loudly. "That what those little scoun'els got into? Where'd they get it?"

Steve told him as much of the story as he knew.

"You been having after-forty aches and pains?" the doctor taunted.

"Not yet," Steve assured him.

"Wouldn't be taking that Pinadex anyhow, if I was you," Dr. Mims advised. "In this heat, and under that garage roof it'd probably bald you."

It was Elizabeth who suggested that Steve call the drug store.

"Pinadex?" the druggest shouted. "Say, did *you* get

that box? I thought it had disappeared into thin air."

"Who should have had it?" Steve asked.

"The other one. Methodist preacher over at Bitter Creek church. Brown, one of the foremen at the mill, had taken some and it seemed to do him a heap of good. His parson had had a virus and didn't seem to pick up the way he should, so Brown ordered him a case. I reckon I just told my colored boy to take it over to the Methodist preacher's."

"I'm afraid I can't send it all back to you," Steve apologized. "We—haven't got some of it any more. But I'll pay for what's missing."

The druggist laughed. "Was that what the young'uns got into yesterday? Forget it. My carelessness."

Steve smiled at Elizabeth who had been straining her ears to listen. "Looks like to me, anyway you take it, we Methodists are mixed up in this binge."

CHAPTER X

CLAIRE'S little maid with the shy smile met Steve at the door that evening.

"She in the livin' room, sir," she directed and disappeared quickly.

And he found Claire sitting at the far end of the long room, eyes downcast, hands folded in her lap like a good little girl. For that moment when she did not look up at him, Steve remained in the doorway, the roses he had brought for her under his arm. The silence tightened almost to breaking. At last Claire raised her eyes slowly to his and as if their meeting had generated an electricity which drew her from her place, she rose and moved toward him, hands outstretched and quick tears on her face.

Steve dropped the long green box and it burst open, scattering golden buds all over the black carpet. The two of them met in the middle of the room, went into each other's arms and kissed, and laughed, and kissed again.

It was Claire who saw the roses over Steve's shoulder. "Darling," she scolded softly, "they're much too beautiful to treat like that!"

He grinned. "I forgot all about 'em."

So the two of them knelt to pick up the flowers, she crooning of their fragrance, their rich color, the length of their stems.

"My favorite flower in my favorite color. Oh, Steve!"

Then they were in the small, immaculate kitchen where Claire tied an apron about her waist and filled a tall jade-colored vase with water. Steve watched her slender, scarlet-tipped hands taking up fern or bud, placing each, standing off an instant to see the effect, then changing its position by a fraction of an inch, for symmetry of line. And watching her, he was content.

He had not really known until this instant what the outcome of the evening would be. He had been torn still— "How can I give up my life work?" and "How can I live without the woman who is my life?"

But seeing her now, aproned, her hands busy with this homey and feminine task, he felt centered, completely satisfied. He was no longer of two passions, two desires. Claire was all that mattered.

And just as he was savoring that release she turned

to him, holding out the vase. "There! We'll put them on the table in the living room and feast our eyes all evening. And we'll talk."

Automatically he took the flowers, but stood between her and the door, making no move to return to the front of the house. His dark blue eyes were almost black, and serious as she had never seen them but they had lost their torment and their uncertainty now. His whole body had relaxed into a look of eager sureness.

"Claire, will you marry me?" The question was blurted happily.

She took the vase from him, placed it carefully on the drainboard, then turned and lifted her face to him.

It was much later when she said to him once more, "Now we must talk."

He laughed at her. "Talk? Why? We've settled everything of importance already."

Tonight it was he who bubbled with laughter and she who was tremulous and uncertain. "I think perhaps *you* have, Steve. Certainly you seem sure enough of what you're doing. But I have to know some things, have to satisfy myself that everything is going to be all right. Please."

He shook his head at her. "It seems foolish to me to come down out of heaven merely to be practical but since you want it—" He lifted her and placed her in a chair, brought one of her big green cushions and laid it on the floor at her feet. When he had dropped down on it and arranged his long legs so that they were comfortable, he found her left hand and cradled it still in his between her knee and his cheek.

"Now!" he commanded. "Fire away."

She sighed but did not speak at once. Steve was right.

The night was too beautiful to spoil for any reason. Yet within her there was a soreness of heart which had been growing since the night of the housewarming. It had become too painful to ignore.

"I keep thinking," she said so slowly that each syllable bore more than its share of weight. "You know, Steve, how strong the teachings of childhood are. You know that we never entirely lose our real convictions. And you don't approve of divorce."

"Approve. N-no. Nor do I approve of surgery. But I know that sometimes both are necessary, my darling. Must we think about that tonight? *Must* we?" He moved her hand from his cheek to his lips and kissed its palm.

Sorrow moved in her. Steve must not be allowed to run away from reality about this thing, even if it broke both their hearts. "I think we must. Anyway I must. One mistake I can grant myself, Steve, but never two. I can stand hurting you once. I can bear hurting Bruce. But I *cannot* hurt you again."

His laugh was nervous and there was a break in his voice when he spoke, a break which grew from the depth of his emotion and not from any weakening of his new determination. "I shan't let you. Not now that I know you love me, that you are mine. I'll never let you go, my dear."

She shook her head where it lay against the high back of her chair. "The thing that worries me, Steve, the thing I keep thinking over and over, is that in the months to come—after you are legally tied to me, that what your church taught you—what your parents taught you, will seem right; that you will think we are not really—married." She paused and swallowed the thickness in her throat. Then she added, hardly above a whisper, "Only tied together."

He lifted his head and turned so that he could look at her. "Darling, don't torture yourself. I love you."

She sounded weary beyond expression, beaten. "I know what it's like, Steve. Not to be married in one's heart."

"That was different," he protested, "but this marriage —our marriage—will begin with love. I love you, Claire. You love me. And I don't see why we have to ever mention Bruce Winthrop again!"

She put her hand over his mouth, pressed his head back against her knee. "Don't run away from things, Steve. I was married to a fine man, one of the finest. I'm divorced. These are facts and we must accept them."

The joy had gone out of Steve. He sat silent, letting Claire's words echo in his mind, trying to face something that hurt him sharply. "Yes, dearest. I know. Your marriage and its breaking up— You wouldn't have realized all this two years ago. You wouldn't have thought of it. You are wiser, dearer now. More a woman. I wish it hadn't happened as it did, but I'll accept it. I'm sure I can."

They were silent for a while. Then she went on.

"And there's your work— I used to think that anything else would do just as well for you, but now it seems to me that a man's work— I am sure it's different for a woman, at least a woman like me. I was born to be a wife,—but a man's work, if it's the right work, becomes a part of him— And I believe I should die if I found, after we were married, that the ministry *was* your only work, and I had kept you from it."

"If it's the right work—" he echoed softly. "Claire, I

don't know. I have always been afraid that I hadn't anything to offer my people. When they're in sorrow I go to
them but what I say sounds hollow, even to me. I preach
and moralize but do I change anyone's life? Take Mrs.
Phalen. I have been to see her often. Do you know what
she said to me the first time I was there? She had been
telling me of all the good fortune her life had brought
her, and she finished with 'And I have walked with God.'
It nearly stunned me."

"She often says that," Claire told him. "I believe that
if anybody ever did, she does."

"And I believe it too," he affirmed. "I am sure her
blind eyes see God. I am sure that if I were in great sorrow she would know exactly what to say to me to make
a blessing of my grief. I have seen grief turned to blessing. But I—"

He turned his thoughts inward, and was filled with a
sense of his own inadequacy. "Perhaps it *isn't* what I
should be doing, Claire," he said heavily, at last.

"If I could be sure of it. If— Oh, Steve, why can't we
just be happy, like other people?" It was a cry and her
eyes were shadowed with pain.

"Perhaps no love is really like that, darling—all happiness. I think maybe love songs and poetry and fiction
mislead us there. Maybe our love is all the greater for
the separation, for the heartache, for the problems."

She moved her head against her chair in impatience
as an invalid moves his on a pillow. "I don't want it to
be like that, Steve. I want it perfect, the way it was before."

He kissed each of her fingers, then her palm. "It wasn't
ever, quite, darling. Remember? You wanted your sort
of life. I wanted mine."

A sad smile twisted her face. "But I thought it was going to be so easy!"

"We can work things out, Claire, make our marriage into something pretty near perfect, and all the stronger because we built it together. Come. Believe it. *I* do. And I'm going to spend the next months convincing you."

He was on his knees, smiling at her cajolingly. She put her hands about his face and leaned toward him, smiling a little before she kissed him.

"There's still one thing," she said after a while. "Sit down and let's finish, now that we've got this far."

He settled back down. "What now?"

"Elizabeth. And Bobby. She doesn't like me, Steve." Claire's voice was not so tragic now, but it was still serious.

Steve thought this over. He could not deny Elizabeth's feeling. Yet he did not want to say the wrong thing.

"Elizabeth loves me, too, Claire. You hurt me very deeply and she—resents it. Any sister would. But when she sees— She'll come to love you in time, Claire. Elizabeth is a loving person, a fair person. She'll change."

"I don't blame her, Steve. I really don't. But she didn't like me before I—before we— She has never liked me. She thinks I'm bad for you. And perhaps I am."

He denied that with violence, and kissed her. Then he slipped the big seal ring of his fraternity from his hand and put it on her third finger.

"I know it's one you gave me, honey, but it's only temporary. I'll get you one that's all yours, one not as big and important as the one Winthrop gave you but—"

She shook her head at him. "You aren't in competition with Bruce, Steve. A wedding band, absolutely plain, will be fine. Or even no ring at all." She looked at the

signet ring she had given him for graduation, heavy
and loose on her hand. "You've worn it. All this time,"
she said softly.

"It was all I had to remember you."

"Oh, Steve, we *are* going to work it out. Make me believe it."

He took her in his arms, kissed her and held her close.
"Yes, my darling, we are. And we're going to do it together."

Even in the morning he believed it, and all through
the night when he was too happy to sleep. Claire would
be his. They would solve their problems as though they
had never existed, any of them.

It had been drizzling rain when he came out of Claire's
small house the night before. Now it was raining hard.
The unbroken heat of the summer had lightened and he
wanted to get out of doors. He made the excuse to Elizabeth that he was going to the post office.

"Looks like it was going to rain all morning. Can I
bring you anything from town?"

She looked at him strangely and shook her head.

He was glad afterward that he had gone. The walk
in the rain had been refreshing and among the mail in
his box were two letters which raised his spirits almost
beyond bearing.

The first was from the Union Sermon Service:

"When you were in theological school you did a series
of sermon outlines for us. They were very popular and
we would like to have a similar series if you can see
your way clear to doing them. For the six outlines we
are prepared to pay two hundred dollars."

It was a small thing. Certainly two hundred dollars

was no sum to make him believe that he could support a wife, but it was a straw in the wind.

Further down in the pile was the second letter. It was from an Atlanta radio station, from a program man whom he had known at the university, and it too brought an offer which involved money. The station was instituting a devotional for the early morning.

"We want something a bit different, yet something that will appeal to the conservative person who listens to such programs. I thought of you and wondered if you would like to make a try for it. There wouldn't be much money at first but if it caught on we might find you a better hour. The sponsor will raise his ante if the program proves popular. Will you come in and talk to me about it?"

Steve's heart almost stood still. When he had decided as a high-school senior to study law instead of the ministry, he had been called into the army. When in India he had decided that his faith was insufficient for the strain of offering it to others, he had been transferred from his division to assist a chaplain at another base. When he had decided to give up and marry Claire after he finished college, she had married Winthrop. He had half expected some great obstacle to be placed in his way now that he was considering quitting his profession once again.

Instead, the very morning after coming to a decision, he had two offers of work which would bring him in money, work which was in an allied field to the ministry, work he was sure he could do.

"Oh, God," he prayed in thankfulness too deep to be expressed in words. He only stood there in the empty post office filled with joy and wonder.

CHAPTER XI

STEVE had read a poem in high school which ended something like this: "There's nowhere to go from the top of a mountain but down." He knew neither the author nor exactly how the poem broke into lines but during the days which followed he remembered the idea and his life became a sort of ledger, balancing the credits against the debits.

He had never driven himself so hard. He rose at five now instead of seven, went to his office to select and type outlines of twelve sermons for the Sermon Service, adding illustrations and fitting quotations. They turned out very well, for along with the check to pay for them, came a request for twelve more.

This brushing up sermons which he had already preached was child's play compared with the radio program. At the university he had taken a course in radio speaking. And so he knew he should weed out s's and other hissing sounds as much as possible, and similar odds and ends of radio technique were familiar to him, but writing an original program proved difficult. Eventually he decided on the character of an early Georgia circuit rider who was to preachers what Johnny Appleseed was to apples, a man who did grafting, and studied the stars as a hobby. Nights on the circuit he spent with pioneers along the road and drew lessons of a simple and homey nature, read Scripture, and joined in the singing of hymns. Painfully Steve wrote out nine such programs, to cover a period of two months and then sat down to wait for the decision of the sponsor.

Even Claire was not an unalloyed joy. She had accepted his fraternity ring but refused another; she did not want their relationship known.

"Let me wear this one on a chain about my neck and hidden, Steve. It's our secret for a while and sweeter that way. Besides it'll be better if the church doesn't know that we plan to marry before you're ready to leave it. Honestly, I'm right about this, darling."

And he had to admit that she was.

Still he was with her whenever he could be and this fact created a certain amount of talk among the people of the congregation. Steve heard none of it but he could sense it in their curious and contemplative looks.

And there was Elizabeth. She did not speak of Claire again, seeming to know that nothing she could say would make any difference, that some crisis had been reached and passed. Instead she had become silent and withdrawn, almost brooding. Steve watched her with uneasiness, tried to joke with her, to rouse her to conversation. All his efforts fell like a jarred angel cake. Even Bobby seemed to move about on tiptoe, as if waiting for disaster.

Nor was Steve's pastorate going well. His conscience held him to longer hours spent in preparation of his sermons, but his mind tended to wander, and when he rose to preach, there was a lack of conviction which had not been there before. Too, he had allowed himself to cut his pastoral calls in half. Afternoons except Monday it had been his custom to make nine calls, setting aside three hours for them. In the morning he had usually made ten brief telephone contacts.

"Missed you from the congregation Sunday. I hope none of your family were ill?"

Or, "I see by the paper that your daughter is to be married. May I wish her every happiness?"

Or again, "So you are going to read a paper at the advertising convention. Congratulations!"

He had always thought this kind of contact with the congregation an important part of his ministry but now, writing endless letters in the interest of changing his work, writing sermon outlines for the Sermon Service and planning radio devotionals, he argued differently with himself.

The people of Kinsman needed nothing from him. They were church people, normally religious. His visits were really social affairs. If he made four calls instead of nine who would care or know the difference?

And no one seemed to know. He met J. G. Kinsman several times but the mill owner was lost in his own problems.

"Something's gone wrong with the market. The government isn't ordering what it was and this synthetic stuff is underselling us. And outselling us, too, for that matter. These first years I haven't much margin, and with notes falling due—" He would shake his head worriedly.

Only Mrs. Phalen seemed to sense a difference in Steve. "Something worrying you, Stephen?"

"Why, no, Mrs. Phalen," he answered, believing it.

She made a small murmur of disagreement, then went on with words. "You aren't relaxed. You're absent-minded. You seem—perhaps older."

He laughed. "I am, if that's all. I'm very happy, as a matter of fact."

She did not probe further but he could feel that she was not convinced and as a result he began to look for differences in himself.

It was almost two weeks after Claire had promised to marry him that things came to a head with Elizabeth. Late one afternoon he found her with red and swollen eyes, more silent even than usual, and busy over the preparation of the evening meal. Of late he had been irritated with Elizabeth because she could not accept his happiness as her own. She seemed to him just plain selfish.

But at the sight of her puffy face a great tenderness welled up in him now. Poor old girl, she hadn't had much of a life any way you looked at it. She had always loved Bob Marsden from the time she was a little girl of fourteen worshipping a high school senior. She had had exactly two weeks of marriage to him before he had been shipped to Germany during the closing weeks of the war. He had survived that and they had written happily back and forth, anticipating his return home before the birth of the baby. But little Bobby arrived while his father was still abroad. Then a date for Bob's transfer home had been set. Steve still remembered the letter Elizabeth had written him in India.

Nor would he ever forget the cable which had followed close on its heels. "Bob killed in airlift operations."

Her parents both dead, her brother half a world away, her baby too young to help in any way except to demand much of her waking attention, Elizabeth had faced her problems alone and had come through calm and self possessed.

All of this ran through Steve's mind now and his hand on her shoulder was tender. "Anything I can help with, Sis?"

She burst into tears at this show of sympathy. They had been further apart since their coming to Kinsman than during the years he was in India.

"It's nothing r-really. It's a lot of things. It's B-Bobby coming home today and saying Bobby is a baby name and he must be called B-Bob from now on."

Steve blinked. Such strange things upset women. They were a sentimental lot. "But surely— You can explain to him, or I will, about that being his father's name and why it upsets you to call him by it," he offered.

She was as surprised as he, surprised enough to stop her tears for a moment. "It's not *that*. I don't mind his being called Bob, if that's what he wants. It's his not *being* a baby any more. It's life rushing by, slipping away from me—" She was sobbing so that she had to sink down on a kitchen stool and hand him the long fork to turn the meat.

He had never felt more helpless. "But—but everybody gets old, honey. Older all the time."

She shook her head without lifting her face out of her hands. "I don't mind getting old," she said in a voice so muffled that he could scarcely understand. "It's— drying up instead. Like—like an old maid daughter who —who goes on looking— Not old but— Oh, Steve, like a rose that never opened and just—just withered. I'm like that, Steve."

The whole thing was beyond him. He did not know how to deal with the situation. And while he tried to figure out a way, Elizabeth went on woman-like to something new. "All these years I have tried to convince myself that I had my place, that I was useful to you, that bringing up Bobby was enough. And now you're going to marry Claire Winthrop and quit the ministry and—" The words had come in a flood and now they were lost in fresh tears.

"But who told—how did you—?" Steve stammered, utterly astounded that his sister knew so much of his affairs.

She lifted a wet, scornful face to him. "An idiot would have known. You're as transparent as window glass, Stephen Elliott. You come home without your fraternity ring, Claire is wearing a new gold chain about her neck, with the end of it carefully hidden. You disappear every evening as soon as your church duties are over. You whistle about the house. You— I'll bet every man, woman, and child in Kinsman knows all about it."

Steve turned his back on the meat he was supposed to be tending. "But—"

Elizabeth sighed deeply. "I've thought and thought. I've tried to convince myself that I'm wrong about Claire, Steve. I've tried to make myself think that she's right for you. I've accused myself of being selfish and jealous, of disliking her because she's undermining my security. But while that may be a small part of it—you see I'm trying to be absolutely honest—I'm still positive she'll ruin your life."

Steve had not really heard the last part of that sentence. He had closed his ears after Elizabeth's self accusation. Now he cleared his throat gruffly. "Sis, you don't have to worry about yourself and Bobby. You're my family, my responsibility, part of my life. I—"

"So's the ministry and you're planning to throw *that* over," she accused him fiercely.

"Claire thinks you don't like her but we both want you with us—wherever we'll be, always."

"That's likely!" she contradicted him. "I suppose Claire's all right for her type, but I don't like the type. And she doesn't like me any better. Bobby and I'll make our way. You don't have to worry about us!"

"But Elizabeth, I couldn't give up Bobby. He's—like my own son. I— And he needs me. A boy needs a man." The seriousness of his feeling was emphasized by his calling her by her given name. He rarely did that.

She shook her head sorrowfully. "Don't be foolish, Steve. If I had married you would have lost Bobby as much as this way. Claire and I can't live together. We couldn't if we *liked* and *understood* each other. Any woman has a right to her own house. And it isn't Claire, really, that worries me. It's this notion you have of giving up your work. Steve, every time I think about it, when I pray about it, I'm sure that some day you'll realize that you've—given up your birthright for a mess of pottage. You'll hate Claire, then."

Steve's heart thudded forbodingly. That was what Claire had said, too. He was sure that they were both wrong but— "I'm not giving it up, really, Sis. I'm going to do radio parsons, and maybe some social service jobs and—I'll still be working for and with people—"

Elizabeth jumped to her feet. "Steve, you've let the chops burn and they were a dollar, fifteen a pound. Oh—"

And there was the weather.

Since the night when Steve left Claire's in a slight drizzle and arrived home with damp feet and hair, there had not been a day which was not marked with more rain than sunshine. Sometimes there had been only the thin mist from a pewter sky. Occasionally a diluted sun would peep out apologetically, then after a brave try, disappear again. And sometimes there would be sheets of rain obscuring the house across the street, the road before you.

At first all the town was glad to see it. "This'll keep me from having to start from scratch with my lawn. It had just about dried up. And the weather's cooler. Why, last night I slept under a sheet, and this morning I woke without that dull headache I've been having lately. It's wonderful."

And raincoated and under umbrellas, the townspeople would go their way blithely through the downpour.

But one week of rain gave way to another; then a third began. The river was up three inches. The weatherman promised no relief. Now housewives met their families at the door with bedroom slippers.

"Take them off there on the porch. I can't have you tracking that mud in. It's bad enough to have to hose off the porch at least once every day. What a year! We spend the first half of it without even a decent dew and now we are about to be washed away."

Mothers sent small fry on errands to get them out of the house. "Honestly, they whine all day. 'What can I do now, Mom?' Will I be evermore glad when Labor Day's over and school starts."

Steve's unrest was back, not so urgent as before, but he suffered from a slow, aching depression that threatened his breathing and his heartbeat.

"It's the weather," he kept assuring himself. "When the sun comes out once more we'll all feel better."

CHAPTER XII

BUT THE SUN showed no sign of coming out for more than a brief appearance. The river inched its way up to the high point of its banks and an unwilling patience settled itself over the town.

Steve had been out later than usual on one of these dreary, late August nights, and had returned home wet in spite of raincoat and umbrella. He had taken a hot shower, rubbed himself until he was red from the friction, and crawled unhappily into bed. He was just beginning to relax when the phone rang.

He lay there for a moment, reluctant to go into the hall where the phone was; more reluctant to be waked entirely. But the bell was insistent, almost scolding. He rose, reached for his robe, and went barefooted toward the sound, still rubbing his eyes.

"Is that you, Steve?" a feminine voice asked.

Steve searched his mind. The voice seemed familiar but he could not place it. "Yes, Stephen Elliott. What can I do for you?" It was difficult to make his voice sound cordial. Almost anything anybody wanted at this time of night would mean going out into the wet.

"It's Joel Kinsman, Steve. I—I've been in an accident," the small, discouraged voice went on.

"Are you hurt?" Steve asked, relaxing somewhat when she replied in the negative.

"I hope you weren't asleep," she continued apolo-

getically. "I wouldn't have called except that J.G. and
Paula are out of town and I—I don't have any money
and my car's wrecked. Maybe I should have just waited
until morning—" Her voice bogged down and stopped.

Steve stiffened his backbone and made the only possible decision. "I'll be right along. But it may take
awhile. It's pouring cats and dogs and I'll have to creep.
Don't want to pile up somewhere. Now tell me how to
get there."

After a brief conference with someone close at hand,
she gave him minute directions. She was at a state patrol
station.

"All right," he said then. "Keep your spirits up. I'm on
my way."

Elizabeth's door was cracked open and as he turned
away from the phone, she came out into the living room,
tying her dressing gown about her.

"What is it, Steve? Mrs. Phalen? I hope she isn't—"

"Nothing like that," Steve assured her, and went on
to explain about Joel.

"Poor child," Elizabeth sympathized. "Paula and her
father both away and—"

Steve snorted. "Poor child, indeed. Do you know it's
almost two o'clock? Decent people have been in bed—"

Elizabeth giggled for the first time in weeks. "Watch
it, son. You've just come in yourself, remember?"

He grinned sheepishly.

"Don't be too hard on her. She's just a youngster and
I like her," Elizabeth said. "Want me to go along?"

Steve patted her shoulder. "You get your sleep, honey.
No need for both of us to trail about all night. Maybe
you'd better let me have what money's in the house. My
pockets are about empty."

Elizabeth laughed again. "I couldn't go anyhow. If Bobby were to wake up and find himself alone he'd be frightened. Get along with you, parson. If you're going to rescue the poor little rich girl, you can't stand here all night gossiping." She disappeared to get her pocket-book.

Outdoors it was as wet and unpleasant as Steve had expected, but the brief passage with Elizabeth had dissolved some of his moodiness. Again he felt the same curiosity he had had about Joel when he had first come to Kinsman two months ago. He had hardly thought of her lately. She did not come to church, and he had not seen her anywhere else.

She was a puzzle beyond his solving. He remembered how she had been that first afternoon, gay, unaffected, stimulating. He had never so much as glimpsed that facet of her personality again. The over-dressed, sulky girl he had seen at Claire's the same night seemed to bear no relation to the one in his car. The silent, fierce-playing golfer was still another person. And tonight she had been a frightened, apologetic child obviously most uncertain of his aid even though she was asking it.

He shook his head and peered out into the rain at the nearly obscured road. He certainly wished she had taken another time to unveil this fourth Joel but then, a minister's nights were not his own.

It was nearly two hours later that, almost by instinct, he found the tiny police station, drove as near to the lighted entrance as possible, and dodged into the little room with its antiseptic, institutional odor. He took off his hat and shook it, looking about for Joel.

She sat alone, sagged in a chair, her face cast down

and almost hidden. He thought she was sleeping until, feeling his eyes on her, she looked up.

Immediately she was on her feet, running toward him, all her calmness deserting her, so that she sobbed bitterly and made no effort to wipe away the tears which streamed down her face. Steve took her in his arms comfortingly and was surprised to learn how small she was, how almost fragile.

For a long time she did not say anything, hiccoughing sobs like a child which has cried itself to sleep.

The state policeman left his desk and came over to where they stood. "It was a wreck, Reverend. Looked like her fault. Others pretty bad hurt," he explained.

Steve went on patting the shaken shoulder. "She was alone in the car?"

The policeman frowned. "That's what she said. One of them others—in the other car—thought— But like I said, they was hurt."

Steve disengaged himself from Joel long enough to sign papers and accept the responsibility for her appearance at court, then wrapped the girl's raincoat about her and led her, still shaking and crying, to his car.

Her eyes were wide and staring. "It was awful. We— I—"

He started the engine which coughed wetly. "Don't talk about it. Don't even think about it if you can help it. Here. Put your head down on my shoulder and go to sleep. We'll get through the mess somehow."

Rather to his surprise, she obeyed, little by little relaxing against him until she fell asleep. All of a sudden he felt such pity as he had never known welling up in him. She was so little, so helpless, so alone. And he was surprised afresh at that idea. He had never thought of her like this before.

After awhile she wakened and said in a small, humble voice, "I didn't even say thank you."

He chuckled. "I've always heard that actions speak louder than words. I wasn't in a great deal of doubt that you were glad to see me though nobody but a woman would indicate her delight with such a flood of tears."

She raised her head from his shoulder and began to make little feminine dabs at her hair. "Don't tease me, Steve. I—I guess I'm fresh out of snappy comebacks and I'm not up to hunting new ones."

He smiled at her. "I'm glad you had a nap," he said gently.

"I did, didn't I? I was sure I couldn't. Did you realize that I've started calling you Steve? I never did before, but J.G. and Paula do. And—Claire." She paused before the last words as if she had almost not said it.

"I certainly don't mind," he answered. "Why should I? We're friends, aren't we?"

"I—don't know," she admitted. "Friends—I'm not at all sure I have any."

"Don't be cynical, Joel. Don't ever be cynical. We *have* to *believe* in people."

Neither of them spoke for a little. The rain drummed on the top of the car, made rivulets on the windows, and satiny black pools on the pavement. It was she who spoke at last.

"Steve, where are the happy people?"

He was reminded of Bobby at the age of three, asking, "Uncle Steve, where's God?" He had answered the child with, "Everywhere, son. God is everywhere." But now he was puzzled by the girl's question, hardly know-

ing if she expected an answer. While he wavered in
perplexity, he repeated her question.

"The happy people?"

"Yes," she said, hardly above a whisper, and then
after a little pause she went on to explain, still in a
child's idiom. "The ones who live happily ever after.
Those who smile with their eyes even when their lips
don't. Those who look contented even when they don't
know you are looking at them. Where are they?"

He frowned and did not answer. He did not know
how to answer. He thought of Elizabeth weeping because life was leaving her to shrivel away. He thought,
too, of his own dissatisfaction. "Aren't you happy, Joel?
It seems to me that you have everything."

"No," she told him. "And it seems to me I've been
looking for them, the happy ones, all my life."

He was still hunting for an answer to her query, and
more important, trying to decide what her query really
meant, what lay behind it. She waited a moment politely, then went on in a tired voice.

"J.G.'s rich. He's got a job he says he loves. But—he's
always hunting something, trying to make more money,
worrying for fear he'll lose what he has. Paula—wishes
she'd stayed in New York and starved for her voice.
I could go on all night, naming the people I know. And
none of them's happy."

He could not contradict her.

She drew a deep, sharp breath. Her voice had turned
bitter. "And I—I have everything."

He almost stalled the car at her panicky tone but he
was still wordless. She rushed on without altering her
expression.

"You knew that my mother and father were divorced?

Did you know that Mother didn't want me, that she left me with J.G. who really didn't want me either? If I'd been a boy— Have you ever seen the kind of boarding schools where parents push off children like me? Have you ever wondered whether people liked you for yourself, or for your allowance? And then *I* had to have Claire."

"Cl-aire!" he echoed.

She nodded. "You're in love with her. You're even willing to quit your job to marry her. You ought to know what I mean. She's too beautiful for this world. And she's charming. Men go down like ninepins when she even *looks* at them. You, and Drew, and that little nonentity Carleton. All of you. I took to not bringing *anybody* home. But that's not much help when you can just look at a man and know that if he did see her, he'd forget you like *that*." She snapped her fingers to indicate how quickly it would be done. "It's Claire who has everything."

He answered quietly. "Claire's not happy either."

"N-no," she admitted. "She's got everything. I've got everything. And something gnaws at both of us. Do you know why I came to church that first morning, Steve?"

He shook his head.

"I thought— I had seen you before, when you were in college. I thought then that you were one of them. I thought maybe you could tell me—"

He had found something for which he had been searching. "Mrs. Phalen is one of them," he said.

She nodded. "I asked about that. She said something about walking with God. I don't know what she meant by it. Maybe you have to be blind, Steve. There's a poem

—something they sing in church. It's about God taking
away eyes so you can see. It sounds silly."

"The Blind Plowman," he supplied the title absently.
He had been hunting the happy people himself and he
had not found them. He was not one of them. He was
as lost as Joel.

"I thought a preacher— It seems to me that a preacher
ought to know about being happy. But they don't. Only
I forgot. You aren't going on being a preacher, are you?"
She was utterly forlorn.

"Did Claire tell you that?" he asked.

"Claire? Of course not. But you're going to marry
her, and J.G. says you can't go on preaching if you do.
I guess maybe preaching is just a job like any other."

He found himself protesting that. "No. I'm sure it
isn't. It's the most important thing in the world. It's being a shepherd, the Samaritan on the road; it's being a
doctor who heals hurts too deep for surgery, it's feed-
ing the hungry. It's the best this world has to offer,
Joel."

"You feel like that about it?" she asked, wonderingly.

"Y-yes. That's what it is, all that and more. It's—"
He fell back on Mrs. Phalen's word. "It's walking with
God. And it's like you said that other time you were in
the car. It's loneliness, and agony of soul, and—" He had
really forgotten her. He stopped to think.

She spoke very softly. "If I even suspected there was
something like that, I'd never stop looking until I found
it. I wouldn't give it up for—for—" She had been about
to say any woman on God's green earth but thought
better of it.

He was turning into the Kinsman driveway. He drove

back to the garage and stopped. As she had on that other occasion, Joel slipped out before he realized that she meant to.

"Thanks for the lift, Steve. I don't know why I talked like a fiend. I don't usually babble. It must be the father confessor in you. Consider it human frailty and forget it. Goodnight."

She flipped a salute to him, turned with an almost military precision, and with her hands stuffed deep in her pockets marched off toward the little guest house hardly discernible against the clouded sky.

Steve watched her go, his mind in turmoil. Finally he turned around and drove out of the estate, figuratively kicking himself for a hundred reasons. He should have walked to the door of the guest house with her but he had been too stirred up to think quickly. He should have told her that she was one of the most intriguing of women, a thousand women in one, a woman to puzzle and mystify a man, of whom one would never tire.

Again he heard her words. "If I even suspected there was something like that I'd never stop looking until I found it." It reminded him of the Scripture he had chosen for the next Sunday's sermon:

"Again, the kingdom of heaven is like unto a merchant man, seeking goodly pearls:" he murmured softly. "Who, when he had found one pearl of great price went and sold all that he had, and bought it."

He eased himself into the garage at the parsonage and went into the house in heaviness of spirit.

CHAPTER XIII

STEVE did not tell Claire of the conversation with Joel on their return trip the night before. He felt that it was almost like a professional confidence. But when she asked him about the accident that evening, he told her what little he knew.

"You mean she was all alone in that car? I don't believe it." Claire was emphatic.

"That's what she told me. And the police backed her up," Steve insisted.

Once more Claire shook her head. "Not Joel. She'd been somewhere with that creature she's so secretive about. For some reason she won't let him come to Kinsman."

And then the whole matter was driven entirely from his mind.

For Mrs. Phalen had been growing weaker and suddenly she was dying. It was Dr. Mims who called Steve on Monday morning.

"She wants to see you," he told his pastor. "Don't let her get too tired. Or maybe that doesn't matter too much at this stage of the game."

"She's—?" Steve made a question of it.

"Any time now. At most, a matter of days."

And Steve, deeply grieved at the imminent death of his friend, got out the car and went up the hill to the Phalen house.

During the recent weeks he had learned to depend
on Laura Phalen. From her he drew a strength which
he needed. The realization that her support would soon
be gone left him feeling desolate.

Lucy's eyes were red when she answered his ring and
even her uniform seemed less crisp now.

"I'm glad you've come, Mr. Elliott. Miss Laura's been
asking for you."

"I heard," he answered softly. "She's—very low?"

Lucy turned away her face. "Yes, sir. Only it hardly
shows. She seems very much like herself. Cheerful. Excited, really. When she's awake, that is. But she dozes a
lot."

It was as Lucy said. Laura Phalen was sleeping lightly
when Steve came into the room. Drew sat beside her,
an open book in his hand, his eyes not following the
printed lines but staring ahead blankly and seeing nothing. Mother and son seemed to realize Steve's presence
at the same moment.

Laura's smile was quick and full of affection. "I felt
sure you'd come if you knew I wanted you, but Dr. Mims
and this boy of mine seem to think I must rest," she said
weakly.

Steve might have been fooled by that bright smile
and by her cordial manner if he had not seen death
among his parishioners before. There was a transparency
about her skin, a tightness over the cheekbones, a gathering together of the lips, which warned him that the end
was near. The hand she gave him was dank, her pulse
feeble.

"This is the first time I haven't found you knitting,"
Steve rallied her.

"The babies Lucy and her doctor bag bring into the

world are going to have to look elsewhere for their sweaters," she answered cheerfully. "Somebody'll knit them."

Drew and Steve shook hands in silence, their eyes meeting sympathetically.

"Son," Laura Phalen went on, speaking with more strength now, "will you go somewhere else to do your reading? I want to talk to Stephen."

Drew seemed to have trouble even now finding words. He cleared his throat, then stooped to kiss her forehead. "Of course, Mama," he answered like a child, and went away.

"Now," Mrs. Phalen said when the sound of his footsteps had died away. "It's still raining, isn't it?"

"Yes," Steve told her. "Only a mist right now, but it's almost four weeks since we've had a really sunny day, a day when it didn't rain at all."

"And the river's up?" she asked.

"Higher than anybody's ever seen it," he assured her.

"That's what I hear," she continued, then changed the subject abruptly. "Steve, I've thought a great deal about you. And I've prayed."

He felt very humble, young and awkward. "Thank you, Mrs. Phalen."

"You must not leave the ministry, Steve. God has called you to it. Never forget that." She was earnest and her voice was strong now, strong and pleading.

"I—" Steve began. Then his throat closed and he could say no more. How had she known, she and Elizabeth, and Joel?

As if she had guessed his thought, she went on, "Sometimes when you love a person, Stephen, you sense things about them. There has been a kinship between us from the first. And as I told you, the blind— Is there a Bible on the table beside you, Stephen?"

Steve took it up before he answered. "Did you want me to read to you?"

"Yes. The twenty-third chapter of Jeremiah."

It was a strange choice for a dying person, Steve thought, as he began to read, then suddenly he knew that the reading was not for Laura Phalen at all, but for *him*. The old woman's utter unselfishness at such a time touched him and enriched his voice as he read.

"And I will set up shepherds over them which shall feed them: and they shall fear no more, nor be dismayed, neither shall they be lacking, saith the Lord."

The rest of the chapter dealt with false prophets, a ringing denunciation. Steve winced as he read, yet was somehow comforted by the fact that the fourth verse kept echoing in his mind. "Shepherds—they shall fear no more, nor be dismayed." It was like a warm hand supporting him.

When he had finished, Mrs. Phalen made another selection. "The twenty-first chapter of John now, Stephen, if you please."

Again he read. It was the story of Jesus' turning to Peter with the command, "Feed My lambs." Steve read it all, his voice steady yet full of emotion.

"Thank you, my dear," she told him and her voice was a mere whisper. "When I'm gone—Drew will be lonely. I'd like to think of your being there."

He took one of her hands and held it in both of his. "I will be. I promise. Whenever he needs me."

"And you'll have the services," she went on and he leaned forward, straining to hear. "The services for me —afterward."

"Yes. I should think so." It was not easy to keep his tones level, unemotional.

The shadow of a smile crossed her pale and beautiful face. "I don't want a tear shed, Stephen. Not one. Read the service as the church has it. Have some triumphant music. Death—triumph! They are one in Christian philosophy."

He swallowed a lump in his throat. "Yes, Mrs. Phalen."

She closed her eyes. "Is it the Spanish who say 'Go with God'?" she asked.

"I—think so."

"I always liked that saying. Go with God, Stephen. Go always with God." Her hands relaxed where they lay and she was asleep. Stephen stooped and kissed her brow as Drew had earlier, and tiptoed from the room.

Laura Phalen died that night and they buried her the next afternoon.

The church had never been so crowded. There were no flowers. Laura had asked that the money be given toward a chapel in the new hospital when it was built. "A little place where people in trouble can go and pray. I'd like that," she had said to one friend and another.

Stephen read the service from his small black Discipline, making his voice triumphant where the hope of resurrection was mentioned, playing down the hints of bodily mortality. It was not easy for him. He could have shed tears for her going himself, but he made himself conduct the service just as she would have wished it.

The double quartet from Atlanta which sang at the Sunday services filled the sanctuary with an Easter hymn composed largely of Alleluias. Its triumphant gladness was heart lifting.

And through the entire service there echoed in Steve's mind the words Laura Phalen had selected from the Scripture: "They shall fear no more, nor be dismayed, neither shall they be lacking." And the three verses from St. John which included the commands "Feed My Lambs," and "Feed My Sheep."

Laura Phalen was buried under a striped awning on which pattered a gentle rain. Then Elizabeth and Steve took Drew home with them for a light evening meal. Not a tear had been shed.

But Steve turned away from the grave with his heart crying out within him until he knew no peace, and the softly spoken verses carried a goad for his conscience. "I shall set up shepherds which shall feed them." Am I, he asked himself, what He has set up, the best He has? Am I their hope for leading them out of fear, dismay, and lack? I, Stephen Elliott, who mean to leave them? He asked himself these questions over and over and found no satisfactory answer.

Then the sterner words of Jeremiah came to him clearly as they had never done before. "Mine heart within me is broken because of the prophets— For both prophet and priest are profane; yea, in my house have I found their wickedness, saith the Lord."

Stephen had become two people. One played the part of host, and comforter, and friend to Drew. The other stood apart, with heart and mind divided. "How do I know myself a shepherd set up? I've had no vision, no voice. I walk in fear, dismay and lack, myself. How can I lead when I cannot even save myself?"

The words rang familiarly for him. They were he finally remembered, almost the exact ones mockers had used concerning Christ. They were, he thought, the ones which belonged to Calvary: "Himself He could not save."

He could not eat Elizabeth's good supper, though he toyed with it politely. He spoke now and again, carrying his end of the conversation, but was thankful for Bobby's endless chatter, for Elizabeth's graciousness as a hostess, for Drew's calm acceptance of his loss.

When the meal was done, he laid the first fire of the autumn and it burned cheerfully on the hearth. The rain outside was quiet and monotonous, shutting them in with an intimate coziness. Elizabeth's voice was soft and slow, Drew smoked his pipe and occasionally dropped a deep baritone note into the conversation. Bobby asked questions and listened wide-eyed to Drew's answers.

Only Stephen seemed upset. There was a coppery taste on his tongue and the back of his neck was sore and aching with tension. He longed to be alone, to come to grips with himself. Yet there was his promise to Mrs. Phalen. He must offer to return to the empty house with Drew.

But it was Bobby who made the first gesture.

"Uncle Drew," he began yawning slightly, "it's 'bout time I went to sleep, I think. If I'm going to spend the night with you so I can get up early in the morning and help you, maybe we better be goin'."

"*Uncle* Drew?" Elizabeth asked, flushing a little.

"I asked him if I could call him that. He said all right. Me and Kinny both," the boy defended himself.

Elizabeth sighed her relief at the inclusion of Kinny. "Well, if Drew thinks so," she agreed. "But this spending the night—"

Bobby nodded importantly. "Uncle Drew is building a boat and he needs me to help him. I thought it'd be better if I was there early so—"

"Did he *ask* you to stay with him?" Elizabeth pressed.

"We-l-l—" Bobby temporized.

Drew spoke up, "I'd like it more than you know, Elizabeth. Will you lend him to me?"

So it was decided, and when they had gone off, Elizabeth made a little joke. "I suppose that boat will be known as Drew's Ark. Three weeks is a little short of forty days and nights, but as I remember, Noah began his building a lot sooner than this."

Steve smiled mechanically, answered when she said goodnight, and sat on by the darkening coals. Like Jacob he wrestled all night but there was no blessing with the morning. And he had come to no decision except that he must go away from Kinsman, must go somewhere where he could be utterly alone.

CHAPTER XIV

ELIZABETH found him still there the next morning when she started to the kitchen to prepare breakfast. She stopped, startled, thinking that he had fallen asleep but he looked up at her, unsmiling, his eyes sunken, his face marked with deep lines.

"Steve," she began in a tone heavy with anxiety, "are you ill?"

He shook his head. "You remember you told me some time ago that I ought to get away?"

"Yes."

"You were right, I should have gone then." His words were heavy and spiritless.

"You mean to go at once? Where?" she asked then.

"I don't know. I'm all mixed up, Sis. I've got to find out some things about myself. Until I do I'm not fit for man nor beast."

She looked at him thoughtfully. "It's up to you, of course. But I hate to see you go away feeling like you do and in weather like this. Come have a quick cup of coffee, then shower and shave. You'll know better then."

He rose to follow her to the kitchen. "When I said at once, I meant this afternoon, if I can get through the things I have to do by then."

She put on water and opened the coffee can. He smiled fleetingly. "That smells good. I thought I wasn't hungry but maybe I am."

But he could not eat when she put his breakfast before him. He simply couldn't swallow food. He drank two cups of coffee black, looked at Elizabeth gratefully because she hadn't asked questions, hadn't insisted that he empty his plate.

The people he had to see were J. G. Kinsman, Drew, and, of course, Claire. He might have selected her first but he remembered that she was a late sleeper. He chose Drew instead.

He found Drew and Bobby at breakfast. The boy was more excited than Steve had seen him in some time.

"We been up so long, Uncle Steve. Come look at the boat we're making. It's a beaut."

"Not this morning, boy," Steve told him gently. "I'll

want to see it one day soon but right now I've got to talk to Mr. Phalen."

Bobby took a great mouthful of grits and scrambled egg and washed it down with milk. "You want I should go somewhere else?" he inquired.

Steve smiled. "No. Finish your breakfast. Drew, I promised your mother something. I told her that when you needed me I would be here. If you were lonely—"

Drew looked away quickly. His mother's thoughtfulness touched him.

"And now," Steve went on, "I find myself needing a few days away—maybe more than that. Anyhow, I have a job of thinking to do and I must be alone."

"I've had times like that, too," Drew agreed. "Don't worry. If Elizabeth will lend me young Bob here, and Paula Kinsman will trust me with Kinny occasionally, I shan't be lonely. Besides, maybe Elizabeth herself will take pity on me once in awhile. Go ahead, Steve, with my blessing."

Kinsman proved a bit harder to talk to. In the first place, Steve had to wait in his outside office until he was free and even then the mill owner was so worried with his own affairs that he had little attention to give to his pastor.

"If it doesn't stop raining, I'm ruined," he grumbled. "I've got notes falling due and it's only by the skin of my teeth that I'm going to be able to pay them. If water gets into my machinery and I have to close down, God knows how I'll ever make it."

Steve found himself thinking of Joel and of what she had asked the night of the wreck. "Where are the happy people?" He did not realize that he had actually said the words aloud until J.G. who had been largely talking to himself, looked up and asked, "Huh?"

"Nothing. Muttering in my beard. But the rain ought to be over any day now. Already it's almost broken a record."

"I don't like it," Kinsman went on with his complaint, "but I guess there's not much I can do about it. If I moved my machinery I'd lose the time just the same. You want something particular?"

"Yes. I need a few days away. Maybe longer than that. I've got some personal problems to work out and I'd like to go where I have nothing else on my mind."

Kinsman nodded. "Take two weeks or even a month if you think you need it. I can get that superannuate from Dalton, old Brother Weeks, to come over and fill the pulpit. Or you can call him."

"I'd rather you just ask him for prayer meeting tomorrow night, first," Steve suggested. "If I can get back for Sunday, I will. I'll phone, or telegraph, if that's all right with you."

Kinsman nodded absently. His eyes were already wandering to the pile of material on his desk. Steve rose and excused himself.

And now for Claire. Steve had been eager to talk to her when he left the parsonage, had felt that her sympathy and understanding would send him off comforted. Now he rather dreaded the interview.

Before this he had thought little of how this new flare-up of indecision would affect her. It had been something only within himself. *Was* he the shepherd he should be? *Had* he something for his flock? He had even begun to question whether he believed *anything* firmly enough to teach it. If this were true, he could not even continue the radio programs which he had planned.

He recalled his promise to Claire. Now as he turned the car toward her house, he thought of that promise and felt bound by it, almost angry because he had to explain that he meant to go away.

This irritation which almost amounted to anger melted when he found her. She was sitting at the kitchen table stringing and snapping beans. At the sound of his voice she called to him gayly.

"Come on back, Steve, and see how domestic I'm being."

He followed the sound and stood in the doorway, watching her hands, skillful and beautiful at their work, met her laughing, welcoming eyes, and was warmed by her as he always was.

"Isn't the weather beastly?" she began, then switched from the half-complaining, half-amused tone, to one of concern. "Steve, darling, what is it? Has something awful happened?"

He pulled up a kitchen stool and sat down. "N-no. Only—I'm going away for a few days. I wanted you to know, first."

She searched his face as if she expected to find written there the answers to the questions she must ask. "But Steve, why?"

Without thought, without actually knowing what he was saying, he blurted out, "To find God."

She stared at him, wordless, shocked. At length she protested. "But, Steve, you're a *minister*. You—"

"I know," he admitted. "It's because of that. You see, Claire, since Mrs. Phalen's death—and before that really —I have been seeing myself clearly, perhaps for the first time. I've been like a child who blithely takes on a tremendous task because he doesn't realize its importance. I've tried to be a prophet when I had no word, a shepherd when I did not know where I was going. I— This morning I realized that I couldn't go on."

She still looked at him. She simply did not understand what he was talking about. He could tell this by her eyes, wide with her lack of understanding. He shrugged his disappointment away, moving his hands nervously. The lower lid of his left eye began to jump with tension. Why should she understand? Why should anyone? He did not entirely understand himself.

"But you've been successful. Everybody says you have. You've been a marvelous preacher, and—"

"It's me—in me, that I've failed, Claire. I guess I can't explain. I took up the ministry the way I might have chosen any other profession. That isn't good enough. I must find the things of the spirit—find God."

His eyes begged for her understanding.

"But if you're leaving the ministry anyhow—" she said hesitantly.

"Maybe it's because I *am* leaving it. Maybe—I don't know, Claire. All I know is that I have to find out if these years have been something for which I must hang my head. I—feel like—like a thief in the night, the shepherd who came over the wall instead of in by the door. I'm ashamed of myself, Claire. And I'm searching desperately for self-respect."

"You're tired. Overwrought," she comforted.

"Yes, I am. But I can't even sleep—or eat. I must go away."

She watched him a moment longer. "Yes. I don't know what you're talking about. I wish I did, Steve. I'd always like to share your—mind, your spirit, but this morning I—I've lost you. But at least I see that you've got to go away."

Slowly she lifted her hand and drew the ring from where it had lain under her breast. Slowly she undid the chain and slipped it off, laid it still warm from her body into his palm.

He jerked his hand away. "No, Claire. That isn't what I want, what I meant. Don't leave me now. I—I couldn't bear it."

She made no move to take back the ring he held out to her. "I'm not going away from you, Steve," she said, her eyes serious and dark. "I'll be here when you come back. You can come to me then if you wish. But one thing I know. You must be free now. You must forget me until you can—cease being divided. Drive carefully, darling. The roads are wet. And you're terribly upset."

She raised her face for his kiss, then urged him on his way. Only when he had closed the door after him did she weep, heartbrokenly and with abandon.

Steve drove toward the Smoky Mountains not so much by plan as because Kinsman was on the highway which went that way. He left the parsonage shortly after noon, having eaten almost nothing and having drunk more coffee. Elizabeth saw him off with anxious eyes but she was too tactful to say anything. The rain was not heavy, still it continued monotonously. He had thought that, once on the road, shut away from distractions he would be able to think clearly of his problems and find some kind of solution. Instead he felt numb and awkward as if he were trying to write with his left hand.

He found himself worrying once more about Joel,

with her talk of uncertainty and unhappiness. There was a great deal of both even in a prosperous town like Kinsman. J. G. Kinsman, successful, wealthy, powerful, feared to lose what he had. Paula grieved for her lost career. Elizabeth for her lost happiness. Joel fretted because Claire was more beautiful. And Claire herself was not happy.

There was general unrest and fear. Would there be war? Was the national economy going under because of the tax burden; or government, because of graft and dishonesty? Were young people largely delinquent? You heard the worry, the uncertainty, the eternal questioning everywhere you went.

But back in Jeremiah God had promised to appoint priests who would save the people from all that. Steve wondered if the promise had been made for Jeremiah's day alone. Or was it for today as well, and had the priests failed once more as they had in the time of Jeremiah?

Steve worried about these questions. His thinking was as mist-thick as the day. He had promised Elizabeth that he would stop somewhere and eat, and he had meant to do so, but hour followed on hour and he had kept moving. Night came early. By then he was half light-headed from lack of food and sleep. He drove slowly, watched the road carefully. Miles of it were behind him. He was in the mountains now, his eyes straining before him, following white lines about curve after curve.

He did not know when he grew drowsy, did not realize that consciousness slipped from him for broken instants. His lights caught at raindrops. His windshield wiper made a grudging sound on the windshield, the steady whine of friction. He nodded, then jerked to attention.

He had left the road. The nose of his car was jammed close to a sign post above a deep ravine. Steve shook his head sharply to wake himself. He did not know where he was. He stepped out into the rain-swept night, fixed his flashlight on the sign post and peered closer to read the legend.

"The City of the Brothers," he read, spelling it out because the sign was so wet it was difficult to decipher. This sounded incredible, like something in a dream, and he read the words again, this time aloud.

Then he raised his flashlight and tried to look about him. He saw nothing, only darkness and a road which disappeared about still another curve. As he stood there, wet and cold, a man with a swinging lantern appeared from beyond a boulder. Steve could not make out his appearance beyond the fact that he was uncommonly big, and his voice, when he spoke, was strong and full of cheer.

"Good evening, Brother. Can I help you?"

"I—seem to be lost," Steve answered. "Can you tell me where I am?"

The man laughed, a gay unrepressed sound. "You've almost dislodged our sign. You're just outside the City of the Brothers."

"It's a strange name for a city," Steve commented. He was sure he was dreaming now. Nothing about this experience seemed real.

The man chuckled, adding dryly, "I guess it's hardly a village, come to think of it. Nine houses, thirty-seven souls. It is very late, Brother. My name is John. Brother John, they call me. Will you rest over night with us?"

"Us?" Steve repeated. Even for a dream, this invitation seemed strange.

"Emily and me. Emily is my wife. And our four children. We would offer you the peace of God for this night, and a comfortable bed, something to eat now and for breakfast. Then bless your journey tomorrow," he promised.

The peace of God! The very words were like a charm.

"If it wouldn't be too much trouble for you and—and your wife," he accepted the strange invitation.

"Trouble? For a friend? You drive along slowly and I'll go ahead with the lantern. This way, Brother."

Steve, still with that feeling that he had left the actual world and stepped into some Never-Never Land of his own imagining, climbed back into the car, backed it and began the slow journey after the lantern.

CHAPTER XV

AFTER the unreality of the world outside, the house was very solid indeed. Brother John opened a heavy door and gestured Steve into a great book-lined room where a fire blazed from unsplit logs. Steve shivered, realizing for the first time how cold it had been out-of-doors.

"Emily," Brother John's big, hearty voice filled the entire place, "I've brought a stranger."

Steve moved closer to the fire. "Maybe I shouldn't

have come without a warning," he said. "Women usually don't like it."

Brother John only laughed; his eyes, gray like rain, like the skies of September, were fixed on the stairs. After a moment they heard footsteps descending and a feminine voice hissed, "John, you great oaf, shouting like that. You'll have four little Indians yelling up there."

She came straight to her husband's arms, kissed him as if they had been long apart, then turned to Steve.

"The peace of God and of our house, Brother," she greeted him warmly.

"Thank you, ma'am." He could not call her Emily and he was not entirely sure that Sister Emily was the correct form of address. The sudden thought that perhaps in the City of the Brothers, she would be called Brother Emily, brought a twinkle to his eyes and a small quirk to his lips. "I am Stephen Elliott, a Methodist minister from over the state line."

He looked at them both, the big man, extraordinarily tall and well muscled, with his white-fair hair and his sun-browned skin; the small woman, merry and round and neat, like a bird, and with a bird's bright inquiring eyes.

"Come into the kitchen and eat," she commanded, linking her arm with her husband's and turning to explain to Steve. "John has been observing a day of the spirit and he'll probably shock you with the amount of food he puts away."

"A day of the spirit?" Steve repeated softly, wondering if she meant the Holy Spirit.

The young woman laughed. "I forgot that shut off from the world the way we are, our terms seem strange to outsiders. When we came to join the Brothers, John wondered whether we should bring—" she made a sweeping gesture about the kitchen with its electric stove, lights, refrigerator, deep freeze, its general feeling of beauty and homelike comfort—"the creature comforts along. We took the problem to evening communion for discussion and prayer and decided that all of these things came from a development of God's general law and we could use them if we held the things of the spirit more important. But every now and then John gets to wondering if he doesn't put the material on too high a plane. Then we have a day of the spirit. It's not so bad in summer but today we've had no heat or hot food and that's tough." She had been setting the table, laying two places; now she stopped and grinned at her big husband.

He grinned back with equal affection. "It shows me that I can do without all those unimportant items—that other things are more vital to me."

She was pouring buttermilk into tall glasses but her eyes grew tender and her smile misty. "I know, darling," she said.

Fried chicken came from the warming oven, then thick crusty, hot biscuit. Fluffy rice with chicken gravy and a tossed salad were equally enticing. Steve who had eaten almost nothing since Mrs. Phalen's death, found his appetite growing by leaps and bounds.

Emily seated the two men on opposite sides of the big kitchen table, herself between them, round chin cupped in her hands, bright eyes fixed on their faces.

"I ate with the children," she explained to Steve.

"Will you bless our food, Brother Stephen?" John asked quietly, and Steve prayed briefly.

There was little talk. Both men ate ravenously and Emily watched them as if she enjoyed it, getting up

from time to time to bring them fresh biscuit or honey
and strawberry jam.

At last Steve sighed regretfully. "I couldn't eat another bite! What a meal!"

John stretched and only half hid a yawn. "This girl
of mine is a pretty good cook for such a little thing.
When she grows up—"

She shook a small fist at her great husband. "I'm big
enough to take you on, you strong back you."

John seized her fist and opened it despite her strug-
gles. "Half-pint!" he teased.

Steve was warmed by their display of affection, by
their complete understanding of one another. Here, he
thought, was a real marriage. Then he remembered the
book-lined room they had left before the meal. He had
been surprised at the selection—classics, and the best
of the new authors.

"Wonderful library you have," he said aloud and some
of his surprise showed in his tone.

John's whole face seemed to twinkle with amusement.
"You didn't expect it of religious fanatics?"

Steve studied the man opposite for an instant, then
smiled, too. "Well, no."

"You'll find a good library in every house here," John
told him. "We're all readers. And not too ignorant,
either. Stay a few days. I'd like to show you." He
stretched his big shoulders and barely stifled a yawn.

Steve suddenly realized that he was sleepy too. "I
might just take you up on that. But isn't it bed time?"

"Way past for people who farm for their living. But
tonight after evening communion John went with
Brother Carl to help deliver a calf. It held him late,"
Emily explained. "May we show you to your room?"

"I usually help with the dishes at home," he suggested.

She shook her head at him. "That's when John and I plan for the next day. It won't take us long. Come, we'll show you."

It was a small room but Steve thought he had never seen a pleasanter one. The furniture was very old, a warm, honey-colored pine and handmade, for the posts at the head of the bed were not exactly matched. The walls were papered with clusters of wisteria in lavender and purple and crisp lavender curtains hung at the windows. A lavender and white coverlid was on the bed.

"The peace of God keep you the night," Emily told him when she had checked to see that everything he was likely to need was at hand, and she had turned down his bed.

"The peace of God, Brother Stephen," John echoed, and they shut the door on him softly.

Steve could hardly get undressed quickly enough. Ever since he had entered this house he had been conscious of his nerves unkinking, of his spirit expanding. There was a feather mattress on the bed. He sank into it, murmuring to himself, "The peace of God and of—" But he never finished. He had already drifted into sleep.

The night passed in a deep dreamlessness and Steve woke to find the curtains drawn and a soft lavender light filling the room. Somewhere outside there was a dull, thick sound coming with the regularity of a dripping faucet. He could not decide what it was and it was a moment before he could even remember *where* he was. Then he smiled, closed his eyes and snuggled his head back into the pillow.

But soon he sat up with a jerk and looked at his watch.

It was nearly eleven. He had slept ten hours. He dressed in almost as great haste as he had undressed the night before.

That heavy sound of wood on wood came clearer when he opened the door. Otherwise the house was silent. He found the kitchen empty and went beyond it to a glassed-in steam-heated porch where he found his hostess seated at a great loom which made her seem smaller than ever.

"Good morning, Mrs.—ma'am," he called over the racket the weaving made. "I'm ashamed of myself for sleeping away the day."

His hostess looked up surprised, then gave him her warm, brilliant smile. "The peace of God for this day, Brother Stephen," she said, turning on the bench the better to join in the conversation. "People call me Sister Emily. I have another row to do here before I start lunch," she added. "You'll find coffee in the pot and bread and butter by the toaster. Or if you're not too hungry, I'll prepare it for you when I come."

"I'm starved," he laughed, and disappeared into the kitchen to forage for himself. He had hardly begun to eat when she came into the room and began to bustle about, banging pots cheerfully, going to the freezer, and the pantry.

"What are you making?" he asked when she settled down at the sink to peel potatoes.

"A rug, today. It's the way I earn my living—rugs, luncheon sets, coverlids, that and the chickens. John runs the farm. Most of the Brothers do more high-brow jobs. There's a painter, maybe you've seen his landscapes, Tod Weatheral. He's really good, they say."

Steve nodded. He had read about Tod Weatheral,

had once seen several of his pictures at the Corcoran
Gallery in Washington.

"He's one of—you?" he asked.

"Oh, yes," she answered with a childlike pride. "And
Martha Pender."

He knew of Martha Pender, too. She was a poet, a
writer of religious verse, not pap, but stuff with sinews
and strength.

"Will you tell me about the Brothers?" he asked.
"Neither you nor Brother John has really said anything
except to answer my questions."

She dropped a potato into a pot of water and started
on another. "It's part of our—code, I guess you'd call
it. We never talk about our faith unless we are asked. I
think the most important thing about us is that we try
to live quite literally by the thirty-third verse of the
sixth chapter of Matthew."

Steve thought for a moment then quoted, " 'Seek ye
first the kingdom of God and his righteousness.' "

"Yes," she agreed. "That's all, really."

Steve took a bite of brown, buttery toast and chewed
it thoughtfully. "Well, that's a big enough order, by itself. How did you and Brother John—come to join the
group? I'd like to hear about it, if you don't mind. You
don't seem—"

He had broken off, embarrassed, and she gave him a
sweet, serious look as she put the potatoes on to boil.
"I hope we don't any of us seem like what you're thinking, Brother Stephen. We're normal people, doing something which I believe isn't usual enough. As we look at
it the kingdom of God isn't something off beyond the
sky, but something we are working for here. But you
asked how John and I came to this place."

She popped meat into the oven and busied herself with green beans which she had frozen herself. "Did you ever hear of John Bischoff?"

"Basketball—and later a coach?" Steve inquired. He had played basketball himself, had hero worshipped the All American player.

"Yes," she said. "Do you remember what happened to him?"

"He—his team sold out. There was a scandal. He's not—"

"Brother John. My John," she answered, lifting her head proudly. "But the story goes back of that a little. We were on our honeymoon. We'd been married at the beginning of the Christmas holidays, and we came into the Smokies because we hadn't much money and it was off season. Well, we were snowed in here." She had begun to make biscuit, sifting and mixing with bare, round arms, and capable, square hands.

"You've no idea how kind they were to us, taking us in as if we belonged to them."

Steve laughed. "Oh yes I have. Indeed I have."

She flushed a little at his praise. "They let us follow our own inclinations, walking in the snow, or reading or— But one night they invited us to evening communion. I can't tell you what it's like. Would you like to come tonight?"

"Holy Communion? The Lord's Supper?" he asked.

"Y-yes. But come and see."

"You have it every night?"

"Yes. We went that time and we never quite got over the experience. We talked about it sometimes. We wrote to the Brothers. We always meant to come again some time only—only life used to hurry us so."

He nodded. She took time out to peep under lids and into the oven. "Then there was that trouble. John was—killed. It did something to him. I thought he was going to have a mental collapse. Finally one day he said, 'Emily, let's go to see the Brothers,' and we did."

She sighed in utter contentment and popped the finished biscuit into the oven.

"A mental breakdown?" Steve asked, smiling a little at the notion of how uselessly a loving woman can worry.

She beamed. "You'd never believe it now, would you? I can't myself. But he's found what he has to have, what he needs."

Steve finished the last of his second cup of coffee and leaned back comfortably. "When I saw you two people together last night, I remembered a question one of my parishoners asked me recently. She said, 'Where are the happy people?' and last night I knew that I had found them."

Sister Emily grew quite rosy but her face was full of pity, too. "But do—I mean where— She must be awfully lost, unloved, and unloving. Can't she look about her? Happy people are—why they're *everywhere*."

He shook his head slowly. "You've forgotten, Sister Emily. A while ago you said life *used to* hurry you. It still does most of us. And harries. Doesn't the City of Brothers have newspapers?"

She looked at him thoughtfully. "You mean the trouble in Korea. And politics, and strikes. Oh, yes. We know about all that. We send boxes to children. We talk about those things at evening communion. We pray about them. Yes. We know."

"But you don't worry and fret," he suggested. "You aren't afraid."

"No," she said quietly, "it's in God's hands, you see."

She looked once more into the oven. Steve watched her with amazement. She had dismissed the world situation as if she had told him that there was coffee on the stove. The world situation; today's situation. He could not accept her casual attitude.

She seemed to sense his disquiet although she went on in the same still tone. "I'm a weaver, Brother Stephen. I tend to think of things in that way. Did you ever think of God's design? The one He has for this world? It doesn't matter whether He began with a grain of dust or with the completed Adam; He put us here, along with His secrets. It's our place to work them out the way I work out the pattern of a coverlid. Dark colors and bright, I use both to make the design. I think it's beautiful when I finish but I've had a plan, a design from the beginning. These little discomforts, heartbreaks, tragedies don't really matter if you measure them in the light of God's time, Brother Stephen. It's all a part of His design, His purpose."

She stopped and looked self-conscious. "I am afraid it isn't a very new idea. Or very well put," she said.

Steve was leaning toward her, his eyes alight, "God's time," he repeated. "Measured by God's time."

She nodded. "It seems to me that if we work *with* God instead of *against* Him—of course we make mistakes and sometimes that part of the weaving must be done over —but we work steadily toward the completed piece. In God's good time." She was very serious, her dark eyes wise and contented.

Steve, looking at her, had a sudden vision of Bobby

lying against his pillows asking if God had punished him
with a headache for taking something which wasn't his.
He had replied that going against God's laws naturally
brought its own punishment. He thought about it now.
It wasn't necessarily as much a personal thing as he had
made of it that day, and he began to realize that he had
oversimplified the matter then. Now vistas were opening before him of which he had not dreamed; he thought
that he would be constantly finding new ones, perhaps
all his life; but now one lay before him very plainly.
When a man moved against the laws he slowed up the
whole movement toward perfection—or to use Emily's
idiom, some of the design must be taken out.

He felt confused yet highly expectant, as he had
sometimes felt at college in one of those rare classes
when learning left dull routine and entered the field of
discovery. An excitement of the spirit possessed him.

For a moment, Steve and his hostess were silent,
thinking, but suddenly that silence was broken. Three
chattering voices were drawing nearer the house, one
deep and masculine, two piping the questions of the
very young. And then they heard the shrill demand of
an infant from the floor above.

"My goodness!" Emily exclaimed, coming out of her
reverie and beginning to set the table in great haste,
"Twelve thirty, and me daydreaming as if I weren't a
busy housewife."

At that instant the front door was flung open and a
youthful cry came to the kitchen. "Mom-mee!"

Four members of the family appeared almost instan-
taneously. Brother John and two small boys of under-
school age, plump and rosy as their mother came through
the back door and a breathless six year old with a reader

under her arm from the living room. The baby upstairs was still demanding attention at the top of his bellows-like lungs. Emily clattered china and silver.

And above all this noise, John gave his usual blessing. "God's peace on the house and those in it."

CHAPTER XVI

STEVE had never spent a more active afternoon. The rain of the night before had stopped and Brother John was sowing a cover crop to stand his slanted fields against the erosion of next spring's melting snows. Steve, who had had some experience with this activity at his grandparents' farm as a boy, chose a plot and did his part. But as he moved about the freshly cleaned fields he was scarcely conscious of their being there.

His mind moved slowly, painfully, out into places which were strange to it. He could almost feel his mental joints creaking, he thought wryly. And yet there were flashes of illumination which startled him.

"The patience of God!" He said the phrase to himself, adding in his thoughts, "That's a miracle if ever there was one. It's *proof* of God, if a person needs it, proof positive. Starting only He knows how long ago with an atom, a grain of dust, something, nothing, in the hollow of His hand, and waiting, guiding, forgiving, going back a way and almost starting over, and only getting the sorry mess we have today. *Only* God, who sees the whole thing, clear to the end, *could* have the patience."

He remembered his mother giving Elizabeth a bit of fancy work to do when she was small. After Elizabeth had complained that it was less beautiful than that her mother was doing, the wise woman had smiled, "But you'll be tired of it a long time before you're through, honey. Take it easy, begin small."

They taught that sort of thing in psychology now, in education courses. "Fit the job to the individual, the task to the ability of the pupil." It was something God had always known, understanding that early walkers must do a great deal of stumbling before they can walk.

"The peace of God! The patience of God!" The two phrases brought a stillness to Steve's spirit. He was weary beyond his own knowledge by the time John called him from the field to the evening meal, and yet utterly content.

When the meal was almost finished, Emily turned to Steve and spoke hesitantly. "You were asking about the Brothers this morning, about our communion. Would you like to go with us this evening?"

His muscles ached, there was a sun and wind burn across his face, and he was sleepy to the point of stupidity. And yet he was excited at the prospect. The Brothers had something he lacked, an inner strength and peace he had found nowhere else. He remembered himself saying to Claire, "I must find the things of the spirit —find God." Perhaps it was here that he would end his quest.

"I should be very glad to go," he answered humbly.

The night air had been cold and sharp. The house where they went was small with only one great bare room. A stove in the center of the room furnished heat,

was evidently used for cooking, and had as well a kiln
for the baking of pottery. Shelves covered every avail-
able bit of wall and even ran across big windows. Here
bright-colored pieces of their hostess' handicraft were
stacked from ceiling to floor. The furniture was rough
and had been handmade but was surprisingly enough,
quite comfortable. It consisted of seven chairs, two small
tables, a work table now covered with a damp cloth,
and a studio couch pulled out from the wall to provide
further seating.

Sister Dorothy, their hostess, was so old as to be
ageless, her bright little eyes like raisins in a ginger-
bread face, her mouth sunken, her short white hair thick
and wild. She wore a long smock the color of mud so
that the blobs of clay with which she had been working hardly showed at all.

She was the only member of the entire colony whom
one might not have called normal in appearance, Steve
decided as the brotherhood assembled, if one accepted
the look of relaxation on every face.

Steve met them all: Tod and Elizabeth Weatheral,
she towering above the small artist; Martha Pender and
her farmer husband Carl; the two bachelors of the place,
Warren Porter and George Benton, who kept the store
and post office; Frances and Peter Morton, who ran the
school; Blanche and Leonard Kemp who had been
actors and were now writing a play; Mary and Frank
Clarke, Mary a pianist, Frank a mechanic working on
an invention the nature of which Steve never learned;
Mary Lenninger whose husband was away with the
army; this completed the list of adults who in turn
greeted Steve with unaffected cordiality. The children
were scattered about the floor; the two babies were

put to sleep in baskets which their mothers had brought.

Brother Warren and Brother George were the last to arrive. They had been the hosts the night before and brought with them now two iron horses and a very long wooden top which became a table to run down the center of the room. They also provided the chairs to seat the eighteen adults present.

Steve caught Emily's eye as she sat down next to him. "Tell me," he asked, "the Brothers—is it a Christian church?"

"Well—John and I happen to be Jews," she answered. "Mary and Frank are Episcopalians. I scarcely remember what the others are. So you can see it's really not a church at all. Not really an organization. We meet in winter, or in bad weather at homes, but in summer we usually meet out of doors. And we have no minister," she explained.

"Oh." He was surprised.

"It's really a teaching of Judaism and of Christianity too," she continued. "Do you remember when Moses went up to meet God on the mountain and He told Moses there were to be no altars, that worship was to be a thing of the spirit?"

Steve nodded silently.

"Doesn't the New Testament say the same—'in spirit and in truth'? The temple was really a concession to the weakness of man, wasn't it?"

Once more he nodded, thoughtfully.

Small glasses had been set before each person present. Now Sister Dorothy bustled about pouring homemade elderberry wine into them and putting a plate of unleavened bread into the center of the table. Then she seated herself and everyone bowed his head praying silently. As each finished his prayer he helped himself to a bit of the bread, then drank the single swallow of amber liquid. Steve, after a glance of inquiry at Emily and her small nod, followed suit.

It had been to him the Holy Communion, the remembrance of the Last Supper but he wondered what it had been to Emily and John who were not of his faith. He wanted to ask but nobody else spoke for a time and he felt, though the silence was unstrained, that he should not.

After a little, speech began again, now one, then another, presenting some small problem for discussion. Some dealt with farming, "which we all more or less do," Emily explained; others with problems of daily living, of child raising, even concerning a cake that had not turned out right. And there were strictly religious questions too.

But it was Frank Clarke who posed the one which gave Steve once more that feeling of the excitement of being on the edge of discovery.

"I was reading today something which puzzles me, something I cannot reconcile. It's from the seventh chapter of St. Mark and should certainly not have struck me so forcibly today but somehow I had always passed it over before, a clear statement that thought of sin is sin itself."

Steve had no need for the actual quotation. It came to him in the very words of the Scripture; "For from within, out of the heart of men proceed evil thoughts, adulteries, fornications, murders, thefts, covetousness, wickedness, deceit, laciviousness, an evil eye, pride, foolishness. All these evil things come from within and defile a man."

His mind was a syllable ahead of Frank's quoting aloud all the way through to the end of that particular passage. Frank was frowning as he finished and he went on in his own words. "I can't accept the statement that thoughts and deeds are one."

Brother John added thoughtfully: "'As a man thinketh in his heart, so is he.' That is how the wise man put it."

There was silence, thoughtful silence. Steve wondered if there was prayer about the table. There were no bowed heads but the atmosphere was fitting for it.

It was Emily, volatile, face alight and sweet with homely wisdom, who spoke first. "I believe it. And I think I know the reason for it. Brother Frank, you are at work on an invention?"

He nodded, puzzled by this apparent change of subject.

"How much thought precedes even the first trial and error?" She was eager, leaning forward, her eyes fixed on his dark face.

Slowly his frown faded and a smile took its place. "It's like an iceberg, Sister Emily. Most of my work I alone can see. Four fifths is in my mind."

"It seems to me that all good things must be that way. The plan precedes the deed. And the planning is the long work, the doing the short one." Emily was still uplifted by her thought, eager, willing him and the others to understand.

"Then it follows," Frank was agreeing quietly, though his eyes shone too, "that evil is the same. The thought and the deed are one, inseparable, the thought being the first and most important part."

Again there was silence and thought. Now and again

someone nodded his agreement. Leonard Kemp, the actor, burst into speech at last. "But no! That's not fair. Thoughts come and a man cannot always stop them. How can one say then that thought and sin are one."

Mary Clarke had worn an impassive face throughout the entire evening but now she spoke. "I had thought of that. It seems to me that we are not held accountable for passing thoughts any more than we are for strangers whom we pass in the street, but for the ones we hold and make the companions of our bosoms—" she smiled a bit at the bombast of the phrase "—the ones we seek again and again of our own choosing, the ones we study for ways and means— They are the beginning, and the development of evil."

Brother Warren had not accepted the theory either. "But how is a man to control his thinking? It's saints that the Christian teachings are demanding!" He was indignant that so much should be expected of him.

"On the contrary," Martha Pender, the poet, interrupted, "sainthood, as I see it is in the striving, the seeking. It comes in a little insight here, a new light on something there. Sainthood is working toward perfection, no matter how far we fall short of it."

Frank, the mechanical perfectionist, agreed. "That I can believe. God does demand saints of that sort."

Steve was surprised to hear his own voice speaking. "God demands saints. But he forgives sin. To me that is the important thing. He understands and forgives sin. As a stranger, I perhaps have no right to speak—"

He was interrupted by a murmur of assurance that they wished him to go on and he did so. "I discovered today the spirit of forgiveness, the spirit of fatherhood. Perhaps I mean that I found God." He paused at the

wonder of that. He had not known that he was on holy
ground, yet as surely as Moses had come from the mountain with a vision of Jehovah for himself and his people,
he had had his smaller vision, his little clarification of
the God he worshipped. He had finished that vision
here tonight. "I have seen something new to me, a God
who demands saints but forgives faltering footsteps
along the pathway of sainthood as a human father forgives—who asks only that we grow, individually and as
the human race in—in body, and spirit, in favor with
Him and with man." He fell silent. There was silence
about the table.

After a while there was further discussion. Steve did
not enter into it, did not hear it. He was lost in the
implications of this new vision which he had seen. That
God had a plan for individuals he had always believed,
but it was a new thought that the whole of mankind
moved to a design of His making. It was his duty, then,
to try to find that plan and his own part in it.

"As a small child turns to his father who knows him
as the child cannot know himself, and knows the world
as the child cannot," he thought.

Perhaps here in the City of Brothers, with these who
sought that plan above all else, he too could find his
place.

The clock on a high shelf struck nine thirty and the
adults about the table began to stir, to gather up children, to put on coats and make preparations to go out
into the night. Steve woke from his thoughts with a
start and moved with them, still slightly dazed. All
about him there was a clasping of hands, the murmur
of, "The peace of God go with you." Even after they
were outside the murmur seemed to linger in the cold

clear air as he walked home with John and Emily and their children. Surely here he might find what he sought.

That second night in the small bedroom Steve slept without waking. Only with the dawn and the first birds came consciousness that others in the house were stirring. He rose and breakfasted with them, and afterward went out to mend a fence, his thoughts still far removed from his immediate world. It was as if, during the long night and the busy morning he prayed though no words came. Only his spirit, completely at peace, stretched out to find the way for him to follow, and toward noon he reached a satisfactory conclusion.

The way of the Brothers was not for him. He could not remain here secluded, seeking his own salvation. His call was elsewhere, though just where he could not be sure. A phrase from an old hymn came to him. "One step enough for me." He could live like that, for now he felt the certainty that when the time came he could see that step. His life would be like the road which he had taken to the City of Brothers, with the lights of his car picking out only a little way ahead, yet enough for him to keep the road. For now he would lift his hand up and put it in God's and follow as he was led—for now, back to Kinsman.

When the midday meal had been eaten he explained all this to Emily and John.

They accepted his verdict gravely.

"We are not people of creed, as you have seen," John told him. "Each follows his own thoughts, seeks in his own way. Yours may take you far from us, then bring you back as it did us. Or it may never bring you back. The peace of God go with you, Brother Stephen. And bring you back to your friends here if God should see fit."

Emily too gave him her hand, her wise and tender smile. "The peace of God, Brother Stephen."

Stephen's car went chugging down the mountain toward a telegraph office where he could send a message to J.G. that he would be back in his pulpit on Sunday. By that time he would have readied a sermon. Meantime he would take the road slowly, arriving home Saturday night. He felt as if he had been struggling against the tide all his life and that now he had turned and was going with it. This then was what all the farewells had once meant—"God be with you" which had become good-bye. "Go with God" which he suspected the Spanish said with as little thought as to its real meaning. "I commend you to God" which had become the French "Adieu," and now, the peace of God. The very words were a stillness of spirit.

CHAPTER XVII

DREW would have found the house on the hill empty without his mother even if the weather had been beautifully sunny, but with the atmosphere running the gamut from gloomy and merely damp, to gloomier with a downpour, it was almost unbearable. He and his mother had been unusually close and during her illness of the last year, her dependence had made her doubly dear.

Lottie, the cook, had never lived in. Dread of the empty house and the steady drip of rain stayed with him all day and by the time the factory closed at four thirty he had a plan. A few minutes later he was picking up Bobby and Kinny who was at the parsonage. They would work on the boat, and, provided Paula Kinsman gave her permission, remain for supper.

Arrangements having been made thus far, Drew turned back to Elizabeth with a look of sudden remembrance.

"But then you'll be all alone here."

"It won't matter. I can have one of those sissy meals by the fire and read or sew," she told him.

"Tea and toast," he scolded. "Or something equally unnourishing. I know how women behave when no man is about. Here. Into raincoat and rubbers you go and come along."

She smiled, making no move to obey. "I am expected to sit and watch you three male creatures build an ark?" she asked, amused.

He held out the coat firmly. "You can if you like, though I imagine you'd be bored to death. But you *can* do a job for me that I would really appreciate. I have dreaded the thought of packing mother's clothes to give away. Would I be imposing if I asked you to do that?"

She rose, her eyes damp with sympathy and understanding. "I'd love doing it, Drew. I know how hard a thing like that can be."

And she did enjoy the task, especially handling Mrs. Phalen's dresses of soft, rich materials which were both colorful and excellent in line as well. The room where she worked was delightful, with a fire crackling in the fireplace and making shadows on the wall. The radio played quietly and she joined in occasionally with a snatch of song or a hummed chorus.

It was after six when Drew and the boys appeared at the bedroom door. Bobby was bursting with importance. "Mom, Uncle Drew let me use his tools. He let me use a saw that goes—" He broke off to make an earsplitting sound.

Elizabeth clapped her hands over her ears and smiled at Drew. "Should you? Tools like that cost a lot of money and a boy of nine can be mighty destructive."

The two boys looked from one adult to the other with pleading in their eyes. It was Kinny who voiced their anxiety. "We're as careful as anything, Mrs. Marsden. Honest we are."

Bobby contented himself with, "Aw, Mom, geezil."

"They really are careful," Drew assured her. "And I'm there to see that nothing happens to them. I do hope that you haven't been bored to death, or gotten too tired." He looked about at the boxes packed and piled. "It's a thankless job."

Elizabeth smiled. "I've loved every minute of it. I had begun to be exceedingly weary of my own four walls and hadn't realized it."

"Well, you three made my coming home this afternoon possible. There's a bath right behind you, and if you want to primp, I believe you'll find the makings in the dressing table. Dinner's in half an hour, Lottie says. I'll take the men with me." He smiled and was gone.

When dinner was over Elizabeth insisted that they should return home. "It's nearly bedtime for the boys and Bobby was up very late last night."

Drew made a sorry face at her. "I was hoping you would sit by my fire and talk to me."

She could understand his loneliness, even had a matching loneliness of her own. "Perhaps you could sit by my fire instead," she suggested.

And it was thus they compromised, talking quietly of unimportant and comfortable topics.

"How long has Bob—that was his name, wasn't it? —been gone?" Drew asked her after an unhurried silence.

"Forever. Nearly ten years, though he's been dead only eight. I have some letters but he never was much of one for saying things, much less for putting them on paper." She looked into the fire and remembered those boyish, unsatisfactory scrawls. She had never really been in touch with Bob after he had gone away to war.

"It must have been hard on girls like you," Drew said softly.

Elizabeth swung her eyes about to meet his. "You know I used to dream, before Bob was killed, that he came back and I didn't even recognize him—a nightmare that I dreamed over and over. I could name off the color of his eyes and how tall he was but—there were times when I couldn't remember what he looked like, not to picture him in my mind. After we had grown up together! I've never told anybody else that, Drew."

He met her eyes gravely. "And you've been punishing yourself for it all these years. He probably had times like that, too. Adjustment would have been hard. Sometimes people have found it impossible."

"I've never wanted anybody else," she told him defensively.

He laughed then. "I have. My girl married while I

was overseas. I couldn't blame her. It was a long time and I had to get my education after I came back. I had a spell of falling in love with every girl I met after I got home. And falling out."

She laughed too. "Delayed puppy love, it sounds like to me. A great big boy like you."

He grinned impishly. "It was fun though."

Bobby broke in at that moment with a plaintive cry from his bedroom. "Mom, can I have a drink of water? Can I? I'm awf'ly thirsty."

Drew looked at his watch. "Do you realize it's twelve-thirty? I'll take the boy his drink and go home. It's been a wonderful evening, Elizabeth."

"You don't have to *raise* Bobby," she told him, then flushed, "just because he has a crush on you."

"I have a sort of crush on him too. I'll water him and tell him goodnight, since he's awake anyhow."

It was good, she thought, to have someone else do the things which were really her duties. It was wonderful. "But don't get any notions, Elizabeth Elliott Marsden," she warned herself. "You're twenty-eight years old and a widow with a son. Besides Drew's already told you that he's an in-again, out-again sort."

But she listened to the water running in the kitchen, Drew's footsteps on the way to the room she shared with Bobby, to their voices in comradely conversation. A moment later he was back, a big man smelling pleasantly of tobacco and tweed. He climbed into his raincoat and grinned at her again.

"He's quite a kid, that one," he told her, adding, "Know how long old Steve will be gone?"

Elizabeth shook her head. "When a person is—running away from himself— Drew, you are a most upsetting person. I keep saying things I didn't mean to say to *anybody*."

"It's chemistry, or radar, or something," he told her. "Don't worry about it. I knew he was all stewed up about something so you haven't given away any secrets. And don't worry about Steve. When it comes to anything important, he'll have both feet on the ground."

Suddenly Bobby appeared in pajamas, blinking at the light in the foyer. "Uncle Drew, can me and Kinny help you with the boat some more tomorrow?"

"I'm counting on it," Drew assured him.

"Don't let him get to be a nuisance, Drew," Elizabeth protested. "And back to bed with you, my fine fellow."

"Just a minute," Drew said. "It seems to me that I saw a circus poster on the Atlanta road yesterday. It said Saturday, and that's my day off. Would you two and young Kinny, if you want to include him, like to be my guests and stay in town for dinner? I don't know when I've seen a circus."

Elizabeth looked at Drew but his eyes were on Bobby who shouted like a young savage and began a war dance into the living room and back out to them again. "That'd be really keen!" the boy cried. "We'd *all* like that, Uncle Drew."

Drew looked at Elizabeth now, a question in his eyes. She laughed. It seemed to her that she had been laughing all evening. "Fine," she told him. "You're very good to us, Drew."

There was something in the tone of his voice, in his eyes as they met hers, that brought the blood to her face. She was glad the light in the foyer was dim. She felt excited and warm even after she closed the door behind him and she began scolding herself sharply. "Just because he's the first man who's looked at you in ages— He's lonely, and he likes small boys."

"Isn't he keen, Mom?" Bobby was pulling at her sleeve to demand. "Didn't I tell you he was keen?"

Elizabeth nodded absently. "Hop along into bed now, Sonny. It's very late."

But when she had tucked him in and bent to kiss him, Bobby spoke again, quite wide awake. "Don't you think, Mom, since God took my real daddy to heaven, maybe I could have Uncle Drew instead? I think he'd make a keen daddy, don't you, Mom?"

Elizabeth froze half way up from bending over him. Her breath seemed to have caught somewhere about her solar plexus.

"Bobby Marsden, you—" The words were sharp and angry. She caught herself just in time. "Honey, Drew is a fine friend for you and your Uncle Steve and me but— You see, if he were a father for you, he'd have to be my husband. That means that he'd have to love me very much, and I'd have to love him very much. Besides, deciding who is to be his wife is something a man has to do for himself. I— It was your father I loved, Sonny. You must never mention anything like that to Drew, never."

Her voice was sharp once more and she was overwhelmed with a sense of failure. She always tried to answer Bobby's questions without evasion, honestly, as the books said, but she knew that this time she had made a poor job of it. She was still too confused to think things out. She began to undress, pushing back tears that she did not mean to shed.

Joel was parking her car when Drew drove up one day to bring Kinny home from "ark-building."

"Hi, stranger," he called to the girl. "Where've you been of late?"

"Oh, 'round," she answered negligently. "And you?" Suddenly she was embarrassed, realizing that he had been watching his mother die. She rushed on impetuously. "Oh, Drew, I *was* sorry about Miss Laura. Sorry for you and sorry for all of us who loved her."

He nodded quietly. "She was a great girl. I was lucky to have had her. You rushing off to do something?"

"N-no. Going back to my place to take off my shoes and read a good book. Anything I can do for you?"

"Maybe. If you would," he answered. "Lottie scolded me like anything last night because I ate out and left a lot of good food 'layin' 'round unet'. But now it seems like I can't go home and eat all by myself, this first time. Breakfasts are different. I always had them by myself in the kitchen anyhow. Be a pal?"

She looked off in the direction of her little house, unlighted and unwelcoming. She was not much more eager to go there than he was to go into his empty place.

"Lottie'll make it entirely respectable," he added.

She laughed suddenly, a soft, musical lilt of merriment that was all the more lovely for the gloom of the weather. "As if I were scared of you, Drew Phalen. Or gossiping tongues. Your car, or mine?"

"Mine," he told her firmly. "When I take a lady out, I bring her back and do the thing in style. In you go." He went around and got in under the wheel, continuing as if there had been no pause, "Flowers are indicated, it seems to me. A corsage for you and something to go on the table. Candles yet, maybe."

She laughed again. "You know what, Drew? Two years ago, maybe as little as a year ago, I think I would have swooned with delight at the thought of an evening like this. But I would have insisted on going home first and prettying up, and then I would have gone completely female on you."

He righted the car in the street and looked at her, mischief in his eyes. "A year ago? Why not now?"

"M-m-m. Surely you knew that I had the most gosh-awful crush on you? You're not that modest." She hooted at the idea.

"I hadn't suspected it," he insisted.

"Well, I did. And then Claire came back and you started mooning about her. I almost decided to go into a decline. Didn't you see me looking pale?"

"I guess I was mooning in Claire's direction almost too much to notice anything," he confessed. "You must admit that she's the most beautiful thing running loose. But I got over it. This violent and heartbreaking crush of yours, it's entirely in the past?" He was teasing her and enjoying it.

"Definitely," she assured him.

They were both laughing as he drew up before the florist's.

"Oh, Drew, I'm glad you came along. I was that low in my mind. J.G.'s out of town, trying to do something about refinancing the mill, and Steve's gone off on some mysterious errand and— You know I have to appear in court next week about that wreck I had and—I seem to have gone all helpless."

"Nothing could intrigue me more than a damsel in distress. Let me know the hour and the day and science will be forgotten."

She was pretty sure that he was spoofing entirely but it was fun. It was fun even if, seriously, she was no longer pining over him, was sure that she would never feel that way about him again.

CHAPTER XVIII

STEVE came back to Kinsman only a little before midnight on Saturday. He had spent most of Saturday parked in a country churchyard where there were big trees and a well with a bucket, working on the next day's sermon. Only after he had crossed into Georgia just after dark, did he run into rain again, heavy and persistent, almost sullen. There was a night light burning beside the front door of the parsonage, showing that Elizabeth had received his telegram but he went in on tiptoe so as not to wake her and the boy.

His room smelled musty and un-lived-in and he twisted the casements open at once, putting his nose against the screen and sniffing the fresher dampness from the outside. Only then did he turn on the light.

Elizabeth had stacked letters on his pillow, had turned down the covers. He picked up the mail and riffled through it: a bill from the book store for a life of John Wesley which he had not yet unwrapped, a circular advertising religious movies, a postcard from a parishoner on a trip—and a letter from the radio station. He ripped open the latter and unfolded it with rising curiosity. During his stay at the City of Brothers he had

almost forgotten that project along with nearly everything else of his everyday life. Briefly he longed for that
haven of untroubled existence, then he squared his
shoulders, and read:

"Dear Steve:
    The sponsors liked it! We'll start rehearsing October
first and go on the air about the fifteenth. There's some
talk of television. Good luck, fellow.
    I'll be driving up to Kinsman meantime to talk to you
but will call first as I never know when I can get away.
                                    Yours truly,
                                    George Robbins"

    With a curiously detached feeling Steve folded the
letter back in its original creases. He supposed he was
glad his written programs had been successful. Unless
something came up—he corrected that thought carefully— Unless God led him into some other way, he
would go on with them. But the excitement he had felt
earlier when he had written them was gone.
    The thought of the programs presented anew the
problem of Claire. He would see her tomorrow afternoon and talk with her. He was surprised when he realized that he had hardly thought of her at all during
his absence. It was as if he had set up a psychological
block, cutting her out of his consciousness. But he had
thought of Joel, of the challenge which she always
seemed to fling at him. And he had worried about Elizabeth, her loneliness and frustration.
    Now the problem lay before him once more. He could
visualize Claire as he had seen her on that morning before his going away, could see his ring rolling in a half

circle on the kitchen floor. But he could not remember
if he had picked it up.

He sighed and rubbed his hand across his eyes. He
was tired from driving and from the hours he had spent
on his sermon. He was nervous about how that sermon
would be received. He wanted it to move his listeners
as no other sermon of his ever had.

But now life crowded in on him with all its unsettled
problems. He realized for the first time that he had not
decided whether he would continue in the ministry,
had not decided about Claire. Really he was right back
where he had started, he thought in discouragement.

And then it was as if a voice spoke, so clearly did the
thought fill his mind and heart. "But you promised to
follow God!"

He finished buttoning his pajama coat and knelt in
prayer for a long time. When he had finished he got into
bed and was at once asleep.

Sunday school had been well attended. Elizabeth,
with a smile tugging at her mouth had told Steve under
her breath, "I know why—so mamas and papas can
have the house to themselves for an hour. Heavens, how
tired everybody is of everybody in his family, shut up
like we are these days."

But at church service, as Steve had expected, the congregation was small, hardly sixty people scattered about
the church. The young minister joined the procession a
bit impatiently. It seemed ostentatious in the nearly
empty place. He had always liked church ritual, had
even, in his college days of serving country churches,
preferred to wear a robe, to follow all the formality of
the service. Now he would have pushed all this aside.

He entered the pulpit and knelt before his choir. Usually at this time he repeated some fitting Scripture as a prayer. Today he gave his own with a deep sincerity, a prayer which he had prayed when he had stopped on the roadside yesterday and begun the preparation of his sermon notes. "Oh God, our father, fill my mouth with *Thy* words, as You would have me say them. And let my people hear."

The choir chanted, "The Lord Is In His Holy Temple" and the congregational rustle of finding the first hymn began. Steve led in the creed, the prayers, the responsive reading, and read from memory the Scripture which he had chosen for his sermon. The choir gave its anthem and solo, the offering was taken and prayed over and placed on the altar. And through it all Steve found his breathing shallow, his hands cold and his throat tight. He never remembered feeling a deeper stage fright before a sermon. He had been unable to identify separate members of his congregation. At last the time came. He stood beside the pulpit, his hands clenched nervously, and announced his text.

"For verily I say unto you, Till heaven and earth pass, one jot or one tittle shall in no wise pass from the law, till all be fulfilled." He closed the Book with a hand not quite steady and lifted his face to his congregation.

"Have you ever," he began earnestly, "thought of the proof that God exists, that God is God?" It was as if he had asked no rhetorical question. He had paused there after that first question as if he expected every member of his flock to answer. There was tension in his hands, in his voice, in his thin brown face.

Then he went on. "We are likely to cite miracles, breaks in the usual performance of the law of God as we

know it, as that proof. We speak of the axehead which
floated for Elisha, the sun which stood still for Joshua,
Jesus raising the dead or healing the leper. These, we
say, are proofs that God is God—He can break the law.
But I ask you this morning to think otherwise of God.
To think of Him as the Maker of our law which is His
law; the planner of our destiny which moves toward
His perfection; the Master of our ways, which He honors
by letting us choose."

It had been Steve's habit to accent his sentences for
the greatest effect, to follow his carefully written notes
so that each thought would fall in its place. But now
he had forgotten all this, had ignored his notes. Only
the deep desire that his people might see the vision as
he had seen it, was in him.

"Have you ever tried to keep a rule which you have
made, perhaps a New Year's resolution, a promise to
correct some small fault? How did those resolutions,
those laws, if you will, turn out, no matter how sin-
cerely you meant them? Have you ever made a rule for
your child? Or perhaps a condition, 'If you do such and
such, I shall—' And did you? Could you?

"Are you thinking, as I did at this point, that it is only
human to err, that no human being is perfect? If it is
human to err, then it follows that the exact following of
the law is divine."

Steve leaned forward, looking into the blur of faces of
those to whom he spoke and suddenly he saw Joel. Her
being there surprised him, jolted him momentarily out
of his complete absorption in his subject. Her lips were
a little parted, her face lifted, her eyes bright. He could
have sworn that she *knew* what he spoke of, that she
understood. He went on refreshed by that thought.

"It has been some days since we have seen the sun here in Kinsman," he said with a brief smile, "but we do not wonder if it rose. We believe—we know—that at the exact moment when it should have risen this morning, it rose. We know also that, more accurate than the best timepiece man has ever devised, it will go down when it should. Has even one of you questioned it in the days when we have not actually seen it?

"Again, I think of the stars, so fixed in the heavens, so exact in their courses that astronomers can foretell their appearances a hundred years apart. I think of our world, whirling and turning in the universe, yet always finding itself in the same place at the same time of the year. Knowing human frailty, your own frailty, does it not comfort you to know that we are in the hands of a God who can lay out a plan like that?"

He paused and looked about him, for the first time really seeing faces, Claire's, Drew's, Paula Kinsman's, Elizabeth's. He took a deep breath and continued. "Perhaps it has occurred to you that a machine is exact, that the higher mechanism is the variable, and that is true, but one other thing I must tell you. Your machine —how long does it last, even the best of them? I like the picture of Him, eternal, unvarying, perfect.

"And this brings me at last to my text which, you will remember, concerns the law of God. I am sure that there are many laws. Some concern the scientist, the riddles which He has set for science to puzzle out, and to me the scientist, giving infinite care to the finding and explaining of those laws serves Him no less than do His other children.

"But what I wish you to recall this morning are two other laws which He has given us. 'And thou shalt love the Lord thy God with all thy heart, and with all thy soul, and with all thy mind, and with all thy strength; this is My first commandment. And the second is like, namely this, Thou shalt love thy neighbor as thyself.' It is the first of these I wish to emphasize this morning."

He was conscious of the unmoving attention of his congregation. It was almost as if they did not breathe. Perhaps he had never had more undivided listening. He went on very quietly.

"Love? I asked myself. The love of humanity, of a single man, for God? What does it mean? We use the word in a human sense rather carelessly but because we are constrained by our humanity I tried to see anew what it meant in a human sense. And I thought first of a longing for companionship. We want, with a desire that never lessens, to be with those we love."

His voice deepened. "Most of you knew and loved Mrs. Phalen to whom we paid our last respects here recently. You have heard her say, as I have, that she walked with God, and you and I knew, whether she said it or not, that indeed it was true. I had never heard anyone else say just that, with no false piety but with reverence and joy. It left me shocked and surprised. But since that time I have asked myself over and over, how is it possible to walk with God? This morning I bring you the answer. You walk in His ways.

"I know as probably you do not, for I have thought about those five words for a long time, how deceptive they are in their simplicity. It is no easy answer, for His ways are the ways of perfection and we are scarcely conscious of our first uncertain steps along that path. As Christ puts it, 'None is good.' Perfection is God's dream for us, and we comprehend it much as a child who takes small bucketsful of the ocean and pours it into a hole which he has dug. As he will never empty that ocean, as he can move only bits of it, so do we understand. The impossibility of that task is a sobering, discouraging thing. We can never in this world walk in God's ways."

Steve had forgotten his people now. He was once more experiencing the exhilaration of discovery and inspiration which he had known during the past three days. "And then we remember that God is a Father, and we have a picture of Him, walking beside us, reaching down His hand, fitting His steps to ours, as a human father does to his small child as he takes those first, uncertain steps. We cannot companion God—but He will companion us.

"He will guide, strengthen, lead. But even He, within the law He has made, cannot take those steps *for* us. So I come to you faced with still another verse of Scripture. 'Seek ye *first* the kingdom of God.' Where more likely that we will find Him? Where more likely that we will discover His laws and learn to live within them?

"There is a very old story of God as the Great Organist and one day when He was not at the organ the wicked angel stole up and tore the divine music to bits and scattered it far over the earth and each played his own bit and there was discord. Only when God had gathered them all together in the last day were they music once more.

"It is the highest challenge which I can offer you, this of seeking the kingdom of God. The voyage of Columbus was small adventure beside it. I bid you— No, God bids you. Seek the kingdom of God. Stretch your mind to the exactitude of His law, your hearts to the perfect love of God, your strength to the ways in which He walks. You and I will never attain it but we can take our small pails to the ocean. We can cherish our tiny bits of music. And in God's good time He will gather them up and make them common knowledge and light for a generation to come after us. I am exalted that He asks perfection of me. I am humbly thankful that He forgives and understands the faltering of my steps."

Steve had come to the end. The church was damp and cold but there was perspiration on his face. He trembled with weariness. The morning program stared up at him from the church bulletin on the pulpit but he did not wish to sing the hymn numbered there, or indeed any hymn. He lifted his hand and prayed in benediction and blessing.

"May the peace of God go with you now and always."

When he lowered his hand and opened his eyes his glance fell on Claire. She sat still in the Kinsman pew gathering her things together. Like most of the rest of the congregation she was silent. But on her face there was a frown and bewilderment, and looking at her, Steve knew that where he had most wanted understanding, he had failed.

CHAPTER XIX

STEVE had never felt so tired after a sermon. The thought of food was impossible and, at Elizabeth's insistence, he drank a glass of milk and lay down. But even then he could not relax. After an hour of trying vainly, and growing momentarily more keyed up, he rose and went to see Claire.

The four Kinsmans were having the noon meal with her and Steve was ushered into the dining room to share the dessert. J.G. was talking as usual when his pastor entered, but he broke off to greet him.

"Whatever happened to you since last time I saw you, boy?" he asked gruffly.

Steve was sorely disappointed not to have found Claire alone but he managed to smile. "Why?" he asked.

"You didn't seem the same man in the pulpit at all," J.G. assured him. "I like a man to take the cool, intellectual approach to religion. None of this camp-meeting, emotional stuff." His eyes were fixed critically on Steve's face.

Paula smiled quietly. "I thought it a very good sermon, dear," she told her husband.

J.G. shrugged. "Oh, for women. But what would happen to the world if working men went for that stuff? I can tell you. It would fall apart. I'm religious, sure. And I'm honest, but I've got to be on my toes every minute or somebody'll be taking everything I've got away from me. This kingdom of heaven thing is all right, but a business man's got to eat, sleep, and live business or he'll wake up in the poor house."

"And a man in the ministry must eat, sleep, and live his religion, J.G." Steve answered softly.

Claire's eyes were fixed on Steve with the same puzzled look she had worn at the service. There was the same little frown between her brows. Steve realized that he had never seen her frown like this before.

"I had you brought here," J.G. went on, "because I thought you were sensible. These days, a man's got to appeal to reason. I never did like shouting and hysterics."

Steve looked at him in astonishment. "I'm sure I never raised my voice, J.G. And I certainly meant my arguments to be reasonable."

J.G. shook his head. "Maybe so. But that's the way the sermon affected me."

Steve chose to change the subject. "Elizabeth tells me you have been away too."

"Yes," J.G. admitted glumly. "Trying to refinance the mill."

"I thought you'd be gone at least two weeks," Claire said.

"Planned to," J.G. said, "but it didn't seem to be any use. They said they'd let me know later, and I decided to do my waiting at home. Now they'll be sending an inspector down here or something of the sort, and me with the biggest stock pile of goods I've ever had on hand. My responsibilities are pretty heavy, I can tell you, what with hundreds of people depending on me for a living, money as tight as it is, and sales falling off. And then all this rain!"

Kinny looked up at that. "What's rain got to do with it, Pop?"

J.G. sighed. "Water's piled up behind the dam now higher than the engineers figured on. More rain than we've any record of and no sign of stopping. Four weeks of it. There you are, preacher, you might put some of this excess religious fervor to some practical use and pray for it to stop. How about that?"

Joel had been silent up to this moment. Now she

laughed. "That would ruin things for Drew. He's building an ark against the floods. You should see it."

"Drew's living depends on the mills," J.G. reminded her sourly.

The Kinsmans lingered after dinner but Steve was determined to outsit them. When at last Claire had gone to see them to the door, he began to wander about the room. It was then that he discovered his seal ring in an ash tray on the coffee table. He was about to speak to her about it but she entered with a question on her lips.

"You had a good trip, Steve?"

He ignored that and went toward her. "You haven't welcomed me home, Claire."

She returned his kiss briefly, then quickly withdrew from his arms and seated herself across the room where there was only one chair. "Tell me about the trip, Steve. All about it."

He tried. He told her of the Bischoffs, the three-hundred-year-old farmhouse they had restored, the farm John ran efficiently, Emily's weaving, their amazing library, their children. He described the others who made up the City of Brothers. He told her of the evening he had spent with the group, their discussions, and even his own thoughts.

Claire listened to him carefully but the puzzled look deepened in her eyes. And when he had finished she sat thinking a moment more.

"But, Steve," she said then, "they sound so normal, the way you tell it. I can't understand why they want to go off like that and— It just doesn't make sense to me."

He tried again. "I've told it poorly, darling. If you could see them, if you could know the peace, the quiet of soul among them. Perhaps we could go there together some time. They urged me to return."

"No," she answered thoughtfully, "I don't think I'd like that. I'd be a complete alien there. I suppose some people have a talent for the spiritual, the religious. I have always thought it was only the ignorant and simple, but the Brothers do not seem to be like that. And of course you aren't. As for me, I am afraid I lack the spark." She was sad, but very certain.

He moved across the room, seated himself on the arm of her chair and drew her to him. "I think it's practice, darling. Religion's new to you. You haven't tried. But you will. For me."

She shook her head against his shoulder. "I don't believe I want to, Steve. All this talk of perfection and striving toward it, it's like a foreign language to me. Just thinking about it makes me tired."

He touched her throat gently. "New ideas are always strange, dearest. It takes years to make them yours. But you would have me to help you."

Her smile was wry. "To hold my hand while I take the first uncertain steps?" she quoted him. "I like my life as it is, Steve. Comfortable, easy, pleasant. And there's a puritan streak in you—something of the reformer, even perhaps, the martyr. It's funny that I didn't see it before."

"I?" he asked, amazed.

"Yes, it—it seems that way. Or perhaps I'm in love with an imaginary man, Steve, and you with an imaginary woman. Perhaps the person each of us loves never really existed. I kept thinking that all during church this morning." She sounded as weary now as he had felt when he had finished his sermon.

"Nonsense," he rallied her. "The weather has you down as badly as it has J.G."

She smiled, not in amusement, but to show that she appreciated his effort. "This kind of thinking is strange to me, Steve. And this morning, while you were preaching, even you seemed strange, different, not at all like the man I promised to marry."

He looked toward his ring where it lay in the ash tray. "So you didn't wear my ring while I was gone. Are you trying to tell me that you don't want to marry me now?" He was hurt and disappointed.

She did not answer at once and when she did her voice was husky with trouble. "I don't know *what* I want, Steve. I was so sure that I loved you but you've certainly changed. Perhaps I've changed, too. Or maybe it's just the weather. I don't think I've ever been so confused in my whole life."

He patted her hand. "I understand, honey. Because I'm like that a lot of the time myself. Let's leave everything until the weather clears up, shall we?"

She buried her face against his shoulder. "Steve, there never was such a patient, understanding man in the world. Thank you, darling."

He glanced at the watch on his wrist. "Honey, it's nearly six and I have a sermon to glance over before I preach. I hate to leave you when you're blue and miserable but—"

She sighed and it seemed to him that it might almost be in relief. "I know," she agreed. "You have a job to attend to. I don't think I'll come tonight, Steve. It's raining and I'm awfully tired. You'll forgive me, won't you?"

He tilted her face up and kissed her. "You stay here and rest, honey. And don't fret about *us*. It'll work out. You wait and see."

That night he preached on the text, "God is a spirit," and stressed the fact that emphasis on the material can set people apart from God. There were only seventeen in the congregation, Joel Kinsman among them, but he preached with the same fire that had possessed him that morning. He was, under God's guidance, priest and prophet to these people. It was his duty and privilege to make them see God.

Monday was Steve's day of rest and he was late getting to his study. The big clock on the main building at the mill was striking ten when he entered the church. It was raining harder than ever and he was not prepared for the small rain-coated figure silhouetted against the clouded window. It was Joel Kinsman and she had her back to him, playing with the control cord of the venetian blind.

"Good morning, Joel. Anything I can do for you?" he asked.

She had been so lost in her thoughts that she had not heard his approach and was startled. "Oh! Good morning, Steve. But that phrase wasn't intended for a day like this, was it? Honestly, I'm so tired of it, I think I'll go away somewhere and cry."

She turned, took the chair he offered and sat there with her shoulders tight and her hands clenched in her lap.

"Something else is worrying you. Want to talk about it?" he asked, after waiting for her to speak.

Then she raised her great eyes to him and they were full of trouble. "I'm not used to bothering other people

with—with my affairs but—" She trailed off and dropped
her eyes again.

"If it's your appearance in court that's worrying you,
I'll be glad to go with you," he offered, feeling about
for the root of her trouble.

She was surprised. "Oh, no. The others in the accident aren't preferring any charges and the trial is going to be a mere formality. Drew will go with me."

"Drew?" he repeated, somewhat piqued. She had
mentioned Drew's boat yesterday, too. Perhaps she and
Drew— For some reason the thought did not give him
pleasure. His voice was rather stiff as he repeated his
question. "But there *is* something troubling you?"

She nodded. "It's J.G. I'd never have bothered you
if it hadn't been for your sermon yesterday but—" Suddenly a mischievous smile lit her face. "Yesterday you
were more like a preacher, Steve."

He met her mood at once. "Haggard and pale?"

She had grown serious once more. "No. But you
sounded as if you really believed every word you said.
Before that— The ministry was just a job."

He nodded slowly. "Yes."

"But I really came here about J.G. Paula says he
walked the floor all night. He talks just as much as he
always did, but he's lost his self confidence. He's not
eating or sleeping. It's not like him. I'm worried about
him."

"And you think I can do something for him?" Steve
asked.

"I don't know. He's been— He didn't like your morning sermon, Steve. He said you didn't know anything
about the world, that a man had to meet business on a
business-like basis. Things like that."

"I know. I was emotional." Steve repeated J.G.'s words.

Her face was grave. "But you *weren't* at all Steve. I never listened to a sermon so hard in my life. It was as if you were speaking to me, just me. I have never been very happy, you know. I've never felt I really belonged anywhere. I thought maybe a job would give me what I was looking for when I finished school last June but J.G. said my working would be a reflection on him— he's been quite sensitive, recently, about such things. Then I got to running around with that Atlanta crowd, and that wasn't what I wanted either. But what you said yesterday, Steve, set me thinking."

"Thank you, Joel," he told her quietly. This was the first time that anyone had ever come to him privately and said, "Your sermon helped me." His parishoners were much more likely to say casually after church, "Another good sermon, parson." The two things were quite different.

"And what I thought was this," Joel went on. "Maybe my importance is to God. I thought about that idea of the world moving toward perfection and I like it. And I hope I'm not being irreverent, but after He has put something into our hands, it seems unlikely to me that He would snatch it back just because we were making a mess of it."

Steve nodded silently but in his heart he was saying, "Thank God, thank God!" He had needed this encouragement, this understanding.

"I thought that we were the hands and feet—and heart, too, to do the things He wants done. It isn't exactly a new thought, and maybe it's corn." She reddened with embarrassment and squirmed a little in her chair.

"Corn?" he repeated. "You know, Joel, we've laughed off all the important things for a long time by calling them corny. I hate sentimentality, but we've laughed off sentiment with it. And the great American ideals, and optimism, and hope, and bravery, and love. We need those things in our lives. We need heroes to worship, we're hungry for them." Suddenly he laughed. "Here I'm preaching a sermon I'm not even getting paid for."

"I like it anyhow," she assured him. "It makes me feel better about my own."

They sat there smiling at each other.

"I'll see J.G.," he promised. "I don't know whether I can do any good but I'll try. It's a thing I've got to learn. You know it was Jeremiah's concept of what a minister ought to be—and maybe yours,—that set me off on this new vision."

"It's a big order," she said. "Steve, what happened to you when you were away? You're—somebody quite different."

That was what Claire had said and he winced at hearing it again. "I met some people," he began. "Some people who take quite literally 'Seek ye first the kingdom of God.'" Once more he told the story of his visit to the City of Brothers.

Joel listened carefully, her eyes fixed on his face. "I think I'd have stayed there. It sounds—marvelous."

"It is. I never saw anything like it. And I thought at first that I'd like to be with them always, but I can't believe that Christians were meant to shut themselves away from the world. The Brothers wrap themselves in their own peace and they don't need any service, or leader."

"Then you're going to stay in the ministry, Steve? You have decided that?" Joel's voice was eager.

"I've decided that it's God's business and I'm doing everything I can to do a bang-up job from now until conference. Then I'm following up other things I think I can do as well. I'm going to do whatever it is that God wants me to do, as near as I can learn it, from prayer, and work, and listening to needs." He stopped and smiled. "I was reading the parable of the Good Samaritan this morning and I got something new out of it. I always thought it was a lesson for a negligent priest and Levite. But this morning I found in it a lesson for Steve Elliott, minister of God. You knew that I had worried about a call, wondered if I had ever had one?"

"You told me," she reminded him.

"It was about that call. I don't need a burning bush, or a voice out of a cloud. All I must have is *need*. Need *is* a call."

She took a little time to digest that, then nodded. "But in Kinsman, Steve. Is there need in Kinsman?"

"Not physical need, certainly, but you brought me one when you came in, remember? You brought me one that night when you asked me where the happy people were. To teach people how to live abundantly is my business."

"Y-yes. I suppose it is. But people in Kinsman aren't interested in religion. Not really. They're church people and all that, but they don't believe it's practical. It's just another organization respectable people belong to, like Rotary or the Women's Club. The comfortable and respectable are pretty difficult to change, Steve."

"I know. But they're my people and I'd like to try," he insisted.

"Good heavens," Joel exclaimed suddenly. "Did *you* know that it was half past twelve?"

"It can't be," Steve argued. "The mill whistle hasn't blown."

Joel laughed. "Of course not, silly. It's Labor Day. The workers, poor things, had counted so on a big picnic and now with all this rain they've got to have it in the recreation building just as if they didn't go there practically every night anyhow."

"I'd forgotten. And I don't see how I could. Bobby has talked about nothing but school beginning tomorrow. One day he's excited that it's going to start, and the next he's bewailing the end of vacation."

"I'll bet Elizabeth isn't bewailing anything. All the mothers are delighted to have the kids out from underfoot, shut in the way they've been. A little more than a month of rain!" She was picking up umbrella and pocketbook, putting the hood of her raincoat over her head.

"I guess the weather has us all sort of low in spirit," Steve said, following her toward the front of the church. "Thanks for coming. I feel better for our talk. And I'll see J.G." He offered his hand in farewell.

CHAPTER XX

LUCY KINSMAN was in the habit of rising early, eating a hearty breakfast and being on the road by the time most people were just getting out of bed. The

Tuesday after Labor Day was no exception. Daylight had come late because fall was already closing in and the continued bad weather made all the daylight hours dark. Even the paved roads were covered with mud and she drove carefully, her mind on the work of the day before her.

There was Mrs. Bates whose children had hookworm and whom she was educating to take the treatment. It was a ticklish job for Mrs. Bates was a white woman and felt it affrontery for Lucy to know more than she did. Then there was Martha Hosea, a Negro girl about Lucy's own age who had lost three previous babies. Now Lucy had eased her along until it was just about her time. If everything went well— She decided to go there first.

The one-room and lean-to shack where the Hoseas lived was perched dangerously on the side of a red hill within plain sight of the Kinsman dam. The roar of it, now that the water was high, came to their ears all day.

"It's company, like," Martha used to say, "when Clem's in the fields. Only now there ain't no call for him to be there. Cotton's done rotted out."

Lucy heard sad news everywhere. The crops were ruined. The whole county was full of families like the Hoseas, wondering how they were going to feed themselves through the winter which was almost upon them. And Lucy worried right along with them.

She parked her car, took up what her patients called her "doctor bag" and started to climb on foot to the little house. In dry weather she might have driven it in the car but now, even on foot, she slipped and slid until she reminded herself of the frog in the well who jumped three feet only to fall back two. Now that she was out of the

car she could hear the roar of water and it seemed to
her that it was louder than on any previous visit.

Carefully she scraped her feet on the grass and then
on the folded sack provided for that purpose at the
entrance. She knocked firmly at the door, calling out,
"Martha, it's Lucy Kinsman."

A long, shaken moan answered her. Lucy caught her
breath, opened the door, and stepped inside.

The little room, scarcely bigger than the double bed
it contained, was pin neat as always, but Martha lay
with her body huddled into a knot of pain, her hands
clenched about the bed's iron head boards and her
chocolate-brown face wet with sweat though the room
was cold.

"Oh, Lucy, thank God," she said and burst into tears.

Lucy put down her bag and began to remove her raincoat. She had delivered babies many times but she did
not look forward with any pleasure to this one.

"Where's Clem?" she asked briskly.

Martha gasped and relaxed a little. "Gone to borrow—
Cotter's truck."

"It's pretty late to be taking you to town," Lucy decided. "Got a fire made up?"

"No. Clem just sot out when I waked him. I—" She
broke off to moan and bite her lips.

"No breakfast, I suppose," Lucy spoke as to herself.
"Well, coffee will make you a bit more comfortable and
I'll get some hot water and— Here. It's only a mild seda-
tive but swallow it."

She disappeared into the lean-to and began to make
a fire in the wood stove which furnished heat as well as a
means for cooking. She filled the kettle and the big
boiler with water, measured coffee acrid with chicory

into a big gray pot. She had just placed it on the stove when she heard the hurried footsteps of Clem returning, and felt the wind as he opened the door.

"God, honey," he began hoarsely, "they ain't there and the truck neither. They ain't *there!*" He flung himself down on the one chair in the place and buried his face in his hands.

Martha bit her lips until another pain eased itself a little.

"Lucy, she come, Clem. Lucy tend to me. You take it easy now. Everything be all right." She spoke like a mother soothing a frightened child.

He dropped his hands and stared at her in astonishment, his mouth hanging open. "Miss Lucy Kinsman? That nurse woman? She got her car?" He got to his feet, swaying like a drunken man, then turned and went into the lean-to, his eyes wild so that only the whites seemed to show.

"Miss L-Lucy, m-ma'am," he stammered.

"Yes," Lucy answered him crisply. "Will you take the bucket to the well and bring fresh water, Mr. Hosea? We haven't enough in the house for—"

His eyes rolled like a frightened horse. "Miss Lucy, we can't be hangin' 'round here. You got your car? We—"

"It's too late to get Martha in to Dr. Mims, Mr. Hosea," Lucy tried to brush him aside. "I've delivered lots of babies. I can take care of Martha all right if—"

"Yes'm, but it ain't that. Thing is, we ain't got time to have no baby. Not now we ain't." He stood in the door motionless, unconscious of Lucy's impatience with him.

"Babies unfortunately don't wait for a convenient time," Lucy told him with feminine contempt. "If you'll get out of my way—"

"I tell you the dam's bustin'. Any time now, it's bustin'," he shouted at her. "We got to get outta here."

Lucy looked at him in startled disbelief. She had known expectant fathers to have fantastic ideas before but none like this. She went over to the side wall, undid the latch and opened the wooden shutter which served as a kitchen window. Out there the dam loomed indistinctly through the heavy rain. Peering with all the concentration her eyes were capable of she thought that the wall of the dam toward the little house held a crack as wide as her arm and that water like ecru lace flew from it.

"There? Is that the break I see?" she asked, forcing herself to speak calmly, and pointing toward the foaming stream.

"Yes'm. That he. We gotta get her outa here, Miss Lucy." He sensed the urgency but was incapable of practical action.

"Yes," Lucy agreed. "Get Martha into her clothes. Wrap her in that quilt on the bed as well and take her in your arms to my car. The back seat." She shot orders at him, put on her raincoat and her galoshes and began to walk down the hill.

Clem, with his wife in his arms, followed closely behind, slipping sometimes in the mud, then catching himself and going on again. Martha moaned, sometimes screaming before she gagged herself into silence with the quilt.

Finally they were in the road again, Lucy driving as fast as she dared. Martha's sharp, animal cries came faster and Clem moaned and prayed and swore. Sometimes the car skidded almost out of control. The road before them was half obliterated by the downpour.

Lucy was really worried now. If the dam broke, the river would flood Kinsman—the mills, the three blocks that made up "town," the lower houses. But before that it would flood Bitter Creek. It was nearer the dam by five miles, at the very head of the valley, and just beyond was the schoolhouse where for the first time that fall, children would be attending school. Why hadn't Bitter Creek let Mr. Kinsman build the schoolhouse on the hill where he had wanted it? The children would be safe now. But there it was, the result of two years wrangling, halfway between the two towns and right beside the river. She must warn Bitter Creek, must let them know at the schoolhouse.

Martha's screams reached a crescendo, shrill and agonized, and above it, Clem shouted, "Miss Lucy, that baby, hit's acomin'."

Lucy drew a long shuddering breath. She was having a nightmare. This couldn't be happening to her. She stepped on the gas, prayed that her reckless driving would not land them in a ditch and began to shout directions to Clem. She hoped that he had a better hold on himself now than he had had back at the house, or—

Round curve after curve the little car sped. If she met another vehicle, she would not see it until too late to prevent their meeting head on. If she skidded, they would all wake up in eternity, and the people in the valley would not have been warned.

Her arms ached with strain. There was a shooting pain at the back of her neck but they were finally coming into Bitter Creek. She rolled down the window beside her, letting in a driving spray of rain. There was no one on the street. She drove into a filling station and shouted.

A boy came from inside looking drowsy and disgruntled. Lucy's words came in gasps.

"Dam's out up there. Call central. Call everybody. Let them know at the school and the mill," she shouted to him.

"Huh?" he asked stupidly.

She repeated herself angrily. A mew like a tiny kitten came from the back seat and Martha settled down to a steady moan. Clem muttered on, praying, swearing.

The gas station boy shook his head. "Phone's out. Can't do it that way. You sure about the dam?"

"Of course I'm sure," Lucy screamed at him. "You got a car? Tell everybody in Bitter Creek. Tell 'em to get out of here. For their lives. I'll warn the school."

She was off again, driving recklessly, racing with the water she could feel gaining upon her, whipping itself up into a muddy, reddish foam, spreading out until it covered everything.

It was three miles—or an infinity of time and space before she finally drove into the school yard and saw without knowing that she saw, the school busses flocked together between trees which whipped in the ever-rising wind. She braked the car as near the entrance as she could get it, left the engine running and stepped out with her doctor bag in her hand, shouting to Clem.

"You get in there and drive on to Kinsman. Tell them at the mill. Then take Martha to Dr. Mims. But you go to the mill first, hear me?"

"Yes'm. Yes'm, I sho' will," he agreed, easing Martha to the seat and putting the baby in her arms. Then he scrambled over under the wheel, shifted gears carefully, and drove back onto the road.

Lucy hurried into the hall, looked about her and decided that the office was on the left. The patiently listening principal and a talkative mother could be glimpsed through the open door beyond. A gum-chewing high-school girl with too much make-up on her face sat behind a typewriter and stared at Lucy blankly until the nurse opened the swinging gate and started toward the inner office.

"Look here, you can't go in there. He's busy," the girl said but did not get up.

Lucy ignored her, moving swiftly into the other room and interrupting the steady flow of the anxious mother's monologue.

"Mr. Beckman," she began in a voice she struggled to keep steady, "the dam's broken. Get the children into the busses and out of the valley as quickly as possible."

For a moment the two stared at her, trying to fit meaning to the words they had heard. The woman understood first and began to babble unfinished sentences about "my baby, my little Agnes." Then she was on her feet, half bent over and running toward the door, her incoherent words rising louder and louder.

If she goes out of here like this, Lucy found herself thinking coolly, she'll frighten everybody and there'll be a stampede. She must be stopped. Lucy fixed her dark eyes on the woman's chin and swung the bag with deadly aim. The face took on a silly, empty look and the woman crumpled to the ground.

Outside in the big office Mr. Beckman was already giving carefully worded instructions to the gum-chewing typist. "Blanche, step across to the study hall and ask Miss Danner to send me six high school boys who can drive cars. Quickly. As quickly as you can."

The girl looked frightened but she obeyed. Mr. Beckman went across and stood under the bell on the wall, waiting. It was only a moment until the boys were back, their callow young faces full of curiosity.

Mr. Beckman was still calm. "Go outside and get into the school busses. Start the engines but don't move until the children are inside. Then head up the hill. Drive carefully but don't waste time. We're in for trouble here and I'll explain as soon as I can."

He turned away and put his finger on the buzzer. Three long peals rang out through the building. An excited burst of voices answered. The study hall teacher could be heard announcing, "It's the fire-drill bell. This class marches out the front door and lines up in the road in front. Two by two and in good order."

"A fire drill? And in the rain? That's crazy," somebody answered. But they were already moving into lines and leaving the big room. Mr. Beckman had taken his place in the center of the wide hall and was shouting so that he could be heard through both wings. "Go outside and get into your school bus. Go outside and get into your school bus." He said this over and over, slowly, carefully. The students looked at him curiously as they came out of their rooms but they were used to obeying and so they only murmured to each other, asking questions or speaking opinions. Teachers glanced anxiously at their principal, straightened up their lines and hurried them along, wondering too but not asking.

Lucy was on her knees beside the pasty-faced mother whom she had recently knocked out, slapping her wrists and rubbing the back of her neck. It was only a moment before the woman began to groan and flutter her eyelids.

Suddenly she sat up, staring at Lucy in anger and amazement. "You—you hit me."

"I did," Lucy answered firmly. "I couldn't have you in hysterics and causing a riot."

"You— Agnes— Why, you—you nigger!" she shouted, scrambling to her feet, then reeling dizzily.

Lucy took her arm. "Stay here and keep quiet if you don't want me to do it again. They're getting your Agnes and all the rest out. They'll be safe as can be in busses in a moment. Then we'll go and get in the last bus ourselves and—"

Frightened and subdued, the woman looked at Lucy out of the side of her eyes. Just then, above the murmur of children's voices and their feet on the stairs, Lucy heard the roar of the river. The woman whom she held in a grasp like steel heard it too and her face whitened with fright. She whimpered and tried to jerk away.

"We'll be drowned. All of us will be drowned. *You'll* be drowned. Don't you care? Oh, let me go!" She struggled this way and that, trying to loosen the girl's hold, and blubbering.

Mr. Beckman appeared in the doorway. His face was strained and his voice was hoarse. "Hurry. They're all out now. Let's get into the busses."

The busses were starting, their engines roaring and popping as they backed out and into the road. The sound of the rushing water was nearer.

Agnes' mother grew pop-eyed with fright. "The cars—the busses are going off without us," she cried and her legs buckled under her.

"Never saw such an idiot!" Mr. Beckman muttered, his patience utterly spent. He scooped up her heavy body and carried her outside, puffing under the weight.

"Come along, miss," he called over his shoulder to Lucy.

She followed them almost to the door, knowing at every step that she was forgetting something. Only as she was about to step out into the rain did she remember. She had left her doctor's bag in Mr. Beckman's office. She turned back, crossed the now empty outer office and entered the one behind it. The roar of the water was in her ears and through the window she could see what looked like a wall of mud descending on her. Logs and trees, a sharply peaked roof, twisted and turned helplessly on its surface. The bus outside roared away—the last bus.

Fascinated, paralyzed, she watched the water come, its muddy spume thrown high, its waves licking out hungrily. Then she shook herself and bent to pick up her bag.

At that moment the water struck the glass of the window with all its force. The room was full of sound, the breaking of glass, the sucking of water into a vacuum. She opened her mouth to scream, only to have it filled with water in which she floundered. The log that Lucy had seen up-end itself a moment before, was driven in through the opening the water had made. Lucy fought for the surface, frantic, hunting crazily for some way out. She hardly felt the blow of the log on the back of her head. Slowly her black bag fell from her hand and settled on the floor of the school office.

CHAPTER XXI

AFTER his talk with Joel on Monday, Steve tried twice to see J.G. and failed. On Tuesday morning, after his breakfast, he went down to the factory and waited for him. Mr. Kinsman was out somewhere in the factory, the harried secretary said. Steve sat there with his damp fishing hat on his knees, wondering what he should say to the mill owner. But when J.G. finally arrived, Steve had no time to say anything. The older man glanced in his direction and growled, "Morning, Steve. Come on in," and led the way into his private sanctum.

Steve cleared his throat in preparation for speech but J.G. anticipated him. "Rain and more rain. Thirty-two days of it! I'm ruined, I tell you, if it doesn't stop. The river creeps up every day and every morning I expect to find it in the factory. The government has cancelled some of its orders and my stocks keep piling up. The union contract runs out the fifteenth and they'll be wanting a raise. I haven't got it. God knows what I'm going to do." He stopped speaking and doodled on the leather-framed desk blotter.

"I've been expecting that man from the bank about a loan but he doesn't come. Those bankers are keeping me on tenterhooks to break my spirit, I'll bet my bottom dollar! And by crikey, they're *doing* it. I'm half crazy with worry," he went on as if to himself.

"Did you ever think of praying that God's will be done, and leaving it to Him?" Steve asked quietly.

J.G. looked up red eyed and angry, shaking his head like a goaded bull. "No, I never did. Such namby-pamby, fool things you say, Elliott! When I first saw you I thought that you had some common sense, but, my Lord, last Sunday, and again now, your ideas are as impractical as—as—" He stopped and groped, but he was too angry to speak. He swallowed and took a fresh start.

"Leave it to the Lord, indeed. If I did, I'd find myself in the *poor house*. Next, you'll be suggesting that I sell all my goods and give it to feed the poor. Socialism, street preaching. That my own pastor—"

Steve was afraid that J.G. might have apoplexy then and there. He could understand why Joel was worried about her father. The veins in his forehead stood out, his hands trembled. He was obviously a sick man.

At that moment, Miss Gates, J.G.'s rather mousy secretary, opened the door a bare inch and spoke through it as if she was afraid that her boss might throw something at her.

"Mr. Kinsman, sir, there's a colored man here who insists that he's got to see you this minute."

J.G. stood up, his lips working. Finally words came out. "Such insolence. Such—"

But Clem Hosea was too frightened to be put off even by J. G. Kinsman himself. He pushed Miss Gates aside not rudely or roughly, but with determination. "You ain't got time to argue, Mr. Kinsman, sir. That there dam, I reckon hit's in little bits by now and the water's movin' in. You better get all them hands outta here an' up in the hills. School and Bitter Creek been told."

He had said his speech and now he turned and rushed from the room as if the waters were right at his heels. Miss Gates looked after him with fright growing in her face. Then she picked up her notebook and pencil and turned to J.G., waiting his orders as she had done ever since he had started in business.

For once J.G. was wordless. He had gone very pale, but he continued to stand before his desk staring at the open door through which the messenger had disappeared. At length a tide of red rose from his collar to his brow. He clenched both fists and raised them to heaven, cursing fate and God and the coming waters.

Steve looked at him a moment in amazement. He had expected the efficient business man to rise to this emergency, to move forward with resolution and quick command. Miss Gates was even more stunned than he. She could follow whatever orders were given but she had no initiative of her own.

Steve did not know how to direct the evacuation of the mill. He hesitated only an instant, then stepped to Kinsman's side and shook him with all his strength.

"Man, the lives of all your workers are depending on you. Pull yourself together. Get them out of here," he shouted.

J.G. stopped his own shouting and looked at Steve as if he had waked from a deep sleep. He shook his head wearily and sighed. "I've always had too many lives hanging on me. I'm tired."

Steve shook him again. "You can't afford to be tired now. You've *got* to take charge."

J.G. nodded. "Miss Gates, have the time keeper blow the whistle. I—I'll come out and speak to them."

Up to that moment, J.G. had been a man in his prime, middle aged and a little worried of late, but still virile and for the most part, self confident. Now he moved like an old man, and his voice when it came over the inter-

com system to every part of the mill, was feeble and uncertain. Yet in those few moments he had figured out
exactly what must be done.

The familiar whistle which blew at six thirty, eight,
twelve, twelve thirty, and four thirty, clarioned three
staccato sounds and when they were finished, J.G. gave
his orders:

"Robert Moss and Vernal Williams, jump into your
cars and warn the people on the flats that the dam has
burst and that they are to go up into the hills immediately. You truck drivers scour the hills for Bitter Creek
people and bring them here, into our homes. Martin
Lewis and Drew Phalen, go to the commissary and fill
your cars with all the groceries you can handle and dis-
tribute them where they are needed. Better get blankets
as well. The rest of you go out quietly and return home.
Don't get excited. You've been warned in time. But get
out as quickly as you can."

He turned to Steve with haunted eyes. "I hope to God
that's true."

But J.G. was making no attempt to leave himself. He
stood there with the speaker still in his hand, his shoulders hunched, his face pale. Miss Gates held her notebook and pencil and waited for him to dismiss her.
Steve himself seemed dependent on the other man's
leadership.

Suddenly Steve threw off his inertia. "We'd better be
getting home ourselves before our women folks become
too worried—while the going's still good. Do you have
your car, Miss Gates?"

She nodded, looking stupid and frightened.

"Are you all right to drive it? Can you get home alone?"
he asked when she made no move to go.

Once more she nodded, put her notebook down at an exact parallel with the edges of her desk, her pencil beside it and went out, taking her hat and raincoat with her.

"Come along, J.G.," Steve urged the older man. "Paula and Joel will be worried."

"Kinny," J.G. started and looked worried. "Kinny was at school."

"That man who warned us, the Negro. He said the school had been taken care of. Bobby was there too."

The two anxious men hurried out, got into their cars and turned up the hill, where automobiles moved ahead of them in lines like ants. Far off they could hear the roar of water.

It was an endless day. Steve found Elizabeth and Bobby watching the raging water through an east window. Elizabeth burst into tears at sight of him.

"Thank God, you're safe," she cried. "Oh, Steve, I was frightened to death."

Bobby looked at her with accusing eyes. "Mom, you *said* Uncle Steve was all right. You said he was just out looking after people the way a preacher was supposed to do and that you weren't worried about him. Anyhow he's here all right now. So why are you bawling?"

Elizabeth, her face hidden against Steve's shoulder, was crying too hard to answer but Steve grinned at him and spoke in a man-to-man voice. "That's the way women are, Sonny. In time of trouble they're as calm as a June morning, telling you that everything is going to be fine. But once it's over, watch for the tears."

Bobby nodded wisely. "I reckon women are funny."

Steve was wry. "You can say that again! But look here, Sis, you can't break down now. Trucks have gone to pick up the people from Bitter Creek. It's been flooded out. They'll be here any minute now and we'll have to have food ready, fix places for them to sleep, and try to supply them with dry clothes."

"F-food," she repeated. "Why, we've scarcely enough in the house for ourselves if this thing lasts three days. But I suppose, if people are hungry and have lost everything they have—"

He nodded. "Luckily it probably won't come to that. Drew will be up here soon with food and blankets. Anything I can do before I go?"

"Go?" she quavered. "You aren't going out again in all that water!"

"Elizabeth, you know I have to do my part." He was almost stern.

She wiped her eyes. "That's right. Bobby and I will be fine."

Just then Drew halted his car at their door and called out. "Groceries! Anything needed at the parsonage?"

The entire family rushed out on the porch to greet him. When Elizabeth had chosen what she wanted from the stock in the back of his car, Drew ran into the house carrying a great sodden bag. He jerked his head toward the rising water behind him.

"Eating up the world, looks like, and the heavens still pouring. Maybe we better hurry up and finish that ark, eh, boy?"

Bobby grinned up at him adoringly. "Yeah."

"But not today," Drew warned him. "Got to get everybody fed first. Any displaced persons here yet?"

"Not yet," Elizabeth answered. "Steve came in to warn us and we're expecting them."

A moment later, a school bus drew up with twelve

people in it, three women, a man, and eight children. Two of the women were desperately worried about their husbands. And three children had failed to find their parents. Elizabeth welcomed them all and took them into the house.

"We run up the hill out of Bitter Creek like they told us," one of the women wept. "I wish I had waited for my old man. Lord knows what come to him. Drowned, like as not."

Drew and Steve allowed their eyes to meet across the room. "I guess I'd better get out and take a sort of census," Steve said. "Then I can carry messages and reunite families wherever possible."

Drew nodded. "As soon as I get through with the grocery detail I'll join you."

Out on his errands, Steve saw the trucks and busses delivering small groups of tired and wet people at the various houses. He watched the river continue to rise, raging and carrying everything before it. Claire had taken two families into her home. More than a hundred were housed with the Kinsmans. All of the Negro section, located at the southern end of the valley, had been washed away and Drew put his house, under the direction of Emmanuel Brown, the Methodist minister, and his wife at their disposal. Others were billeted in Joel's guest house and she went up to the big house to help there.

Steve hurried from place to place, getting additions to original lists, as he saw new loads arrive, taxiing children to hysterical mothers, reuniting husbands and wives, taking messages concerning relatives further removed. The lists grew and grew and when he went with Drew to the Kinsman house at ten thirty that night and checked over the names with the mill owner they were elated.

Drew rattled the pages which made up the list and lowered his voice so as not to wake those who slept on pallets in the adjoining living room. "Seven hundred thirty-three of them," he said, "all safe and sound. I wish we could get on the other side of the river and find out who's there. Three times this number, I imagine."

Steve looked thoughtful. "I don't know. Lots more houses, of course, but not so much room in them."

"There are nearly two thousand people living over there," J.G. reminded them gloomily. "Under normal conditions, that is."

"You checked Joel's place, Steve?" Drew asked. "Is Lucy there? She isn't at my place. Jennie Brown keeps asking and I'm anxious myself. Mother was so fond of her."

Steve consulted his list. "N-no. Some of the Negroes are on the other side."

Drew nodded. "Yes, certainly. You know she was the one who brought the word."

"No. It was a man. A big, stupid-looking fellow I never saw before," J.G. insisted.

"Clem Hosea," Drew recognized the description. "He and his wife and new baby girl are at Dr. Mims. They've named the baby for Lucy. He's the one who told me about it. Lucy drove them in, giving the warning at Bitter Creek, and at the school. She sent Clem on to you."

"She's done a wonderful thing here," Steve said thoughtfully. "I really believe there's almost no one missing."

J.G. was not cheered. "I had the dam built," he said heavily.

Drew looked at him surprised. "Of course you did, J.G. The engineers checked the rainfall as far back as there were records. There'd never been anything like this."

"I brought most of those people here, too. Not the Bitter Creek ones, but the others. And now they've lost their homes."

Paula came down the steps into the hall and spoke to them. "Come upstairs, J.G. You're worn out. I've given your bed to a very old couple, and mine to a sick woman but I've put out two beach rolls for us in the dressing room."

"I can't sleep," he protested.

"Come and try," she urged.

"Do that, J.G.," Steve seconded her. "Drew, your house is full to overflowing. Come home with me. We're like the old woman in the shoe but we'll tuck you in somewhere. There's nothing more we can do tonight. You've been great, J.G., thinking of everything and keeping things going. My hat's off. Goodnight."

Kinsman lifted his hand in acknowledgment but his heavy face did not light up at Steve's praise. "Goodnight," he said.

Wednesday morning brought a glimpse of the sun in the sky and it had stopped raining. By afternoon the clouds had disappeared. The river still overran its banks and people swarmed about irritably in houses which were not their own.

All over the country papers carried descriptions of the flood. The radio crackled with it. Newspaper reporters nosed about asking questions, taking pictures.

Steve and Drew and Dr. Mims were busy night and

day, running errands, seeing to people and their needs.
J.G. was everywhere with sleepless, bloodshot eyes, directing what should be done by the telephone company,
the power and light, answering questions to which there
were no answers, asking his own pointed questions, giving firm indisputable orders.

Thursday morning the day was as bright as if there
had never been a rain. The world was a place of thick
adhesive mud and the river was still out of bounds but
receding. It was Saturday morning before things began
to be normal enough for the damage to be checked.

By this time Lucy's father and two brothers had come,
and her mother, who sat humbly in a corner of the Kinsman kitchen, her gloved hands clasped, her lips trembling and her eyes swimming with tears.

Mr. Beckman, the school principal, was the first to
actually find the Negro nurse when he walked over to
the school that midmorning. He left her lying there in
the wet silt, locking the door after him and walking back
home hastily lest he be sick on the public street. It was
Mrs. Beckman who called the funeral director in Dalton
and who walked up to Drew's to ask Emmanuel Brown
to tell Lucy's still searching family.

The whole country knew about her by that time.
There had been pictures of her and stories of what she
had done. Clem and Martha had been on the radio, reading statements which had been prepared for them, and
stumbling badly in spite of their careful rehearsals. Steve
had followed them, telling how Lucy had worked to serve
her people and how she had wanted a hospital for them.

They buried her on Sunday afternoon.

There never had been such a funeral in Kinsman, perhaps not in all Georgia. The little C.M.E. church had

been washed away completely, so the funeral was held in the new Kinsman Memorial with Steve and Emmanuel Brown sharing the services. And everyone able to walk had come to do Lucy honor. Half of the church had been set aside for the Negro people. The building was packed as it might never be again and many who came had to remain outside.

Steve read the service as it had been set down in the Discipline and Reverend Brown preached from the text, "Greater love hath no man."

CHAPTER XXII

UNTIL Monday morning, J.G. had been too busy with the human side of the flood to look more than casually at what it had done to the factory, but by that time the Red Cross had taken charge, the homeless were housed in the recreation building, the water was down to what had been the high water mark before the breaking of the dam, families were reunited, and rolls had been checked sufficiently to show that Lucy was the only casualty.

At ten minutes to eight, the exact moment when he always arrived at the main building, J.G. went into the factory entrance instead of the office one and walked slowly, heavily through the door. He did not go close to any of the machinery, did not touch any of the cloth piled in the stockroom. That was not necessary. Red earth, beginning to dry out now, had settled on everything.

Even the most casual glance could detect the rust forming on the machinery. The cloth was stained and circled
beyond any hope of reclamation. It would always be the
pinkish hue of red Georgia mud. Every step toward his
office his body drooped more, his gait added years to
its age.

His office door creaked as he opened it, and bits of
hardening mud fell to the floor with a small thud which
emphasized the utter silence in a place which usually
hummed with sound by that hour of a week-day morning.

Inside he stood once more just looking, not touching
anything, noting the rust on the steel files, the way his
expensive desk had swollen and separated at its joinings,
how the papers had washed up against the walls and
stuck there, how the windows had given way under continued pounding.

As if every joint in his body were sore, he went to the
safe and opened it, his fingers awkward on the dial. Inside it was comparatively dry, but the sheets of the
books which he brought out with him were curled and
the covers were covered with mold. He used an immaculate and monogrammed handkerchief to wipe off
desk and chair, opened the books before him and sat
down. His big head braced in his hands he began to
study, turning pages, sometimes going back to refresh his
mind with something he had seen a little while before.

The hours clicked away. J.G. used the mechanical pencil from his coat pocket for adding, subtracting, multi-
plying. His forehead was crisscrossed with concentration, his knuckles white from the pressure he exerted on
his pencil.

At noon there were no whistles to warn him but he
might not have heard them anyhow. He was writing a

letter which began, "Dear Paula." It was full of instructions about investments, percentages, and brokers. The
letter was entirely impersonal. It might have been a report to a board of directors. No prying eye must see his
love for his wife. When he was tempted to make the
letter a testament of his devotion, he stemmed the words
with an emotional effort which made trickles of sweat
run down his face. Six pages he completed and signed
boldly. It was all he could do for them now—Paula who
had been his joy, Kinny, his pride, and as an afterthought,
Joel. He wanted to do his best for Joel, too, but somehow he had never been able to get close to her.

A hundred and twenty-five thousand dollars in in-
surance and whatever they could get from selling the
mills, this ought to be enough to see them through if
it were carefully invested. He sat on, slumped in his
chair, staring at his signature. After a while he got up
and stooped to pick up his desk paperweight which had
been washed on to the floor by the flood. He placed it
on the sheets of the letter which he had pushed aside.
The letter must not be—soiled when it came to his wife.

It was nearly three o'clock in the afternoon when he
put his hand into his pocket and brought out his gun.
He had been conscious of it every moment since he had
left home—the way it had sagged heavily under his right
arm as he walked, had lain like a stone as he sat at his
desk.

Now, with the sun struggling through the dirty windows and lighting up the destruction of the office, he
studied the pistol carefully. He had had it a long time,
had bought it in a pawnshop because of a sudden whim.
He remembered the oily smile of the pawnbroker as
clearly as if the transaction had taken place yesterday.

J.G. hoped none of his family would find him; he hoped
that it would be someone who was tough enough to forget soon. The phone rang suddenly, shrill in the empty
silence. He decided to hurry.

He raised the pistol in a hand that was almost steady
and fired.

Like almost everyone else in Kinsman, Steve and Elizabeth were cleaning house that morning. Newly washed
blankets and sheets hung on the line in the bright sunshine. Elizabeth ran the sweeper and Steve moved furniture. Bobby ran in and out of the parsonage, bringing
in fresh mud and making reports of what was going on
in the outside world. It was mid-afternoon when the
phone rang.

Paula's voice was tight and over-wrought. "Steve, have
you seen J.G.?"

"N-no. Not since the funeral yesterday afternoon," he
answered.

"He went out at the regular time this morning, the
servants say. I don't usually get up for breakfast that
early but I supposed he had gone to the factory. But
I've called and called there and no one answers. And he
didn't come home to lunch."

"Have you tried Potter?" Steve suggested. "J.G. and
the superintendent are probably down there going over
things and have forgotten the time." He was trying to
reassure the excited woman but he was growing anxious
too.

"Yes, I called there. But Mr. Potter says that when he
suggested that they go over the place this morning J.G.
put him off. He said tomorrow would do just as well because he had something else on for today."

"Could J.G. have gone to Atlanta to see the bank?"

"Without telling me good-bye? He wouldn't do that, Steve. I can't get it out of my head that he's somewhere in that factory. I—I want to go down there and find him but—I'm scared, Steve. You don't know how worried he's been lately."

"I'm in work clothes but I'll go with you if you like," he offered.

He heard her sigh of relief. "Oh, Steve, would you! I'd appreciate it a lot. I'll pick you up as soon as I can get there."

As Paula jerked her car to a halt and stalled the engine, she laughed a little nervous giggle. "I don't know what's the matter with me, Steve. I don't usually get in such a tizzie. J.G.'s a grown man and knows how to take care of himself. I guess I'm just silly." She was trying to convince herself against her own better judgment.

"Woman's intuition," Steve jeered not unkindly, but he too felt his heart beat with premonition. J.G. had been terribly worried about the mill even before this final disaster.

Paula halted before the office entrance. "Will you—go in?" she asked, drawing herself up small, her eyes dark with fear.

But the office entrance was locked. Climbing over the debris in his path, Steve went along the side of the building and around to the other door. The sight of J.G.'s car parked there increased his anxiety but he was relieved to find the door sagging open, and footsteps making a clear path in the mud toward another door at the far end of the long room.

He hurried through it and the stockroom beyond, then slowed as he approached the closed office door. No sound came from it. He knocked and there was still only silence.

J.G. could be anywhere in the building, or in one of the other buildings, for that matter, he argued with himself. But somehow he was sure that the mill owner was behind that door. He put out his hand and slowly turned the knob.

It was as if he had seen it all before, the crazy disorder of the room, the desk and files looking as if years had passed over them, and most vivid of all, the slumped body of J.G., his head resting on one corner of a closed, leather-bound day book, his right arm flung out empty handed, the pistol shining on the floor near his feet. Steve was acutely conscious of every detail of the place, was sure that he would be able to describe it on the last day that he lived.

"J.G.," he faltered. He should have expected this. He should have been with J.G. today.

He stepped closer, put out a reluctant hand to touch the man's cheek, and even as he did so, noticed the slight flutter of the top page of a pile of papers under a bronze paper weight. It was J.G.'s uncertain breath which had stirred it. His cheek was warm under Steve's fingers.

"Thank God!" he prayed, reaching for the phone and dialing Dr. Mims' number. "Let me be in time. Let us save him, dear God in heaven."

By some miracle, the doctor was in his office and answered immediately.

"It's J.G. He's at his office. He's shot himself," Steve reported breathlessly and hung up.

Then he did not know what to do. The crimson stain on the desk was widening slowly. Paula was out there in the car and ought to know.

But Paula had waited as long as she could. Now she stood in the office door, her clenched fist pressed to her mouth, moaning.

"He's alive, Paula. He's still breathing," Steve reported.

"He—shot—himself," she said slowly. "Here—by himself." The words forced themselves painfully from her throat. Then she turned to a frenzy of movement. "Don't just leave him there. Here, ease him into my lap." She dropped down on the floor, oblivious of the slime which covered it.

J.G. was heavy and inert, but Steve managed to move him. The artery at his temple had been jammed with the corner of the leather book, and now he began to bleed in spurts from the wound which ran along the side of his head. The sight of it made Paula feel faint but she held him in her lap, forced her eyes to the wound and put her thumb against the artery just below the gaping skin. Once more J.G.'s blood oozed irregularly, making a small stream down her skirt.

Steve went to the phone once more and called the ambulance in Dalton. He was sure that they would want to take J.G. to the hospital there. That done he called Claire. Paula would want her, he felt, and Claire would expect to be called.

When he had identified himself and told her what had happened, he heard Claire draw her breath in a sharp whistle. "I'll be right there," she said.

Apparently Paula had been talking for some time. Steve had not been fully conscious of it but now as he turned away from the phone he knew that he had been hearing her out of one ear. She was speaking softly, almost as if to herself, yet at the same time to Steve, and to the unconscious J.G. as well.

"It was a game I played with myself, a terrible, foolish game. I knew there in New York that I was never going to make the grade, never going to amount to anything as a singer, no matter how hard I practiced, no matter how I worked. But I wouldn't admit it to myself. I really married to get away from the failure that I knew was coming. I let the family think that I did it for Mother and so the other children could have things. And I let J.G. think I had sacrificed my career."

She raised her voice a little and spoke directly to Steve. "Will you press your thumb here on this place for a bit? My hand is cramped and I can't hold it as tight as I should."

When he knelt and complied she went on with her monologue. "All these years, J.G., I must have loved you the way I do now, the way I know I do now, but I wouldn't let myself be happy. I went on pretending that if I had kept on in New York, kept on studying, I would have been a star. And you wanted it that way, J.G. You helped me to go on pretending because it flattered you to think I might have been famous. And so I never gave myself to you, or to Kinny, or to the town of Kinsman.

"I could have interested myself in the mills. I could have kept on with my music, taken lessons, given pleasure as an amateur. But, no. I had to sulk, to grieve for something that never could have been anyhow." She moved Steve's hand away from her husband's temple and put her own back, looking her pastor squarely in the eye.

"Do you suppose God will give me another chance?

If—if he lives—Steve—I'll know when things are bothering him. I'll go to the mill and watch the machinery work, and I'll get to like it. I really will."

Steve, still on his knees, answered her gently. "I think J.G. was driven to this because he was afraid that there wouldn't be any mills, that he couldn't provide for you and the children any longer."

"You mean—that we may be really poor?" Suddenly she smiled. "Did he think I would mind that? I'd really *like* it. Because I'd be useful again."

Dr. Mims was at the door and Steve rose to let him in. He too knelt on the floor. His long fingers examined the wound, then he listened to J.G.'s heart, to his breathing.

His face was grave when he looked up. "The wound itself is not so serious," he told them, "but he's lost a lot of blood. I've got to do a bit of sewing here, Mrs. Kinsman. Would you like Mr. Elliott to hold your husband?"

Paula's lips went as white as her blouse but she shook her head, and she sat there quietly, holding J.G.'s head steady between strong hands, watching with her heart in her eyes to every rise and fall of his chest. Only when it was over did she go limp and after a tiny struggle for consciousness fall beside the inert form of her husband.

Steve had seen Claire appear in the door, but he had waved her away until the operation was over. He realized too that the ambulance had driven up and he motioned the attendants to wait. Now they came in with a stretcher and took J.G. away.

Claire hurried in, wept at the sight of Paula, and began to rub her hands and face and croon endearments. Steve picked up Paula Kinsman in his arms and followed the doctor to the ambulance, with Claire at his elbow.

"How is he? Is he going to be all right?" she asked.

Dr. Mims shook his head. "I don't know, Mrs. Winthrop. If he lasts until we get to Dalton, we'll give him a transfusion. That's all I can say."

"I'll follow you in my car," Claire promised. "Tell Paula I'll be there when she needs me. Do you want to go with us, Steve?"

Steve shook his head. "I'll find Joel and tell her—about this. I'll bring her along to the hospital. And I'll take Kinny to Elizabeth. Don't worry, I'll try to think of everything and attend to it."

The two cars moved away, Claire's following the ambulance. Steve saw that a strange man was driving her and he wondered who he was. He remembered suddenly that Claire had said, "Do you want to go with *us?*"

But he was too busy now to worry about that. He must find Joel before she heard about her father, Joel and Kinny, too.

CHAPTER XXIII

LIKE everyone else, Joel was taking advantage of the sunny weather to clean house. Steve found her hanging out a newly washed rug in her back yard and whistling "Blacksmith Blues."

"Hi, there, Preacher. Does the sun make you feel as good as it does me?" But by that time he was near enough for her to see the expression on his face, and she asked quietly, "What's wrong, Steve?"

"J.G.'s had an accident."

"He's tried to kill himself," she guessed at once. Then she swallowed and asked, "Is he—?"

"No. I think he's going to live. Dr. Mims has taken him to Dalton. Do you know where Kinny is?"

When they had found the boy and delivered him to Elizabeth as Steve had promised, they were on their way. Joel had been very calm, very quiet and Steve looked at her anxiously, then asked a question. "Do you want to talk?"

"I'd rather pray, Steve. And I wish you'd pray, too."

Steve merely nodded. He had already prayed for J.G. but he prayed again.

They found Paula and Claire in the dreary waiting room at the hospital, not talking, just staring into the distance. They looked up at the newcomers and shook their heads. It was Claire who said, "no word yet."

"They've given him the blood transfusion?" Steve asked.

Again it was Claire who said yes.

And so they sat and waited, their hands idle, their minds empty or jumping from regret to regret. It grew dark and at Steve's insistence they went out to eat, then rushed back for fear that they had been needed. It was just after midnight when Dr. Mims, looking haggard and weary, came to the door and smiled.

"He's going to live. That is, if he *wants* to. Go home all of you."

Paula and Joel looked up and spoke in one voice. "May we see him before we go?"

"He's asleep. But you can come and stand in the door for a moment."

J.G. was not doing well when Paula returned to the

hospital the next morning. He just lay there, a white bandage about his head, his eyes closed, his body lax and unmoving, his breathing shallow, not answering when he was spoken to. After a while she burst into tears and went away lest she disturb him.

In the afternoon, Steve brought Joel to the hospital in his car, and once again they were silent throughout the ride. The girl went into her father's room alone and sat down beside his bed. She did not know at first whether he were sleeping or awake but after a little he sighed a long jagged sigh and she spoke to him.

"J.G., it's Joel." There was no sickroom sound in her voice. She spoke out loud, and there was anger in her words.

His face twitched and after a moment he opened his eyes and looked at her as if she were a stranger.

"You know," she went on in the same hard, untender tone, "I've never liked you very much. I've thought you were a failure as a husband and a father. But I never thought you were a coward. Now I'm ashamed. I've never been *ashamed* of you before."

He was listening now. His hands no longer lay relaxed on the spread.

"Coward?" he repeated.

Joel faced him squarely. "I used to think, 'Anyway he's got guts. In a crisis, he never knows when he's licked.' That's what I used to tell myself and I was proud. I told it to Kinny, too. But now you've let us down."

J.G. was breathing more heavily, his face was flushed with anger. "There's nothing I haven't done for you children. Nothing I haven't given you."

"Oh, *things*," she answered contemptuously. "You've given us lots of things. But never any thought, never any of yourself. You never had *time*. You were always too busy making money, making cloth, to act like a human being."

"You don't understand about business, girl. None of you women do. You think it's something that can be attended to in eight hours and put aside. Business is a twenty-four-hour-a-day proposition."

"There. You see," Joel said, quickly looking away from him. "You wanted a boy. You gave me the name you meant to give *him* but you never called me by it. You never called me *anything* but 'girl.' Sometimes I wonder if you ever even thought about me." She had turned away and was standing at the window, tearing her handkerchief into shreds.

For a long time J.G. did not speak. He was looking at Joel's slender back, her miniature but beautifully proportioned figure and seeing another girl who had said many of the same things to him twenty years ago. "You don't even know you have a wife and a child," she had stormed.

"A man can't be everything," he had defended himself. "I'm going to be a millionaire before I'm through. And that takes time—all my time."

Joel turned back to him now, a questioning look on her face. "Did you say something, J.G.?"

"I was thinking of your mother. You don't remember her, do you?"

She shook her head. "Just that she went away and left me and never came back."

"Sit down—Joel," he said. "It wasn't quite like that. We quarreled from the day we married. Before that really, though those quarrels were— I don't quite know how to explain."

"I know. Obstacles that made you want her even more. That's the way you've always been."

He thought that over, then agreed. "Something like that. But her ideas of what life should be were very different from mine. I was ambitious, wanted money in my pocket, to have people say, 'That's J. G. Kinsman. Started out with nothing and look at him now.' She had had money. She thought it didn't matter. Before you were born we quarreled more than ever. I got to hate the idea of a child. Maybe she did too."

"And you used me to hurt each other," Joel took up the story. "I have heard often enough how I was named." Her husky voice was bitter.

J.G. looked surprised. "I didn't mean it to sound like that. But I guess you're right. Only your mother was crazy about you. I beat her down. I made her let me keep you."

"I—see," Joel said. And she really did. She knew her father's inexhaustible energy, a certain brutality that was in him when it came to getting his own way. She herself had been a victim of it. "You—do you know what became of her?"

"No," J.G. admitted. "At first I thought that we would make it up. Then I heard that she had remarried. That hurt my pride and I wouldn't let myself think about her any more."

They sat silent a while. "I always thought that she didn't want me," Joel said in a very small voice. "And you didn't want me, either."

He looked at her with sorrow. "I was very busy when you were small. After the divorce, I was more determined than ever to show the world what a big guy I was. And you reminded me of your mother, kept me thinking that

I had failed in one place at least. Besides, you were such a self-sufficient little thing, right from the first."

"Didn't you realize that I *had* to be?" she asked.

"No. I thought that you didn't like me. That I had failed with you just as I had your mother. And I guess I did." His face was strained and white.

"I wonder why we've never talked like this before? Never in all our lives?" Joel asked as if she were thinking aloud.

"Probably because I never took the time," J.G. said wryly.

"And I was away from home so often," Joel went on with her thinking. "And if I was there, I was hurt, and angry, and proud."

"Hurt?" he asked.

"Yes. I was your daughter. But you gave Claire everything that you gave me. I almost hated Claire." Her voice had turned from sorrow back to bitterness.

"But Claire—she was my responsibility, too, honey, she and Paula's brothers." J.G. was plainly puzzled by this new turn of his daughter's thoughts.

"It wasn't what you *did*, J.G. I had all I needed of *things*. But nobody would have known, even Claire her-self, which one of us was your daughter. And she was prettier!"

"Did that matter so much?" J.G. asked in a gentle voice.

"I think it wouldn't have, if—if I had been sure that I belonged anywhere." She blinked her eyes hard to stop their stinging.

J.G. turned his face to the wall. "I wanted you and Kinny to have everything. I wanted you to be able to hold up your heads."

"And we wanted—to be loved. *Your* father had time to *talk* to you, to *know* what you were thinking." She had not succeeded in banishing the tears.

"Kinny, too?" J.G. asked.

"Kinny, too," Joel answered. "And Paula, I am sure, though she's been too loyal to say so."

"Paula—married me for my money," he said heavily.

"She thought she did," Joel said. "But she's gone all to pieces over your—accident. She feels it's her fault. She says she's been a poor wife."

They were silent for a long time. Early dusk came into the room and the nurse entered to put on the light. When she had gone, J.G. sighed.

"We've all made a sorry mess of things, Joel," he said.

"Yes," Joel answered. "But you know it doesn't have to stay like that." For the first time that afternoon she smiled, and after a moment J.G. smiled back at her.

"You know that we're probably going to lose the mills?" he asked her.

"And you'll be forty-nine your next birthday. You've got time to make another million if that's what you want."

"We-l-l," he said. "But first, I'd like to take you and Kinny fishing, and spend an evening at home with Paula, finding out what she thinks."

"What she thinks right now is that she ought to learn more about the making of cloth," Joel told him.

"Bless her! Isn't she the most beautiful thing on God's green earth?" he asked boyishly.

"You tell her that, Dad," his daughter advised. "You were pretty rough on her this morning."

"You never called me Dad before," he said wonderingly.

"And you've never called me Joel until this afternoon."

They sat there with tears on their faces, looking at each other and smiling, until the nurse bustled in. "Visiting hours are over, Miss Kinsman."

Joel leaned down and kissed her father. "Goodnight, Dad." She thought that he looked very tired but alive to his fingertips.

"Goodnight, Joel."

Steve, who had been running errands in town, was waiting for her in the reception room and at sight of him she began to weep.

"I was brutal to him, Steve, but he's snapped out of it. He's going to be all right."

He put an arm about her shoulder and let her cry a while, then offered his handkerchief.

"Let's get home and tell Paula," he said.

"And Kinny, and Claire, and everybody," she answered.

CHAPTER XXIV

IT WAS STEVE who took the good news to Claire. She had said that she wanted to see him and until now it had been impossible. Steve entered the house with a feeling of impending change which was deepened by her turning her cheek when he kissed her.

"You aren't angry? I haven't done something to hurt you?" he asked her.

"No," she said. "It's a long story, but I want you to listen carefully, Steve."

"We are always so—serious these days," he said with attempted lightness.

"Yes," she admitted. "I *am* serious tonight, Steve."

He thought the living room more dramatic than he had ever seen it though he could not be sure that there was anything changed about it except that there were vases of yellow roses everywhere, roses which he had not sent. He thought fleetingly of the man he had seen in her car yesterday.

When they were comfortably seated, not close together as they usually sat, but apart and with an indefinite formality, she spoke in a breathless yet final voice. "I'm not going to marry you, Steve."

He did not answer. He was too confused, and yet not at all surprised. It was as if he had known it was going to end in just this way. He felt numb, but relieved too that the thing he had feared had happened, and he had nothing left to fear.

"I have been thinking about it ever since the night you and Elizabeth were here for dinner and the housewarming. I'm sure that I'm right; it never would have worked. Maybe if we had married right after we finished college and had these last two years together, things would have been different but—" She broke off and shook her head.

Steve still had difficulty finding his voice. "Claire, I—"

She smiled at him a little sadly. "I was really your first girl, wasn't I, Steve?"

"Y-yes," he admitted rather reluctantly.

"I can't remember when I didn't have a beau—more than one, really. But you were so different."

"Perhaps just inexperienced," he offered.

"Yes, but it was more than that. And we were so *wise*, Steve. We had taken all the courses. We knew what made the happy marriages, and what made the unhappy ones. We could quote all the books and all the statistics, we knew all the answers. Do you remember the sessions our gang used to have about marriage?" Her eyes were dreamy with thinking of it.

"We settled all the problems," he said, remembering.

"All of them. But we broke all the rules, ourselves."

"Oh, no, Claire. We took the tests, we talked out our problems, we—"

"I know. But we loaded our answers, we ignored a thousand things, we never knew a thousand others. In short, we were in love."

"We loved each other," he said, meaning to agree with what she had said.

"No," she insisted sharply, "that's something different. We were *in love*. We were blind and deaf and dumb. Particularly to each other."

He still would not agree. "It wouldn't have lasted like this for both of us if it had been just an infatuation, Claire. I'm sure it wouldn't."

She smiled again like a woman smiling at a child who would some day be wise. "Have you heard Paula talk recently, since J.G. hurt himself? Do you know how long she has lived on a dream—a dream that she really knew was false? I think we did the same thing only we didn't know it."

"A dream," he echoed.

"It's like a childhood disease. After you're grown measles hits you hard, they tell me. Your puppy love was like that, Steve. You went through it at twenty-seven when you should have had it at fifteen, or seventeen. You looked at me and thought I was beautiful and—"

"But you were. You still are," he interrupted.

"Yes, I know," she said matter-of-factly. "But you thought because I *looked* like your ideal that I had *all* the virtues. The woman you need should have the strength of the pioneer woman who traveled in a covered wagon and shot at Indians, Steve. I want life kitten soft. I know exactly what I want—"

He sighed. He had no argument to put up against what she said.

After a while she went on. "Bruce knows me the way I am, the real me. And he loves me just the same. You'd be disillusioned when you found that I was selfish, and lazy, and a little stupid, Steve."

"Bruce Winthrop!" Steve said slowly. Suddenly he realized that it had been Winthrop in the car yesterday. He had come back into Claire's life, had been here in Kinsman.

Claire's voice was very gentle, her eyes misty. "I'm going back to Bruce, Steve."

Once again it was as if he had known this for a long time. He nodded without saying anything.

"I didn't want to tell you this. I wanted to run away. I've always been a bit of a coward about hurting people. Not that I think I'm *really* hurting you, Steve. You haven't been in love with *me* ever. But you may ache a little at first. I do right now. Because I feel as if I had grown up all of a sudden."

She was more beautiful than ever, Steve thought, looking at her. She would be a beautiful mother (and he could think about that without jealousy and almost without regret) and she would be a beautiful old lady.

"I guess I'll have spells of missing you all my life," he said.

"I know. Sometimes I think everyone has a dream of

something perfect which never becomes quite real. With Paula it was music. With us it was each other. I feel— philosophic and very wise tonight." She smiled at him rather sadly.

"Tell me about Bruce," Steve asked. "He was here during the flood, wasn't he?"

"He heard about it over the radio, the flood, I mean," she began. "He was worried about me. Bruce loves me very much, Steve. He came as near as he could on the road and after that he walked in the rain across the hills. He got here in the night Tuesday. You never saw anyone so muddy, so tired. Bruce isn't very young, Steve. He's almost forty, and he's used to sitting in an office, not hiking all over strange places where there are no roads or even paths. He certainly wasn't a romantic figure."

"He was in the car when you drove down to the mill yesterday," Steve said.

"Yes. And I'm going to meet him in Atlanta tomorrow night, Steve. He's waiting there for me and this time it's going to be—" she stopped and smiled girlishly "—for real."

Steve felt empty, as if he had not eaten for days. He stood up and held out his big right hand. "Believe me, Claire, I hope from my heart that you'll be very happy."

She blinked as she put her hand into his. "Thanks, Steve. Thanks very much."

But he felt, too, the rightness of her decision. Now that he faced reality, he knew that the aching want of her would grow less and less; that it would never be so acute again.

He had prayed in the City of Brothers, "Thy will be done, and may I be shown the way I can do it." He prayed it once more now, humbly, as he walked toward the parsonage, adding, "Keep her happy, Lord. And the Kinsmans, and all of the lost, and misguided, and contrary. All of us are so—so—" He could think of no better words than "Stupid and weak." He wasn't satisfied but he was sure God knew what he meant.

CHAPTER XXV

STEVE woke the next morning with the sound of Elizabeth's singing in his ears. She used to sing about her work but lately the house had been silent unless Bobby and his friends were romping about. He lay there thinking how good the bright, autumnal sunshine and Elizabeth's singing voice were, until the morning odors of coffee and bacon roused him from that drowsy contentment and drove him to shower and dress.

Full wakefulness brought Claire into his mind once more, and as he dressed, he thought of her going to Atlanta that night and back to Bruce. She had seemed very happy about it and he hoped that she would continue to be. There was still a feeling of emptiness in him, of suspension, of waiting.

"My, but you sound cheerful this morning," he greeted his sister.

She smiled, half shyly. "I suppose it's the weather—the flood being over and the sun out, but I feel as if we were on the verge of something wonderful!"

He looked out the window at the newly washed blue of the sky, and the unbelievable white of the scattered

clouds. "It *is* a beautiful day. All but perfect. Makes
you think of picnics, and fishing, and hill climbing."

"Steve," she exclaimed, having just made the discovery, "you have on your ring."

He lifted his hand and looked at it. "Yes. I suppose it's
no secret but perhaps you ought not to mention it until
somebody tells you. Claire is going to Atlanta about noon
today to remarry Bruce Winthrop."

Her eyes lighted and she began, "How mar—" then
broke off conscience-stricken. "I hope you aren't too awfully *sick* about it, Steve. If you are hurt about it the way
you were before—"

He shook his head wonderingly. "It's a funny thing
but I'm not. I don't know how I feel exactly. My mind
tells me that it's all for the best, but I feel sort of—
drained."

She went over and kissed him, an expression of affection which was rare between them. "I want you to
have everything to make you happy always, Steve. Always."

Embarrassed by this show of emotion, they busied
themselves with the serving of breakfast until Bobby,
still in pajamas and with his hair unbrushed, appeared
hungrily and joined them for morning prayers.

"Geezil, I wish school would start," he grumbled over
his oatmeal. "There ain't *nothin'* to do and—"

"I wish it would, too," Elizabeth told him. "Maybe
teachers could do something for your English even if
your Uncle Steve can't."

In the midst of this speech there came a knock at the
front door and on its heels Drew's voice calling, "Anybody home?"

The parsonage family shouted a hearty welcome and

Drew walked back to the kitchen. He looked about for a chair, pulled it up to the table and grinned at them, as Elizabeth poured him a cup of coffee.

"They tell me J.G. is going to pull through," he began. "He certainly surprised me when he shot himself. Never thought he'd do such a thing."

"Neither did I at first," Steve agreed, "but the more I think about it, the better I understand why the tycoon is likely to break under stress. I suppose each of them presents a little different problem, but it all boils down to the foundation on which they build—themselves, success and money." He grinned suddenly. "If anybody needed a demonstration of what happens next, we've had it here. Literally, 'the rains descended, the floods came—and beat upon'—all our houses. 'And great was the fall thereof.'"

"Such an early hour for a sermon," Drew jeered affectionately, then added seriously, "still I guess we need something a good deal stronger than ourselves when we get in real trouble. But what I came about this morning was the meeting we had at the union hall last night. Nearly everybody in Kinsman was there, executives and laborers alike. We decided to go down and see about clearing the mud out of the mill. It will be some help toward getting back to work, anyhow."

Steve's face shone. "I think that's fine. I'd like to come along."

"I thought you would," Drew said. "Joel was telling me something else pretty wonderful last night. She says they've been getting letters from all over with checks and money in them, to start a memorial hospital for Lucy. It makes me want to cry."

Steve began to feel about in his pockets. "I've received

several contributions myself. Here's one from a little
Negro girl, with a dime in it."

Bobby swallowed a prodigious mouthful and announced, "Preacher Brown got some, too. I heard him
talking about it up at the post office."

They were all silent for a bit, thinking about Lucy.
Then Drew spoke briskly. "Want to go along with me,
Steve?"

"Thanks. I'd better take my car, I suppose. Preachers
never know when they can come and go. I might need it."

"*I'd* like to go with you," Bobby offered. "I could walk
back, if Mom'd let me. But I got something I'd like to
talk to you about." He was very solemn.

Drew was just as serious. "I'd be very glad for your
company, if your mom agrees."

Elizabeth laughed. "You two combine against me.
But it's all right if you finish your breakfast, Sonny, every
last bite."

In Drew's car, Bobby sat silent, his hands clasped
tightly in his lap, staring straight before him.

Drew looked at him for some minutes with amusement, then spoke in the man-to-man voice which had
endeared him to the boy. "You had a piece of business
you wanted to discuss with me?"

Bobby still did not look directly into Drew's face, but
at the spot where his tie was knotted at his throat. "It
ain't—isn't business exactly, I reckon. Only she said it
was something men had to make up their minds about
by themselves."

"She?" Drew questioned.

"Yep. Mom."

He made no move to continue and Drew asked an-

other question. "And you and I are to decide about it as
two men?"

"Yes, sir. You see, my Uncle Steve is going to marry
Miss Claire. My mom is sure he is. And then Uncle Steve
won't need us to keep house for him any longer."

Drew, beginning to see where the "reckoning" of his
young friend was leading, felt as if he had been kicked
by a mule, and impelled to laughter as well. He said
nothing and after heaving a deep sigh, Bobby took up
his duty to his mother once more.

"And I thought you didn't have any mother, or sister,
or wife, and I didn't have any father. I thought I would
like you to be mine." He finished his proposition and
raised his eyes to meet Drew's.

Drew gulped and gasped. "Why, thank you, Bobby,"
then added after a moment, "And what did your mother
say?"

"I guess you weren't listening," Bobby said in a re-
signed sort of voice. "Grown folks mostly don't. But I
done told you that once. She said it was a thing men
had to decide. But first she turned awful red and
sounded like she was pretty mad. And after that, she
said something about two people having to love each
other a lot, and something about my father that I think
I forgot."

"Robert, my lad, you never wronged an adult more,"
Drew assured the boy. "I never hung on anybody's words
more breathlessly."

"Are adults grown folks?" Bobby asked and when
Drew had told him that they were he went on, "Half the
time I don't understand 'em. What you just said, did it
make sense to you?"

"Not much of it," Drew told him.

"Did it mean that you would like to marry my mother and be my new father, or that you wouldn't? I have to know because I'd like you better than anybody else but if you don't want to, I've got to start looking about for somebody else."

Drew patted his thin little knee. "Your mother's a wonderful woman, Bob, but she's wrong about what she told you. It's a thing a man *and* a woman have to decide. I can't think of anybody I'd rather have for a son than you. I think you'd *just* fill the bill. But suppose you give me a little time on this."

Bobby considered, then nodded. "O.K."

"And women are funny, just between us men. I don't believe your mother would like your talking about this to me. If I were you, I wouldn't mention it to her."

"Sometimes she asks," the boy answered.

"You tell her it was just man talk and she wouldn't understand. But whatever you do, don't tell her anything we've discussed."

Bobby solemnly made a cross mark above where he supposed his heart to be, adding aloud, "Hope to die. You can let me out here, I reckon."

Drew had been taking his time about the courting of Elizabeth. She wasn't, he felt, the sort of woman one could hurry. Yet if Steve was really going to marry Claire, Elizabeth was much too proud to linger in Kinsman and if she went away, she would in all likelihood be lost to him forever. He thought about the problem through the long busy day while he shoveled dried mud out of the mill building, while he broke remnants of glass out of windows to make ready for the glaziers, while he carried bolts of cloth from the stockroom to hang on an improvised line to dry.

As Bobby had suggested, he would ask her to marry him at once, but not today. When today was over he would be too tired for what his young friend referred to as "any of that silly love stuff." Already his back ached and his muscles cried out that tomorrow he would scarcely be able to move.

It was almost dark when the mill workers got through. Ordinarily they would have protested at the injustice of the long workday which they had just put in, but that evening they turned home with light hearts and tired bodies, calling back and forth to each other with impertinent friendliness.

Drew climbed the hill in his car and stopped at the parsonage.

"I can't come in," he said in answer to Elizabeth's invitation. "Nobody was ever dirtier. But I wanted you to have dinner with me tomorrow night.

"Tomorrow night?" she echoed. "You mean all of us?"

He shook his head smiling. "I mean you, Elizabeth Marsden, just you."

She was deeply surprised. Once during the time that Steve was out of town, she had thought that Drew might be interested in her, but he had usually visited with the whole family, been equally interested in them all. And recently he had talked a great deal about Joel.

"There's an old farmhouse just off the Atlanta road where they serve the kind of meals I come home and dream about in front of a big fireplace. I thought we might go there, if you like. And may I call for you about five?"

Elizabeth found herself thinking wildly of excuses,

that it would be hard to leave Bobby, that she did not know what Steve's plans were; but what she said was, "Tomorrow at five? I'd love it."

The Farmhouse was one of those exclusive places known only to the initiate, who could call and make reservations twenty-four hours ahead. As the name implied it was an authentic farm place, a house old when Sherman's army had marched by, taking horses and provender. It had changed little since that time, and the menus in which it specialized were from ancient Southern recipes. The dining room was a big, high-ceilinged room with a fireplace, Elizabeth said, "as big as my bedroom at the parsonage." Once the fireplace had been used for cooking, but tonight two huge oak logs burned in it, furnishing the only illumination. A small rosewood table had been drawn up before it, covered with thin monogrammed linen and coin silver.

Elizabeth never remembered eating so heartily, nor having food so good. She and Drew had laughed, had talked about everything from their childhoods to the possibility of the new hospital.

She was glad that she had dressed with extraordinary care, was aware that she had never looked better. For the time being she forgot Bobby and Steve and all of her duties at home. She felt like the girl who used to go dancing with Bob years ago before the war.

"You were a very dilatory Mr. Noah, it seems to me," she teased. "What with the flood and your boat only half finished! For shame!"

Drew smiled at her. "I've never known you to look so beautiful as you do tonight, Elizabeth. You're like—"

"I feel like a kid," she broke in, blushing. "I don't know when I've had such a good time."

"You could have had lots of fun like this, if you only would. Why didn't you let yourself go, Elizabeth?"

"I don't know," she answered slowly. "It seemed silly because I'd been married and had a child. Undignified."

"Is that bad?" he laughed at her. "But you know what I've been telling myself? I've been trying to convince myself that all this time you were waiting for me."

Her eyes widened and grew dark as he looked at them.

"You—wait— But, Drew—" she stammered.

He smiled tenderly at her evident confusion, then looked about them. "You don't think that I provided all this carefully contrived background for a casual date, my dear? But you're going to be Mrs. Noah, aren't you?"

Suddenly, unexpectedly, Elizabeth laughed, a merry, entirely youthful sound. "She was the worst kind of scold if I remember the way the story goes."

Drew laughed a little, too. "I guess I picked a poor name, but—Elizabeth, didn't you feel it the night you were at my house? Weren't you sure that you belonged there? It seemed to me as if you had been there always, moving about in that quiet way you have, getting things done, sitting at the head of the table. You know you felt it, too."

"Yes, Drew. Yes, I did." Impulsively she reached across the table to touch his hand. "And I'm so happy that Bobby will approve. He will, you know—?"

"You think so?" Drew grinned.

CHAPTER XXVI

J. G. KINSMAN was well enough on Friday to be irritable with everyone who came near him, to storm at doctors, nurses, and members of his family. He wanted to go home where he could eat ravenously and make plans for the future.

At three that afternoon, when visiting hours began, he was quarreling with Paula. "A whole week of it, slop for food, no proper salt, waking me up at daybreak to wash my face. It's more than human flesh can stand. I don't believe you all *want* me to come home."

"Dr. Mims says that we ought not to move you until Monday, J.G. It doesn't matter to him where you are except for your own good."

"Probably gets a percentage from the hospital," J.G. grumbled, half humorously.

A nurse, so intimidated by J.G.'s violent manner that she came no farther than the door of his room, announced, "There's a Mr. Smith to see you, Mr. Kinsman."

"Smith, Smith? I don't know any Smith. Here I lie, helpless, for any stranger to come and look at me as if I was a side-show freak. Smith, huh!"

The man was round, and florid, and entirely equal to the occasion. "I'm a stranger, Mr. Kinsman, but I do have a reason for my visit. I'm a representative of the Mutual Safety Bank. The last three days I've been inspecting your properties at Kinsman with reference to refinancing it."

J.G. sat up suddenly and glared. "Well, why didn't you say so? And you certainly took your time about getting here!"

Paula smoothed her husband's counterpane and made soothing sounds, then turned to their guest, smiling, "When an active man is confined to his bed, it does something to his manners, Mr. Smith. I am Mrs. Kinsman."

The visitor smiled in recognition of this truism on human nature and shook hands with each of the Kinsmans. Then he sat down and opened the brief case which seemed almost a part of him.

"Your superintendent was kind enough to show Mendel and me over the plant and we've talked to both workers and executives. I thought you might like to know how we feel about the mill."

J.G. settled back and looked grim. He supposed he could stand being turned down on that new loan. It was really no more than he had expected.

"One of the reasons for our delay was to discuss with the government the possibility of rebuilding the dam. We have a commitment from them to defray half of that expense, which we consider very good." He sat there nodding and very pleased with himself.

"What does he want to build me up for a let-down for? Why can't he just come out and say they aren't going to do it?" J.G. thought angrily.

Smith went on as if he were addressing a board meeting. "We found the labor-employer relations unusually good. On the day after our arrival we found every man employed at the mills in whatever capacity, doing manual labor, cleaning up after the flood and—"

J.G. sat up suddenly, his eyes afire. "The heck you say!

Who told them— Who gave them—" He blustered to cover his emotion.

"It seems it was the wives of the union members who suggested it. They met with the bosses and the plans were made. It's perfectly neat now except for the cloth in the stockroom and the machinery," the report went on.

J.G. groaned aloud. He had been trying to forget those two items.

"The cloth is being bleached once more," Mr. Smith continued after a glance at the papers in his hands, "then re-dyed. It can be sold, not at top prices, but sold so that there will be no loss."

"But the machinery," J.G. burst forth. "I have seen it like that, only not so bad and it took eighteen months to blast the rust from it. In eighteen months the mill will be bankrupt!"

Mr. Smith still nodded and smiled. "But there is a new process now, developed in Britain. Seems the rollers are dunked in five successive tanks and they come up shiny new. Takes only two weeks and it's comparatively cheap, too." Smith had the air of a man who had not only invented this miracle but who executed it as well.

"Another thing that impressed Mendel and me was the efficient handling of things when the flood occurred. I understand that there was only one death?"

J.G. disclaimed any credit for that. "I had nothing to do with it. A Negro girl who was a nurse here gave the warning. She was the one who was killed. Great grandmother belonged to my grandfather before the war and they took our name."

Mr. Smith beamed about this as well. "Yes indeed. I heard the whole story on the radio. Most impressive."

Then he became grave and business-like once more. "It is because of all these things that Mendel and I are in accord about our report. We shall most heartily recommend that the bank accept the plan that you worked out with them when you were in New York recently. You understand, of course, that our recommendation will not guarantee the loan. It is only a recommendation and the directors will have to pass on it."

J.G. cleared his throat with a great "har-rumphing." "I understand that, certainly. Thank you for telling me about the report, Mr. Smith."

The genial little man closed his brief case, stood up and shook hands all around once more. "I've a train to catch in about an hour and Mendel will be waiting for me. It is most pleasant meeting you both." He bowed himself out genially.

"Well!" J.G. exclaimed when his visitor had gone.

"That report of his, is it really true that it means so little?" Paula asked.

"So little! He knows and I know that it means I'll get the whole refinancing deal just as we laid it out at the bank two weeks ago. I must send for Potter. You tell him, Paula, that I want to see him tomorrow afternoon at the latest to hear all about this British rust-removing outfit, and that I'll want the figures on costs. Why I don't even know whether they come here and do it or if we have to ship the machinery. I'll want all the figures on the bleaching of that cloth, and the re-dyeing as well. Tell him that I want to know what's going on, with figures on everything."

Paula made a small protest. "Dr. Mims wanted you to stay quiet for a while, J.G."

He snorted. "Rest. Be quiet. Nurses, doctors, my own

family. All of them repeating it like so many poll par-
rots. I never heard anything so stupid in my life. Lying
here and not knowing what's happening in my own business. I won't have it, I tell you."

But he had quieted down somewhat and was explaining what he meant to do now that the worst of the financial stress was removed, when Joel and Kinny arrived a
little later.

"Hi, Dad," Joel greeted him and kissed his cheek rather
self-consciously. "You're looking quite steamed up for an
invalid, with that old fire back in your eye."

"I'm as well as I ever was. Better. And they won't let
me out of this infernal hole. I need to be at the office
with my fingers on things. I'm completely in the dark.
Completely. Even old Potter going behind my back to
make contracts when maybe they're cheating us and—"

"You know very well, J.G.," Joel said, smiling, "that
Mr. Potter can't sign any contract without your knowing it. And I bet he hasn't the power to sign anything
under any circumstances. Huh?"

"Well, no," J.G. admitted rather sheepishly. "Hey, boy,
did you hear the good news? The mills are going to run
again."

Kinny had turned his back on the room and was playing with the tieback of the draperies. He made no reply
to his father's announcement.

J.G. was immediately hurt and gruff. "Manners, boy.
It's customary to speak when you're spoken to. You were
friendly enough when you were here day before yesterday."

Kinny turned on him, his face stubborn and red with
anger. "When I was here last time you wuz talkin' about

takin' me'n maybe Bobby Marsden huntin'. You promised. And now you can't talk about *nothin'* except that
ol' office." He kicked the foot of the bed in his distress.
"Bobby Marsden's looking for a new father. I guess
maybe I'll get me one, too."

J.G. sat up, his eyes fixed on his son's tear-stained
face. "Look here, son, wouldn't you just as soon go hunting with—with a man who's a professional hunting
guide? He'd know a lot more about it than—"

Kinny scrubbed his cheek with an embarrassed fist.
He hadn't meant to cry, particularly not to let anybody
see him. "Hunting is for fathers. Bobby Marsden thinks
so, too," he said.

"You see," Joel told him softly. "It's like I told you."

J.G. turned his eyes on Paula. "And I promised you
that we'd go to New York for the opening of the opera
season if we could possibly afford it."

She nodded. "But I knew you'd get busy and—I really
didn't expect it, J.G."

He shook his head puzzled. "I simply don't know why
any of you should want—"

"Family life, J.G.?" Joel suggested when he paused.

He squirmed. "There you go calling me J.G. again," he
protested.

She grinned at him. "There you go acting like J.G.
again," she echoed him.

He grinned back. "Well, I guess—I'll have to have help
if I'm to teach an old dog new tricks. But I'll keep those
promises, every last one of them. See if I don't."

Kinny came suspiciously to the foot of the bed and
looked at his father. "Cross your heart and hope to die?"

J.G. met the boy's searching look, remembering back

through the years when the formula had been a part of his own life. "Cross my heart and hope to die," he promised.

Steve had been to visit J.G. every day of his illness and saw no reason to make an exception of Sunday but he was rather late in arriving now.

J.G. looked up over a welter of letters, notes, books and advertising matter. "You preach another of those street-corner sermons this morning?"

"Street corner?" Steve echoed.

"Yep. Ranting. And a lot of crazy notions."

"Perhaps you would have considered it so," Steve admitted. "I preached on the importance of intangibles."

"In-tan-gi-bles," J.G. pronounced it as if each syllable were a separate word. "Now there's a fine word for the world—or even just Kinsman—to ponder on. And what do you have when you've got 'em?"

Steve looked thoughtful. He found himself handicapped by his preparation for the sermon. One did not speak to an individual as one spoke to a group. Certainly one did not speak like that to J.G. Kinsman.

"Perhaps all the things that matter," he said finally. "Home, and love, and courage, and patriotism, and—"

But Kinsman broke in there, grinning. "Hell, and hate, and cowardice, and treason," he completed the contrast.

Steve nodded. He was not surprised. He had mentioned this sort of thing that morning, too. "And you think those things don't matter?"

He had J.G. there. The older man sat thoughtful a moment, then said slowly, "Maybe they're the things that have us in the mess we're in—that the whole world is in."

"Those and others. Greed. Selfishness. I suppose you could go on naming that kind of intangibles all day but I'd rather spend my time on the others, the ones that are God's gifts."

J.G.'s brows were questioning and Steve explained hesitantly, as if he himself were still thinking these things out loud. "I guess all my sermons, for a while at least, will be about the law of God, J.G. All my thinking seems to turn that way. I don't pretend that following that way is easy, any more than the law of music, or science, or art— Nothing that you give yourself to utterly, is easy. I used to practice scales on the piano. Never got much beyond that, and it was drudgery. Much of anything, much of everything is. But giving yourself to *something* is inevitable."

J.G. nodded. "I choose tangibles. You know where you stand with 'em."

"Do you?" Steve probed. "Did you last Monday?" He watched a flush creep up under J.G.'s skin and did not wait to salt the wound. "You've a talent for business, J.G. As I see it, it's the way of business that you should follow, remembering that you are following His way as well.

"To me, the important thing is the search. I think if we seek, God will take care of the rest. And this I believe with all my faith—seeking will give us peace of mind, and heart, and soul; the peace that passeth understanding."

J.G. thrust out his chin stubbornly. "I'll still stick to the tangibles, young fellow. Know what I was doing when you came in here? I was figuring. I'm pretty glad to be alive and back on my feet with the mills. I thought I'd do something about that cloth that's been re-bleached and re-dyed. I'm going to give away my profit on it. Four and a half per cent I'd make after everything was taken care of. I'm going to set aside that much and give it to—to—well I haven't figured it out yet but to some-body who needs it. Still don't see what connection you made between intangibles and the law of God in that sermon this morning, Steve. You didn't make that very clear to me."

Steve shook his head, smiling. "I guess it doesn't mat-ter too much, J.G. You stick to your tangibles."

CHAPTER XXVII

SEPTEMBER went by quickly for Steve.

J.G. came home from the hospital and the mills were going full tilt once more. The first morning he was back in his office he sent for Steve.

"You know anything about all this money that keeps pouring in here for a hospital?" he demanded as if it were some conspiracy which Steve had dreamed up behind his back.

Steve grinned at him. "As a matter of fact it doesn't *keep* coming. It's just about quit," Steve told him.

"Then you *have* been getting some. That's what Paula said," J.G. accused.

Steve nodded. "Twelve thousand, three hundred, seventy-two dollars and fifty-one cents," he reported.

J.G. lifted his head with a certain pride. "I have almost twenty thousand. A lot of it was in dollars, folded into letters that said more or less, 'to help that brave woman's dream come true.' "

"Preacher Brown got change wrapped in paper, with letters like that," Steve told him. "I guess people are hungry for heroes. Look at the way they took on over Captain Carlsen who stayed with his boat. Maybe humanizing our leaders isn't such a good idea after all."

J.G. looked at him sternly. "Steve, you're getting so that you talk all the time in sermons."

Steve was unabashed. "In other words, like a preacher. Well, you talk like a cotton-mill man!"

J.G. snorted. "I didn't ask you to come here to preach at me. I wanted to have the figures on this hospital deal. I'd like to build the thing if we can get the money together." He shook his head doubtfully. "Building's expensive. Terribly expensive."

The Negro preacher had been sent for too, and he arrived now, a dignified man with a long serious face.

J.G. shook his hand, asked him to sit down. "Hear you have some money for the Lucy Kinsman hospital?"

"Yes, sir. Nearly eight thousand dollars," Preacher Brown said. "Brother Kinsman's church in Atlanta contributed four thousand. A Negro organization sent five hundred. Most of the rest was in little bits, a lot of it in silver."

J.G. whistled a long slow whistle. "Forty thousand dollars! All unasked for."

The Negro minister turned big dark eyes on J.G.'s face. "No, sir. It was asked for all right. Miss Lucy prayed for that hospital every day of her life, and then she payed for it *with* her life. It was asked for, all right."

J.G. was abashed. "I reckon we ought to get started

on it. I'll have to see what we can get a building for, one that will do at all." He rubbed his face with one hand and added, "Maybe I could squeeze out something. Money's tight with me, though."

"Mr. Kinsman, sir," Emmanuel Brown suggested with a mixture of humility and pride, "don't you think the folks hereabouts ought to be allowed to make contributions, all of them? Seems like, with Miss Lucy warning them and saving them the way she did, they'd all want to do something."

J.G. nodded gravely. Certainly everybody in Kinsman owed the girl a deep debt. His own Kinny had been at that school where the water had trapped the girl.

Steve was excited about the idea. "Why don't we have a mass meeting at the church on Sunday afternoon— Everybody, the way it was for the funeral." He turned to the other preacher. "You could let your people know. I'll call the other two white ministers, and I'll get in touch with all my parishoners. We ought to almost match the sum we already have."

And so it was planned. The people of Kinsman and the country surrounding it turned out in full force. It was a break in the somber life following the flood. Steve prayed briefly, and J.G. told them why they had come together.

"We were sure that you whose lives, whose children's lives, had been saved, would want to do something to keep Lucy Kinsman's memory among us."

Preacher Brown spoke next. "There should be two wings, for our state law requires segregation. I mention this feeling I have about the hospital because many of the letters we have received have asked for a Negro hospital. But Miss Lucy was a friend to us all. She wouldn't have wanted it that way. That is, unless you white people feel—"

Drew was immediately on his feet. "I have here a check for five thousand dollars. It is from my mother's estate, and I give it for her because she loved Lucy very dearly. Mr. Chairman—is one of you a chairman?—I move that our hospital have two wings, according to the law, but that the Lucy Kinsman Hospital serve both races."

The talk, the contributions filled the long afternoon. It was late when Clem Hosea lumbered to his feet. "I ain't never been one to say nothin' in meetin' but seems like I can't stay still any longer. Me an' my wife Martha, and my baby Lucy Kinsman Hosea, wouldn't be here alive this afternoon, if it wasn't for Miss Lucy. Looks like I ain't got a dime to change an' rub two nickels together to feed my family this endurin' winter, but I got a strong back an' times I laid brick an' times I toted morter. I could give *work*, ever' bit as long as needed."

That brought on a storm of work offers and at last Steve had to raise his hands. "I am sure that what we've been doing here is more important than most church services but it is almost time for our evening service. All of you, black or white, are welcome to stay and worship with us, but I believe we had better close up this business. I've got pieces of paper for you to write work offers on, or money pledges if you want to put them into writing. We'd like to know how much we can count on. Thank you for coming. Thank God for Lucy Kinsman, and for people like you. The peace of God go with you."

Joel couldn't wait for the hospital. She bought books on child care and simple hygiene and studied them like a beaver. "I know nothing, absolutely nothing, Steve," she protested, angrily. "But I'm going to learn."

She had taken over Lucy's visiting, and spent many days scouring the mountains to help those who lived there.

"It would probably be more efficient for you to take a part of your allowance and hire somebody who knows all about this sort of thing," Steve told her.

"I'm working on that, too," she confided. "But just anybody won't do. I want somebody who'll love those folks like I do. Just going out and telling 'em—they're proud people, Steve. They wouldn't listen. They listen to me, most of 'em, but I don't know enough."

"Maybe you could go away and study nursing," he suggested.

She looked at him speculatively. "I've thought about that, too. But I don't think I will until I'm sure about— I don't think I will just yet."

The legal investigation into her automobile accident had been postponed because the three in the other car were still in the hospital. When, in late September, court convened again, Steve went with her.

The proceedings were simple enough. The judge called to his desk Joel and the three people who had been in the other car and began to question them and the patrol officers who had arrived at the scene almost immediately after the accident.

"It was raining cats and dogs, your honor," the driver of the other car explained. "Couldn't neither of us see good and Miss Kinsman, she skidded. She coulda been drivin' a mite fast but—night like that, I ain't certain. I ain't sayin' it was nobody's fault an' Miss Kinsman, she paid the hospital bills and got us a new car. First new one we ever had."

Joel hung her head. "I was going a little fast," she said.

"Costs. Twenty-five dollars," the judge decided. "Rain's no time for driving fast, young woman."

"No, sir," Joel agreed.

And it was over. Outside and in his car with Joel sitting beside him, Steve looked at her and smiled.

"Who was actually behind that wheel, Joel?"

She looked at him with wide, surprised eyes. "Why, I—"

He was still smiling. "I'd hate to turn my most sympathetic parishoner in for perjury," he scolded half humorously.

"I didn't *say* I was driving," she protested.

"Not today, you didn't. But when it happened—"

She sighed. "It was Bert Craft. You know that gang I ran around with this summer. At least you saw some of them. I met them through a girl I knew at school, one who seemed to think a good deal of me. That night I had been to a dance with the usual crowd. I was in the ladies room and several others came in. They didn't know I was there and Helen—she's the one I knew at college— was saying, 'No matter what we want to do, Joel will pay for it. Doesn't she always?' You'd have thought she hated me, Steve, the way she said it." Joel shuddered a little remembering.

Steve made a sympathetic sound with his tongue and the roof of his mouth, and she went on.

"I asked Bert Craft to drive me home. We were hardly on the road before I realized that he was drunk. I suggested that I drive and he wouldn't listen, only speeded

up. It was then that it happened. Neither of us was hurt.
But the poor people in the other car! Bert didn't say a
word, just looked at me, then ran off.

"I must have been an awful kid, Steve, to be taken
in by that gang, but you know how—unsettled I was. I
wanted to find my own friends, people who had nothing
to do with the Kinsman name."

"It's all over now," Steve comforted her.

She sighed. "And not too tragically. Those three Mer-
cers are all right and they're proud of their new car. And
I never meant to lie about the accident, Steve. Or to
shield Bert either, I just couldn't bear for people to know
that I had been out with such a skunk!"

Elizabeth and Drew were married the last week in
September. They had planned to be married at the parsonage, very quietly, but as the news spread, woman
after woman came to Elizabeth and asked that it be in
the church.

"There's never been a wedding in the church," they
said. "Everybody in town loves you both and would like
to be there."

And so it was arranged for six o'clock the evening of
the thirtieth of September. There were a great many
candles and ferns and white flowers. Elizabeth wore a
suit of coppery brown with cream accessories, and her
flowers were a corsage of tawny-green orchids. Steve,
reading the ceremony, thought he had never seen her
look half so lovely.

An army friend of Drew's had come to serve as best
man, and Joel was maid of honor. She wore green velvet
the same color as Elizabeth's orchids which brought out
the tinge of red in her dark hair.

Bobby entered with his mother and when Steve asked, "Who giveth this woman in marriage?" he piped out a very dignified "I do," and retired to the Kinsman pew where he sat during the remainder of the ceremony beside Kinny.

Afterward there was a short reception out under the great trees in the churchyard. There had been no formal invitations but everybody in Kinsman had been asked and everybody came. There were laughter and good wishes enough for three weddings, and when the brief hour was over, Elizabeth and Drew left for the three-month tour through South America which was the Kinsmans' wedding present to them.

Lottie, the Phalen cook, was to look after Steve and Bobby until their return, and Paula Kinsman, who had sung beautifully before the ceremony, would see that things went well.

Steve and Bobby stayed until all the guests except the Kinsmans had gone away.

"Come home with us," Paula had urged. "Your house will seem very empty just now. Come and spend the night too."

Steve was tempted but a glimpse of Bobby's weary and rather pathetic face changed his mind. The boy, he felt sure, would be less miserable at home. So he declined, thanked them, and with his nephew turned toward his car and the parsonage.

"Will you hear my prayers, Uncle Steve?" Bobby asked in a not quite even voice.

"Of course, fellow. Every single night until your mother comes home."

Bobby plodded on to the car and climbed in. For most of the ride home neither spoke. Then the boy broke the

silence. "You know," he said, "I never would have asked
Uncle Drew to marry my mom, if I'd known he was going
to take her so far off."

CHAPTER XXVIII

OCTOBER and November were busy months indeed.
Steve worked on the new hospital doing unskilled labor
one day each week. He was not particularly apt at it.
Still he felt that he got to know people in a way he had
never known them when he had visited them formally in
their homes or preached to them from behind the heavily
carved mahogany pulpit.

He continued with his family counseling two mornings weekly at the recreational building. Here again he
found that he was closer to his clients than he had been
before. Once they had been cases. Now they were *people.*

When Mattie Rometka, a Georgia girl who had married a New England Czech, wept and told him that she
was going to have to leave her husband, and that there
was a baby coming, he didn't point out, as he would have
four months earlier, that mixed marriages were rarely
successful.

"How old are you, Mattie?" he asked instead, and
didn't mark her answer down on a card with her there
looking at him as he would have done a short time ago.

"Sixteen," she sniffled. "I—I thought—Pa never give

me nothin' pretty, an' onct he beat me for smokin' a ciga-
rette. I—thought— Mike used to give me presents."

Steve looked at her, her swollen, common little face,
her pale blue eyes, her fine, white blond hair. "You pret-
tied up when he was coming then?" he asked her.

She nodded, wordless.

"And now?"

"I'm that tired. And I don't feel so good. Throwing
up, and with the baby comin'," she defended herself.

"How about the house? Do you keep it clean? And
feed Mike three good meals every day?"

She dropped her eyes to her hands which lay in her
lap. "He swears at me," she countered.

"I'll bet he does," Steve thought. "Look, Mattie, a
hungry man's mean. You feed him."

She shook her head stubbornly. "It fair turns my stom-
ach, food does, me feelin' like I do."

"Are you planning to go back to your father when you
leave Mike?" he asked then.

"I heard tell there was places in town where they'd
keep you until after, and then give out your baby to
people and let you—" she was full of the plan, her eyes
alight.

"Be a girl again?" Steve asked with pity. "Be like you
were before you married?"

She nodded, a little of her expectation gone out of
her now that her thought had been put into words. She
could see how impossible her dream had been. "My ma
had nineteen. I'm the youngest. I ain't going to live like
that, Mr. Elliott."

"No. You talk to Dr. Mims about it when you see him
next time. But right now you go home. You live next door
to Mrs. Roberts, don't you? You tell her what you've been

telling me. Tell her I said you were to ask if she'd help you to fix a really good man-size supper. You see how she does it. And get the house a little straight. And you sweet talk Mike a little. A pretty Southern girl like you will know how to do that."

"Mrs. Roberts says I'm poor white trash and don't wear enough clothes," Mattie explained with a fresh flood of tears.

"Mrs. Roberts is lonesome," Steve told her. "All her children are grown and gone away. She and Ben sort of knock about in that big house of theirs. You try asking her help, Mattie. You try loving her. And try loving Mike."

After that he went to see Mrs. Roberts. At first she was contemptuous of Mattie. "A littly whitey, hook-wormy, string of a thing, Mr. Elliott, that's all she is."

Steve grinned and offered the snobbish woman the formula which he was only just learning himself. "Try loving her, Mrs. Roberts, instead of criticizing. She'll soften that hard old heart of yours."

Mrs. Roberts sniffed again but finally nodded. "Do what I can," she promised grudgingly.

Mike proved to be a harder nut to crack. "She won't do *nothin'*. She's no wife for a real man. She won't cook, won't clean, won't wash, won't iron. One thing she will do. She cries." He spat in disgust.

"You're about thirty, aren't you?" Steve asked. "How responsible were you at sixteen, Mike? You didn't want to be tied down, did you? I bet you wanted to kick up your heels when it came night. Take her to a movie, Mike. Buy her some candy. Pet her a little. You've got to love a wife, especially a little young one like Mattie who's scared to death because she's never had a baby before."

Mike chewed stubbornly on his pipe for a bit, then a slow grin lighted his somber face. "Don't see you doin' nothin' like that, Reverend." And having gotten off this great joke on Steve, he was less angry himself.

Finally Steve talked to Joel. Her response was immediate. "She's a sleazy little thing, but she does have an eye for beauty. That house they live in is horrible. I'll go up and help her with some curtains and things. And I'll take her the government bulletins on child care while I'm about it."

Most of the people he met at the clinic were more or less like Mattie, bewildered, unhappy, misunderstanding and misunderstood. Steve took great pains with them and usually he found himself ending up by talking them over with Joel.

And many of these people from the clinic began to come to his church. Not in the mornings, for at that hour the place was filled with the stylish, the better paid and better educated of the community. But at night they came in flocks and listened to Steve with a sort of breathlessness that pleased him immensely.

J.G. sneered at these night services. "Slumming in my fine church, are you, Steve?"

But J.G. didn't awe Steve as he had earlier. "I preach to whoever comes to hear me in *God's* church, J.G., morning and evening."

The great man nodded. "I see that they know their places. None of them *joining* Kinsman Memorial."

"N-no," Steve told him quietly. "But if one of them wanted to, I'd take him in."

J.G. frowned. "Don't go too far, Stephen Elliott," he warned.

Once again Steve answered with the same quiet confidence: "Only as far as I have to go."

Thanksgiving morning was clear and cold. Steve and Bobby walked up the hill to the church, striding along with their hands in their overcoat pockets, and entered the cloisters between the church and the educational building.

"Do you suppose you can find Mrs. Kinsman and the rest of the junior choir?" Steve asked the boy.

Bobby, looking at him with the patient contempt that the young reserve for stupid adult questions, said, "Well, a'course," before he ran off to join the others.

In spite of the fact that it was almost time for him to don his robe, and that the weather was nippy, Steve lingered under the open arches, looking down into the flats at the half-completed hospital, and the mill, silent for the holiday.

From them he needed to raise his eyes only a little to find the small house of the Hughes who, through an arrangement he had made with the Methodist orphanage in Macon, had taken a brother and sister ten and twelve years of age to rear as Baptists.

Mike and Mattie Rometka lived higher up the hill. They were having Thanksgiving dinner with Mrs. Roberts, whom they already called "Granny" because that's what they planned to teach the baby to call her. But just now they were probably driving back from Dalton where they had been to Mass. Steve's heart warmed as he thought of these "Other sheep—not of this fold."

But there were those of his own congregation whom

he had served and who had gained his affection. He thought for a moment of Mrs. Phalen and the rich memory she had left behind her, of Drew who would soon be making a home in the house she had left behind, Drew and his sister, Elizabeth, of those quiet, sturdy friends the Potters, and at the top of the hill, the Kinsmans. He had had some small part in their building a happier family, he thought.

But he did not have to call Joel to mind; she was always there in his thoughts.

He turned and went into the warm vestry, entered into the chatter, the laughter, the general holiday spirit, donned his robe and lined up at the end of the procession. The organ prelude came to a close and the organ burst forth with the introductory phrase of the processional hymn. Paula Kinsman gave the signal and the choir, selected members of the congregation and unpaid since the flood, took up the words.

> "Come let us tune our loftiest song
> And raise to Christ our joyful strain;
> Worship and thanks to Him belong
> Who reigns, and shall forever reign."

Out ahead of him, Steve could see Paula Kinsman in her white robe. There was a glow about her, a new softness. Her eyes sparkled and there was a faint color in her cheeks. Perhaps she had gained a little weight. He wondered, as her soprano voice rang out, if she were not pregnant.

> "And saints on earth, with saints above,
> Your voices in His praise employ."

The children's choir sang with the others, their voices sweet and piping. Steve followed them through the chancel gate and took his place before the center pulpit chair, kneeling to pray. Usually on such occasions he prayed in silent words, that his sermon might be the message that God would have him speak, that the congregation would go away closer to God for his having spoken. But today his prayer was wordless, like a spring overflowing because it held too much. As he rose to his feet, his eyes sought Joel's face and found it. How *dear* she looked, and how young, her head tied in a gay-colored babushka, her eyes serious and bright on his face.

"She's one of the happy people herself," he thought tenderly.

As he announced the first hymn, he wondered if this were perhaps the highest form of prayer, this outpouring of one's spirit toward God, if this were not the ultimate intimacy, the meeting of eyes in complete understanding.

"We'll begin the service by singing number three fifty-five, 'Sing Praise to God Who Reigns Above, The God of All Creation,'" he read from the hymnal, and let his eyes travel about the well filled room.

He knew in his heart that when conference came next June he would not be coming back to Kinsman. J.G. wanted somebody he could manage, someone who would agree and admire. Steve was no longer that man. Yet as he began to sing, he thought how much he owed to J.G. and to Kinsman Memorial. The little church was perfect and he had always loved beauty. But that was the least of it. He had come here five months ago unsure of himself and even of God.

"Within the kingdom of His might,
Lo! all is just and all is right,"

he sang lustily, and believed it as he sang. He remembered Mrs. Phalen once more, and smiled to think how uncertain he had been of her meaning when she had summed up the blessings of her life with "And I have walked with God."

He might lose this church, but that would be because God willed it. And he would go to pastures that were of God's choosing. It was amazing the security that knowing he was in God's hands gave him.

The hymn, and the Apostles' Creed, ended and Steve prayed briefly, mentioning the things which the congregation, and the community had to be especially thankful for, the Kinsman Church, preservation from the flood, the prosperity which had followed, the not yet completed hospital. "And for each personal blessing, Father, in the name of Him who taught us to pray, Our Father—"

The junior choir had the first anthem and Steve sat listening, watching their rapt, young faces as they sang the old, childhood chorus. "Praise Him, Praise Him, all ye little children, God is Love, God is Love." It was then that he decided to change his sermon. Before he had come to Kinsman he had had a favorite sermon which he titled "Love Everlasting." He would preach it again today. What had anybody to be thankful for more than God's eternal love?

God's love—and Joel's. They had not talked of it, still it lay there between them warm and perfect.

But J.G. was not going to like the marriage and Steve had wanted to give the new feeling between father and daughter time to grow before a new discord came be-

tween them. That Joel's father would fight her marriage
to a man without financial security they both recognized.
But that, too, had not been mentioned in so many words.

Suddenly, in the midst of the Thanksgiving service he
knew that he could not put off for one day longer telling
Joel that he loved her, hearing her say the proper words
to him. Again his eyes met hers, clinging, all but speaking.

He had to clear his throat before he could begin the
first reading, for happy expectation had made it husky.

"I will praise thee, O Lord, with my whole heart; I
will show forth all thy marvelous works."

He watched Joel's lips form the words of the response,
"I will be glad and rejoice in thee; I will sing praise to
thy name, O thou Most High."

The responsive reading done, he joined the Gloria
with his people. That had been what he had been trying
to say when he knelt as he first entered the church. He
had sung it a thousand times but never so wholeheartedly
as now.

"Glory be to the Father, and to the Son, and to the
Holy Ghost; as it was in the beginning, is now, and ever
shall be, world without end."

Then he stood at the lectern, the small, limp Testament open in his hand which trembled with the emotion
that was in him. His eyes sought Joel's, found and held
them.

"I shall read from the First Epistle of John, the fourth
chapter, the seventh to the twenty-first verses," he said
slowly.

And then his voice broke slightly as he began to read.
"Beloved, let us love one another, for love is of God, and
everyone that loveth is born of God, and knoweth God."